JAKE

KEITH BOND

Michael Terence
Publishing

First published in paperback by
Michael Terence Publishing in 2019
www.mtp.agency

ISBN 9781913289751

My grateful thanks to John, for all his patience, help and encouragement whilst I was writing this book…

Introduction

For many years I have thought that I would like to write a novel, not necessarily this novel, any novel! I just felt that somewhere deep inside me there was a book trying to get out! What kind of book would it be though? Some would advise an author to stick to what they know, life events, your own experiences, but that might not be interesting enough to grab people's attention. No, I felt I had to let my imagination run wild, embroider on some real events, make up a few fictitious ones, get lost in the whole process, dress it up and have a ball! So that's what I did, I hope you enjoy reading it.

Prologue

He was in the depth of the wood, a place that he often played in, he loved its smells, the way that the sunlight filtered through the canopy of the trees and created moving patterns on the leafy ground. There were always new treasures to find and interesting things to see, a pine cone, an iridescent crows feather that shimmered blue, black and green, a clump of snowdrops like an island in the snow of springtime; a puffball fungus that he could smack with a stick and send clouds of what looked like yellow smoke floating in the air. He had always found that a stick was an essential tool for a lad to have as it was invaluable for beating down prickly thorns or nettles that were in your way, or poking, prodding and generally knocking things down!

The wood was both a place of fascination and fear to him and most of the time he would delight in hearing familiar sounds of birdsong or the pitter ta pat of raindrops hitting the leaves, or the wind making rustling sounds as it played through them, but occasionally he was suddenly startled by a strange noise and like a frightened animal alarmed for its safety, he would tense and bolt, frantically fleeing to escape the unseen menace that he believed was pursuing him. Once he felt that he had outrun this threat and his heart had stopped pounding in his chest, he would then return to his explorations, but always, after such events, he would avoid the denser darker woodland areas that were a bit scary and harder to run through, he would stay on the beaten tracks or go to the camp he had made on the outskirts of the wood, nearer to where he lived.

Sometimes this was a good place, a happy place, but other times it wasn't so, it was a place to come to for escape, solitude and bitter tears. Jake was proud of his camp, it was his secret place that no one knew about, he had chosen the perfect spot to build it amongst a big clump of mature 'Japanese Knot Weed', he kept all of his treasures here, as it was strong and fairly weatherproof. It had taken him a few weeks to complete as he had to cut through some of the thick stalks to use them for reinforcing the outer walls. It provided a great vantage spot as he had made places for looking out into the wood from three different directions, He could hide out in here, if he heard any strangers in the wood he could look out and see if they were heading his way, if they did get close he could watch what they were doing, but he hardly ever saw anyone, that's why he liked it.

He had chosen this particular spot because there was a solid natural hedge behind him that didn't require any work or maintenance, he occasionally had to straighten things and tidy up inside where an animal or a bird had got in and made a mess, but apart from that, it all looked after itself. He was proud of his camp and he didn't want anyone else to know where it was, least of all his dad, he certainly didn't want him to know about it.

Chapter 1

Bill Wiggins was a stocky, muscular naval man, he was an able seaman in The Royal Navy. He had met Vera Evans at a dance in Hanworth when he was on leave, she was with her friend Ivy Newton and he liked the look of her as soon as he saw her standing the other side of the town hall dance floor. She was slightly taller than him, very attractive with brown eyes and brown hair which was styled in a 'Victory Roll', it was March 1947, the war had ended two years ago on the 2nd September 1945. He went over and asked her to dance thinking that'd he'd get the 'brush off', but she had said yes and they had hit it off together straightaway and had nearly every dance together until the local band played the last romantic tune which was 'All of Me' a current hit by Frankie Lane. Then Bill had asked Vera if he could walk her to the bus stop to catch the last bus home to Barton. She had said yes and on that walk he had asked to see her again before his leave ended, Vera said yes to that too and they arranged to meet again the next day in Crowsthorpe which was the next village to Barton and only three miles away, so weather permitting she would be able to cycle there.

Bill kissed her just as she was about to get on the bus.

"You will be there tomorrow, won't you," he asked earnestly?

"Of course I will silly," she replied and climbed on to the bus, waving him goodbye as it set off. She sat next to Ivy Newton on the bus home and they chatted and giggled about how they'd enjoyed their evening, apparently Ivy had met a corporal from Diddington Barracks called Dave and she was seeing him again next week.

Vera started out for Crowsthorpe early as she didn't want to be all hot and sweaty when she met Bill again. They had agreed to meet at the village square outside of the 'Green Man' pub. Vera was fifteen minutes early so she leaned her cycle against the back of a bench and sat on the seat to wait for Bill. It seemed like she had been waiting for an eternity and he was twenty minutes late, perhaps he wouldn't turn up at all she thought.

A minute or two later she looked up the hill towards Hanworth and she saw him walking down the road, she couldn't get over how handsome he was with his dark Brylcreemed hair, navy blue blazer and grey flannel trousers. They greeted each other and kissed, a long lingering kiss of promise, they started walking up the road and Bill put his arm around her waist pulling her tightly into him. They agreed that the canal towpath would be a pleasant place to walk.

They walked along the path for some distance, several brightly painted coal barges had passed them, and they found a nice spot to sit down. After a while, their kisses became more passionate and Bill's hand was fondling Vera's breast so they moved further back on the grassy area until they were under a clump of trees and hidden by some bushes, and here they made love. Later at the pub Bill told Vera that he had never met anyone as nice as her before and asked her if she would write to him, she wanted to of course, so they exchanged addresses and talked about when they would meet on Bill's next leave as he was due to report back to his ship at Portsmouth docks tomorrow.

The next year was going to be the darkest period in Vera's life. She found she was pregnant with Bill's child and as she was living with her parents, her pregnancy became obvious to her step-mother even before she began to show, due to Vera's bouts of morning sickness. She was treated very coldly and told in no uncertain terms what the situation was going to be.'

"Don't think yer'll be staying under this roof to ave it cos yer won't mi gal, I ain't avin tongues awaggin at me in the village, you'll have to go away sumwer an drop it!"

"Where will I go Flora, Bill can't help me he's away at sea?"

"Well, yer shudda thought a that afore ya spread yer legs for ya saila boy, yer little slut!"

"I'm not a slut, so don't you speak to me like that."

"Whar are yer then, bringin shame on yerself and this famly, yer can thank yer lucky stars that dad ain't taken the strap to ya, we've read is letters?"

"You've what, how dare you, you had no right to read my private letters!"

This was all too much for Vera she burst into tears and ran to go to her bedroom.

"An tears aint gonna help yer none either, seventeen years old and yer've gone and ruined yer life," Flora shouted after her. Flora was now at the bottom of the stairs and shouted up.

"N I s'pose yer think he'll marry yer, yer liddle fool, don't yer know sailors have one like you in every port!"

Vera flung herself onto her bed and sobbed into her pillow, the thought that her dad and step-mum had read Bill's letters to her was more than she could bear.

What on earth was she going to do, she thought, but determined, she resolved that she wouldn't stay here a moment longer than she had to.

The next day after Vera had told Ivy Newton she was expecting and swearing her to secrecy, she told her what her step-mother had said to her and Ivy told her she would take the day off work tomorrow and go with Vera to Hanworth Town Hall to see someone and make enquiries as to what she could do.

The clerk they saw at the town hall was extremely helpful and very sympathetic to Vera's plight, she had a list of mother and baby homes, nursing homes and such like and was able to telephone the different places to check if they had vacancies and find out if they would accept Vera and when. Luckily, one of the mother and baby homes did have a vacancy and because of her circumstances would take her right away, unfortunately, it was forty miles away just outside of Stratford Upon Avon and Vera had no idea how she would get there, but she was sure that by hook or by crook she would. The clerk a Mrs Thorburn booked a place for her and made all the arrangements with the 'Sitwell-Derwent Nursing Home' as it was called, Vera had two days to present herself otherwise she would lose her place there. Mrs Thorburn typed out a letter of introduction and gave it to Vera wishing her well. Vera and Ivy thanked her very much for all her help and left feeling more hopeful, even though Mrs Thorburn had told Vera that being at the home certainly wouldn't be a picnic, she would be expected to work and earn her keep until the time arrived when she would have her baby. She also said that unmarried mothers had a lot of pressure put on them to have their babies adopted. When Vera got back home she went straight to her room and began to pack her small suitcase as Ivy had come up with a brilliant suggestion. There was a dairy farm at the edge of the village and once a week the milk churns were collected and taken by lorry somewhere. Ivy said she would go and ask the farmer if the lorry went anywhere near Stratford Upon Avon and say she had relatives there that she needed to visit and she was hoping she could cadge a lift. Farmer Jim Ellis was a tall muscular man with a full head of curly ginger hair, he looked to be in his mid-fifties. He was wearing a cream and brown checked shirt which was slightly unbuttoned and showing a hairy chest, he had on a pair of baggy old brown corduroy trousers held up by braces. He smiled when he opened the door and saw this pretty young woman standing there.

"What can I be doin for ee then young woman?" he asked amiably.

"I hope you don't think I'm being cheeky but I live in the village and I was wondering if you could tell me where your milk lorry delivers your milk to," Ivy replied feeling herself blushing in embarrassment.

"N why would ee be wantin to know summat like that then?" he asked, bemused.

"Well an aunt of mine lives in Stratford Upon Avon and she's written to say that she's ill and would like me to go and look after her," she lied, blushing again.

"I see, well c'mon in and we'll see what we can do, he saw the reluctance on her face so he turned his head slightly and leaned back into the room a little and called out, Madge can you pop here a minute?"

Madge Ellis appeared behind him and he introduced her.

"This is mi wife, Madge," he said with a smile.

"Oh pleased to meet you," Madge said surprised.

"Invite the young woman in Madge, she wants some help from me," Jim said patting his wife's shoulder fondly, "I'll be back in a jiff."

The woman beckoned Ivy to come in and showed her into the kitchen where the most delicious smell of home made bread filled the air, "Sit down she said, would you like a cup of tea?

"That's very kind of you, yes please," Ivy said.

Mrs Ellis went over to the range, took the kettle and filled it with water and put it back on to boil. As she was doing that Jim Ellis came back into the room holding an envelope, handing it to Ivy he said.

"If you c'n be at yard gate by five o'clock t'morra morning you c'n have a lift pretty much all the way, just give Fred the note, n don't worry you'll be safe wi im he's a good chap!"

"Will there be room for my friend as well," Ivy asked sheepishly.

Mrs Ellis pours a cup tea, "Do you take sugar dear?"

"No, thank you," Ivy said, taking the cup of tea.

"Aye spose so," Jim said lighting a big briar pipe, "it's a big lorry n Fred'll enjoy the company I'm sure."

Ivy finished her cup of tea, she had enjoyed chatting to Madge and Jim who were really friendly 'down to earth' sorts. As she was leaving she thanked them again for their kindness in helping her and as she walked from the door saying goodbye, Madge said:

"Don't be a stranger now Ivy, anytime you're passing call in and I do hope your Auntie will be alright, bye bye."

Ivy had hated lying to them, but it was strange, she felt as if they had seen right through her, put two and two together and made five, thinking that perhaps it was Ivy herself who was in trouble. They couldn't have been more kind, bless them and Ivy felt sure she would visit them again.

Now she had to go straight to Vera and tell her the good news and tell her to get a good night's sleep as they had to be up at the crack of dawn and be at the farm gate by five o'clock.

Vera gasped as Ivy told her the news, she gave her a great big hug, thanking her and telling her that she was the best friend in the world.

Chapter 2

Fred Haynes was driving along the road towards the Ellis farm and was surprised to see two young women in his headlights standing by the five milk churns outside the gate, one of them had a suitcase as if she was off on her holidays. He brought 'Big Bertha' as he called his lorry, to a stop, switched off the engine and jumped down from the cab, making his way round the front of the lorry to where Vera and Ivy were standing. "Morning ladies," he said lifting the peak of his cap, "you goin sumware are you?"

"We hope so, Vera said handing him the sealed envelope that had the note in, Jim Ellis asked us to give you this."

Fred took the envelope and tore it open, but it was too dark for him to read the note inside so he opened the door of the cab, reached in and found his torch. He shone it on the note and said:

"Aah, looks like you young ladies have got yourselves a lift then, he took Vera's case and put it behind the seat, you climb in; I'll load the milk onto the lorry and we'll get going!" Ivy helped Vera up into the cab and then pulled herself up to sit beside her, they smiled at one another clasping their hands together, they were really cold as they had been stood waiting for at least half an hour, but the cab was quite warm and they would be on their way soon.

There were some loud bumps and metallic clangs as Fred loaded the milk churns onto the back of the wagon before he came and jumped into the driving seat with a cheerful grin. He held out his hand and shook both theirs and said, "This is nice, it's not often I have any company on my job." He noticed they were shivering and looked cold, so he reached behind the seats and surprisingly pulled out a fleecy blanket, "Here you are, tuck this over your legs, it's one I keep in here for when the missus comes with me into town sometimes." He watched them drape the blanket over their legs and said:

"There y'are, that's better init, giving them another broad grin, we'd better get on our way, the cab'll soon warm up once we get going," he turned the ignition key and the wagon shook and throbbed loudly into life.

"So, tell me where is it you want dropping off, ladies?"

"This is very kind of you Mr Haynes, we're going to a place called Hiddleton do you know it?"

"Yes I do, it's a few miles this side of Stratford, I go through there." Actually, it wasn't on Fred's route at all, it was five miles out of his way, but he didn't mention that to Vera and Ivy. How could he possibly leave two young women stranded out in the wilds on their own at the prey of God knows who might be on the road!

"I've a few pick ups to make on the way but all in all we should have you there in about three hours or so."

Vera and Ivy couldn't believe their luck, "Thank you, Mr Haynes," they said cheerfully in unison.

"I can't have you calling me that all the way, he said, just call me Fred." The two women smiled and thought what a nice man he was. They were guessing that he was in his mid to late forties. He was of medium height; solidly built and very muscular, probably as a result of the job he did with all its heavy lifting. He had sandy coloured hair that was a mass of soft curls with long sideburns and he was wearing a pair of faded navy overalls. He was a gentleman and managed to keep Vera and Ivy's spirits up throughout the journey with witty tales about his wife and family, despite the fact that the whole purpose of it wasn't a good one for Vera, she was scared and still reeling from the arguments and recriminations she had experienced with Flora and her dad, she didn't know how she was ever going to forgive them for the things they'd said and done, after all it wasn't as if they had led exemplary and blameless lives. When Vera was only eight and her mum Lily was lying upstairs terminally ill, her sister Flora who lived with them was having relations with her dad Nathaniel; after Lily died the two of them married, so Flora became Vera's stepmother.

Fred had been a Godsend, he was true to his word, they arrived in Hiddleton at eight-thirty, Fred had asked them where they wanted dropping off, so Ivy, thinking quickly said, "There's a pub in the village, that's where we're going, and then she realised that he might ask her what it was called so she added, its got a funny name, I can't remember it.

Fred smiled to himself and said, "Ok."

When they finally stopped outside a pub, Ivy saw that it was called 'The Unicorn'.

"That's it," she said, "that's the one, I knew it had a funny name!" Fred almost laughed aloud then, but thankfully he suppressed it.

Fred jumped down from the cab and went round to the passenger side to open the door and help Vera and Ivy out, he half climbed back in and reached out Vera's case and handed it to her. Shaking both of them by the hand he wished them both luck and said how nice it had been to have their company, he then got back in the lorry and drove away. Further up the road he stopped at the little transport cafe he knew to have his breakfast. This cafe did the best fry up for miles around and Fred always stopped here when he was in the area. While he was waiting for his bacon and egg, he sipped some hot tea from his cup, took the now crumpled envelope from his overall pocket, pulled out the note and read it again.

Dear Fred,

I know you won't mind doing this small favour for me. This young lass Ivy who lives in the village, came to the farm yesterday asking if the milk lorry went anywhere near Stratford as she needed to get there to visit a sick Aunt. When I told her it did she looked so relieved, I thought she was going to faint.

She's a nice lass and I suspect that she doesn't have a sick Aunt at all, but that she's in some sort of trouble, if you know what I mean; she needs to be away from the village for a while and get things sorted out.

Be a good chap and do this for me, and please don't mention this to anyone. There's a good drink in it for you when I next see you.

Thanks

Best Regards,

Jim.

Fred was only too pleased to have been able to help and hoped that Ivy was going to be alright, she certainly had a good friend in Vera, although she didn't exactly say a lot, he might have been forgiven for thinking that Vera was the one that was in trouble as she seemed anxious and on edge, but that was obviously her concern for her friends welfare. Anyway he wished them both all the best as it was not a good situation for any young girl to find herself in. He wondered if the father knew about the girl's plight, and if he did, where was he. He knew for certain that if he had ever put a girl in the family way that he wouldn't hesitate to marry her and save her from the humiliation of being an unmarried mother rather than be scorned and looked down on by family, neighbours and society in general. It was always the poor girl that paid the price, while the chap who was responsible for her being pregnant got away with his feckless behaviour, and some of them were serial offenders, who preyed on innocent vulnerable girls.

He would tell Jim Ellis the next time he saw him that he had delivered his charges safe and sound, and what nice girls he thought they both were, and he would enjoy having that drink with him as he's definitely a good bloke.

Chapter 3

Vera and Ivy walked a little way along the road looking for 'The Sitwell-Derwent Nursing Home', not knowing if they were going in the right direction or not their eyes were scanning both sides of the road in the hope they would see it. Vera put her case down on the pavement and stopped for a rest, just at the moment they saw a postman on his rounds over on the other side of the road. Ivy called out to him and waved.

"Yoo hoo, postman," having caught his attention she left Vera; went across to ask him where the home was. The man pointed up the road and said:

"It's not far, if you carry on down this road for a bit you'll see the war memorial on this side, take the next turn on your left by the church and it's down there on the right."

"Thank you ever so much," Ivy said, crossing the road back to Vera.

"He says it's not very far, it's up here by the church."

"Oh that's a relief," Vera replied, "at least we don't have to traipse for miles, I wonder what it'll be like?"

"I don't know Vera love, but I'm sure you'll make the best of it until you've had the baby, at least you're away from Flora and your dad. The sooner we get there and get you settled in the better!"

They followed the postman's directions and found the house

"Here it is then," Vera said," it's a big place isn't it?"

"Yes it is," Ivy replied.

The house was Georgian with tall rectangular windows, it was set back some distance from the road it had a large porch with white stone columns either side; three large stone steps led up to a black painted door that was flaking with peeling paint, there were pieces of masonry missing on the frontage making it look quite dilapidated. The most striking feature the house was an open balcony running along the front of the building on the first floor which had fancy railings and fretwork details. It must have been a very grand house once upon a time, but it looked a bit run down now.

They walked up the driveway past the overgrown lawns and shrubs; up the stone steps to the front door. Vera pushed the white button doorbell and they waited for someone to answer. Vera had butterflies in her tummy.

"You will come in with me Ivy," she asked with a worried look.

"Of course, I will, everything will be alright," Ivy replied as the door was pulled open.

In the doorway stood a stout very austere looking woman who looked to be in her sixties, her face had a pinched expression as though there was a permanent unpleasant smell under her nose and her clothes were all black apart from a white ruffled blouse. She looked both of them up and down very suspiciously and having spotted Vera's suitcase said with an officious tone:

"Which one of you is Vera Evans?"

"I am," Vera said nervously.

"Come in then, have you brought all your papers?"

"Yes, I have, they're in my case, can my friend come in with me?"

"She can, but she can only stay for a few minutes, we've got Doctors rounds shortly."

They walked into a large hallway with a wood parquet tiled floor and there was a polished cedar chiffonier against the wall and up ahead was a curved staircase. They were led by the woman up the sweeping staircase and to Vera's surprise they were shown into a dormitory with six metal hospital-style beds in it. It had never occurred to her that she would have to share a bedroom. Having overcome the initial shock of seeing the dormitory she was philosophical about it, rationalising that what did she think a nursing home would be like, if not like a hospital, what did she expect, a private room! She glanced at Ivy and gave a little grimace of disapproval.

"Here you are this will be your bed," the woman said touching the metal rail at the bottom of the one at the end by the door, "my name is Mrs Folliett, I'm the Matron, I'll be back in five minutes to show your friend out."

Vera, let Mrs Folliett leave before she whispered to Ivy:

"She thinks she's Queen Victoria, she never so much as cracked a smile, throwing her head back and putting her nose in the air Vera then mimicked a regal sounding voice and said:

"We are not amused," they both burst out giggling and it briefly took away a lot of the nervous tension that they were both feeling. Ivy suddenly embraced Vera and said:

"We haven't got much time lovey, so we'd better say our goodbyes, I promise I'll write to you every week, keep your chin up and don't forget to let me know how you're doing."

"Oh Ivy, love," Vera said feeling her bottom lip quiver and tears filling her eyes, "I don't know what I would have done without you, you've been such a good friend, I'm going to really miss you."

They were both crying now and Ivy said:

"I'll miss you too, I hope everything goes well for you, keep in touch; take care of yourself and you must write to Bill; tell him he's going to be a father and where you are. She leaned forward hugging her and kissing her on both cheeks, then turned away as she was saying, "Goodbye Vera."

"Goodbye Ivy, Vera replied Thanks for everything love."

Just as Ivy reached the door it opened and the Matron appeared, "I'll show you out," she said.

As they were going down the stairs Ivy said to her:

"She's been through a very bad time the last few weeks a..."

The woman cut Ivy's remarks short with, "I'm not interested in what she's been through before she came here, I'm only concerned with what happens in this place!" By this time they had reached the bottom of the stairs; the woman opened the door, stood aside to let Ivy go past and said, "Good Morning to you."

Ivy was so incensed but she bit her tongue as she didn't want to bring any trouble to Vera as a result of her being rude to this woman. She put her shoulders back; held her head high and quickly marched out of the door, down the steps, along the driveway; it wasn't until she reached the pavement and knew that she was hidden by a tall bush that she bristled with indignation and said out loud, "The old bag!"

As she made her way to the railway station she wondered how Vera would get on with the Matron and hoped she would make friends with the other women in the home. She loved Vera and felt so sorry that she had fallen for a baby and ended up having to come to a place like this.

The next few days and weeks were a real eye-opener for Vera, it was all so different from anything she had experienced before. She was medically examined for venereal disease, syphilis, parasites and nits; asked questions about her medical history and general health. She was told that The National Assistance Board could only meet part of the charges to pay for her board and lodging so she would have to work up to her confinement to earn her keep. She was made to feel like she was a criminal who was being punished for her wrongdoing. If she'd had any choice in the matter she would have been out of the door like a shot and not thought twice about it, but she didn't have a choice so she told herself to just accept the situation; do her best to fit in and get along with the other girls. It was hard, there was a strict regime that took a lot of getting used to, she wasn't used to communal, institutionalised living. There were some lighter moments though, she found that she had a good rapport with most of the girls and during recreational periods they would tell each other tales about their past experiences and have a good old laugh together. One particular girl told a story about a girl at school who had a really bad lisp and how the other girls used to make her say things that accentuated her speech problem so they could laugh at her, you know how children can be so cruel?

One girl even went so far as to write a special piece that she got the girl to recite for them in the playground. When the girl who was telling them this story recited the actual piece mimicking how the poor girl spoke, it was greeted with hysterical laughter from them all. This is what she said.

"Thum people thay I lithp but I can't pertheive it mythelf unleth I thay pea thoup, thoft thoap or thomething thimilar!"

Vera had joined in the laughter but later found herself having a real pang of guilt thinking about the poor girl who was made to say it and how she must have had a real complex about it. Still, it had served the purpose of lightening the lives of the girls before they went back to their chores! There was a total of twenty-four girls in the home in all and they were housed in four separate dormitories on two floors of the house. Vera was in the first floor dormitory and she considered herself lucky because the girls in there seemed a nice bunch. There was a maternity unit for when the time came for them to give birth and there was an essential laundry for all the washing of clothes, bedding and the obvious dirty nappies. Vera was glad she didn't work in there instead she had the privilege of working in the kitchen helping the cook, the term privilege was used loosely as some days Vera certainly didn't feel that it was, it was hard work. She had to get up at 6am, get washed and dressed; brush her teeth and hair then make sure her bed was made neatly and her personal things were all put away out of sight in her bedside locker, generally everywhere needed to be spotless as there was a daily inspection by Matron. Vera would then go down to the kitchen, her first job would be to set a fire under the big copper that stood in the corner and light it as this was the only source of daily hot water for the kitchen. She would then begin peeling the vegetables for the main meal that she had taken from the storeroom the day before under Mrs Maguire's instruction. Mrs Maguire was a friendly soul, she was a short plump woman with a real Irish 'brogue' and quite ladylike in her demeanour. When she first met her Vera had found it difficult to understand her lilting accent especially if she spoke quickly as she tended to do. Although it was tiring working in the kitchen and long hours Vera worked hard as she wanted to be kept on there and not be sent to do laundry work. Apparently, it had transpired that her arrival at the home had coincided with the previous kitchen helps time for confinement so that turned out to be a lucky break for Vera.

"At around ten o'clock," Mrs Maguire would say to Vera. "Ahh put the kettle on lass n we'll have a cup of tea."

This ritual was deliberately timed, as it was the same time that they had doctors' rounds in the maternity wing upstairs, and Mrs Maguire knew that Matron would be taken up with that.

"The less she knows the better, Mrs Maguire said, what the eye don't see the heart don't grieve," and she gave a little chuckle. She didn't usually get friendly with the helpers that came to work with her in the kitchen, she hadn't liked the last girl as her personal hygiene wasn't up to standard, but she felt there was something special about Vera that she liked, she was a good worker; they seemed to have an affinity. So much so that Mrs Maguire had confided in Vera that her first name was Bridie and that she could call her that when they were alone, but she told Vera on no account was she to call her by her first name in anyone else's hearing. So when they had a work break Vera called her Bridie and it gave them a special bond. It was during one of these breaks that Bridie had asked Vera how she came to be in the home, not the obvious reason of course, but the other circumstances that had brought her there. Vera had told her about Bill being in the navy and the way that her family had treated her.

"Ah, a sailor is he, t be sure," she had said.

Vera had explained that she hoped when he came home from sea that they would get married.

"Ah it'll all work out fa yus, don't ya go frettin, t be sure."

Vera had noticed how Bridie had the habit of starting a lot of her sentences with ah and ending them with t be sure, it was just the way she expressed herself. One morning after Vera had made the tea and she and Bridie were sat enjoying ten minutes break, she took a letter from out of her overall pocket that she had written to Bill the previous evening and gave it to Bridie to read as she wanted to know it was alright before she sent it.

Bridie said, "Are you sure you want me to read such a private letter lass?"

"Oh it's alright, there are no lovey dovey bits in it," Vera said. Bridie took the letter from Vera, put on her spectacles and began to read it.

Chapter 4

My Dearest Bill,

I hope this letter finds its way to you and that you are keeping well. I have been meaning to write for a while but so much as happened since the last time I wrote to you, when I was at home. I know you must be very busy as I haven't had a reply to my last letter yet. I don't know where to begin really and I know however I say it it's going to come as a shock to you but I'm pregnant and having your baby. As you can see by my address I'm in a nursing home for unwed mothers, I've been here three months now.

Ivy helped me to get here, she has been a real friend to me, my only friend. I don't know how I would have managed but for her. Anyway this is where I will have the baby as they wouldn't let me stay at home. Flora and my dad were dreadful to me and said and did things that I will never forgive them for, Flora even told me they had read your letters, I don't know how they could be so cruel and unfeeling. They said I'd brought shame on myself and them because I'm not married, I've never felt so wretched in all my life Bill. This place is a bit like a prison but I get along with most of the girls in here alright, well we're all in the same boat aren't we so we've got to make the best of it. I feel sorry for one young girl here though, she was raped by a gang of men, she will have her baby adopted apparently there's a young childless couple want it. I thank my lucky stars that my baby was conceived in love and I know who its father is, What an awful thing to happen to the poor girl. Under no circumstances will my baby be given up for adoption, I intend to keep it. They do put pressure on you to give your baby up though because they get money for them, they say you can't keep them because you're not married and can't bring it up right if you don't have a husband. They snatch them away from the mothers sometimes too, they don't have a say in it, it's so cruel. I love you Bill and I want us to be happy together I hope you feel the same. I would hate you to think that I'm trying to force you into anything, I hope you feel the way I do and together we can make a home for us and our child. I can't wait until we see each other again and I look forward to hearing from you. Whatever your answer is I will always love you. Please write back soon. Take care, I think about you all the time and really miss you.

All my fondest love,
Vera. xxx

As Bridie read the letter her heart went out to Vera and she was moved to tears, she clasped hold of Vera's hand and said:

"Aah mi poor lass, send him the letter, unless he has a hard black heart, I'm sure he will want ta marry yer, an then I know everyting al be alright."

They were both sniffling, but Bridie blew her nose and said:

"Don't take on so, c'mon now finish peelin dem vegetables. Bridie resolved to tell Vera all about her own experience of motherhood and everything that had happened as a result of it, but she didn't want to tell her yet, there would be time enough later if her plan worked out the way that she wanted it to, She had warmed to Vera from the first day she had come to work in kitchen with her and she soon discovered she was polite, considerate and good-natured as well as being a good willing worker. She realised how much she had brightened her life in a way she regarded her as her own daughter and would be glad when the time came for Vera to be confined, have her baby and leave the home. There were many things she had to sort out first before she could bring her plans to fruition.

Vera was pleased that she had shown the letter to Bridie, she felt now that it was a good letter; it would give Bill a strong insight as to her situation and what she was going through. She hoped she wouldn't have to wait long for a reply as it felt more than ever that her life seemed to be on hold.

Chapter 5

It was, in fact, three worrying weeks that Vera had to wait before she was handed a letter by Matron while she was in the kitchen working, she slipped the letter into her overall pocket until Matron had gone, she appeared to be hanging on in the hope Vera would open it there and then so she could hear what it was all about. Vera had seen Bridie give her a sly wink and a negative little shake of her head behind Matron's back as a caution to wait until later. As soon as she had gone Bridie steered Vera by her shoulders over to a chair and said:

"Aah Cmon lass sit yerself down and read what he has to say ta ya, I'll put the kettle on." t b sure.

Vera nervously opened the letter, her hands were trembling as she started to read.

My Dearest Vera,

When I received your letter I was so sorry to hear about all the things that had been happening to you. I had so many mixed emotions, initial shock, then sheer joy at the prospect of becoming a father, madness and anger at what you have been going through. I can't tell you how sorry I am that I haven't been able to be there supporting you through this very difficult and lonely time. I am currently serving as a sub-mariner off the coast of Newfoundland, Nova Scotia. I have requested that as soon as we return to England whether I can be granted a compassionate discharge from the navy so that I can come home and we can be married, but this, unfortunately, won't be for sometime, very likely several months. Rest assured though love as soon as I can I'll be there. I am disgusted at the way your family have treated you, but so grateful to Ivy for being a real friend in need for you. I hope they are treating you well at the home and that you and our future baby are well? I have enclosed ten pounds so that you can buy things you might need like toiletries, baby clothes, etc. We will, of course, have to think about where we are going to live, I certainly don't want to live with your folks after the way they treated you. The only thing I can think of is that as soon as I'm discharged I could find a job that has accommodation with it, but I can sort that out later. I don't want you worrying about anything, you just take care of yourself and the baby. I love you and am always thinking about you, things will work out once we are together again, we can start our new life together, the three of us.

All My Fondest Love Darling,
Yours Always,
Bill.

Vera couldn't believe the loving words that Bill had written to her, she was half expecting him to tell her that she would have to manage on her own, and that he wanted to stay in the Navy. She was so relieved to know that he felt exactly the same way that she did and was going to accept his responsibility for their baby. There was many a sailor that would have stayed at sea and let a poor unfortunate girl fend for herself, but not her Bill.

When Vera had finished reading it she burst into tears, causing Bridie to rush over to comfort her, fearing the worst.

"Aah there, there, never mind lass, Bridie said, sitting next to her and putting her arm around Vera's shoulder, "it'll be alright sweetheart, t be sure."

Vera passed the letter over to Bridie and as she read it she began to smile, and when she had finished she said.

"There y'ar, didn't I tell ya not ta worry, ya couldn't wish for better than that. I don't know about you, but I need that cup o tea now."

They sat together over their cup of tea and talked about Vera's prospects for the future now that she knew Bill was going to stick by her, she was already three months gone, so she would be at least six months into her pregnancy by the time she saw Bill again. She confided in Bridie how worried she was that they would have everything in place for when the time came for Vera to give birth; leave the home, they would have to find somewhere to live, and a job for Bill.

"We need a miracle really," Vera said!

"Aah, well now miracles do happen sometimes, I'll light another candle for yer," Bridie said softly.

For the rest of that day Vera was on cloud nine she couldn't wait to tell Wendy her news and show her the letter, she was her roommate and had the bed next to her and she had been the only one of the women that she had become reasonably close to. She spoke to the other girls in her dorm and was civil to them but that was as far as it went most of the time. Some of them just wanted to keep themselves to themselves, have their babies and get out of the place. Unfortunately, Vera didn't quite get the reaction she had expected when she showed Wendy Bill's letter, Oh, she said she was pleased for her but Vera felt she detected a hint of jealousy, perhaps she was a bit naive and insensitive in showing her the letter, it might have been better to have kept it to herself.

Vera was right, during the next few weeks she noticed how Wendy was a bit aloof with her and didn't really want to engage in their little chats like she used to so she didn't push herself on her, she thought she'd wait until Wendy wanted her company.

Several days later just as she was going downstairs to start work in the kitchen she met Matron coming out of her office, and Matron said sharply.

"Evans come into my office, I want a word with you."

Vera wondered what was the matter and whether she had done anything wrong, she stood in front of Matron's desk and Matron said with a sneer on her face.

"If you think a letter from your sailor boyfriend is going to stop your baby being put up for adoption, you're sadly mistaken Miss, we require that our babies are placed in stable loving homes."

Vera was absolutely devastated by Matron's remark and for one moment was stunned into silence, but then she bristled at the cruelty of her remark and let fly.

"Let's get one thing straight shall we, this child that I'm carrying is not one of your babies to be sold to the highest bidder, it's *my* baby and it will have a loving stable home, I'll see to that, will that be all Matron."

"No it will not be all miss high and mighty, I, the doctors and the board of governors decide what happens to the babies that are born in this home, not you, you want to be very careful that you don't find yourself thrown out onto the street and end up in the workhouse, you ungrateful little baggage."

"Don't you call me a baggage, who do you think you are?"

"You will find out very soon who I am," Matron said imperiously, "now get on with your work."

Vera was shaking as she walked out of the office, she noticed a group of women had gathered and been listening to the altercation that had taken place. Wendy was one of them and Vera knew by her face that she had told Matron about her letter, but she was not going to give her the satisfaction of acknowledging her.

She went downstairs to the kitchen, worrying now that Matron was going to be vindictive and take revenge on her for speaking out by getting her thrown out onto the street. She got on with her work, lighting a fire under the copper and making a start on the vegetables to try to take her mind of what had just happened. Later when Bridie arrived she saw Vera was all red-eyed and had obviously been crying so she asked her, "Whatever's the matter lass?"

When Vera poured out in between her tears what had gone on earlier, Bridie said.

"Aah well that's it then the time has come!"

Vera didn't know what she meant and looked at Bridie puzzled.

"Come and sit down here beside me Vera, I've been meaning to tell you something for a while now."

Vera sat down and Bridie began to tell her what she had wanted her to know when she felt the time was right. Circumstances had now decreed that this was that time! Bridie didn't really know where to start, but she began anyway.

"Aah mi little darlin, I'm afraid I've been keeping a secret from you!"

"A secret, I don't understand, what do you mean Bridie?"

"Listen darlin, I'll tell you all about it."

She began to tell Vera some amazing things that hardly seemed possible. Bridie said that she had taken the job at the home not because she needed to work to earn money, but because she wanted to do good and give something back. She had chosen the home because it was a cause dear to her heart and borne of a personal experience she had had when she was a young girl; she said that she would tell her more about that later.

Bridie went on to explain that she was a woman of private means and was from a wealthy family in Ireland, Vera's jaw dropped in surprise and Bridie continued.

I had it in my mind when I came here that I would just use my skills as a cook to make the lives of the poor women forced to come here a little more bearable, but I hadn't met you then Vera. It was after you came to work alongside me that a sweet plan began to form in my mind that I hoped you would allow me to make happen. I was going to reveal my plan to you when you had gone into the maternity unit and would have your baby. But what happened to you today has meant that I have to tell you all this now. Be assured that I want you to have the best pregnancy and the best delivery possible and to know that your baby is safe and will not be snatched from you. I think you realise now that that is in jeopardy here. If you will trust me as a friend, I will tell you what I want you to do.

"Will you trust me and allow me to be your friend Vera?"

"I already feel you are a friend, Bridie, since I've worked in the kitchen I've felt a bond between us, you are the only friend I have in this place."

"Then listen, Vera, I want you to be a brave girl, because in a few minutes you and I are going to walk out of this place with our heads held high and you can come to live with me. I will provide private nursing care for you and your baby; you will be my companion. Bill can come and join us when he is able and then you can decide what you are going to do. Now, how do you like that idea, are you in agreement with it?"

Vera sat there speechless, then she said:

"I can't believe it. I don't know what to say."

"Vera the only thing you have to say is yes and then your troubles will all be over and you can escape from this place."

Vera took a deep breath and said:

"Yes Bridie, thank you; she leaned forward and kissed her on the cheek, what do I do now!"

"You go up and get your suitcase and belongings, come back downstairs and we will go to see Matron, seeing the look of trepidation on Vera's face Bridie said.

"Don't worry, let me do all the talking, you just enjoy the show, off ya go wit ya, t be sure."

Vera went quickly upstairs and started packing her case, while she was doing it, who should walk in but Wendy. She saw what Vera was doing and said:

"What are you doing, are you going somewhere?

Vera said, "Not that it's any of your business, Wendy, but yes, I'm going home, goodbye," and Vera held her head up and walked out of the dormitory and down to Matron's office.

As she descended the stairs Vera saw Bridie waiting for her outside Matron's office, Bridie took her by the arm and knocked determinedly on the door.

"Come in," Matron said.

When she saw Bridie and Vera standing there she was quite taken aback, and she noticed that Vera had her suitcase with her. She looked at Vera and said."

"Where do you think you're going. girl?"

Vera didn't answer, Bridie did.

"She's coming with me."

"What, don't be ridiculous, she can't poss…

Bridie cut her off short and said:

"I'm not being ridiculous Woman, She is coming with me, here's what I would like you to do. You tell me how much Vera's care here has cost to date, I will write you a cheque for that amount and we will be on our way. Any money owing to me you can keep in lieu of notice."

"What, you're going to write me a cheque," Matron said sarcastically.

"Yes that's right, Bridie said taking a cheque book from her handbag along with a posh fountain pen, who do I make it out to?"

"This is all most irregular, Matron said huffing and puffing, make it out to The Sitwell-Derwent Nursing Home while I find the figures." As Matron was looking she said:

"Of course you realise that she will be your responsibility now, we won't be held accountable should anything happen to her."

"Aah I do realise that thank you, she will have the best of care t be sure."

When Bridie had written out the cheque and signed it she tore it out; gave it to Matron, put the book back in her handbag closed the clasp, looked straight at Matron and said:

"Oh, by the way, I think you should get your apron on, go down to the kitchen and cook the dinner."

Matron visibly snarled as Bridie and Vera dissolved into a fit of giggles and left.

Chapter 6

They walked arm in arm to the nearest telephone box and Bridie called a taxi to take them home. Vera couldn't remember a time when she had felt so excited, it was like a big adventure. In the taxi, the two of them talked and laughed for the whole journey. Vera said she could still see the look on Matron's face when Bridie said *You'd better put your apron on and cook the dinner*. It was priceless. When they reached Bridie's house Vera couldn't believe it when the taxi drove through some wrought iron gates and up a long drive past trees and grass with shrubs and landscaped flower beds to a massive looking house with large bay windows and a grand entrance with stone columns, Vera thought she should pinch herself to see if she was dreaming.

"Here we are Bridie said as the taxi stopped on the shingle drive outside the entrance, home sweet home," she paid the driver and Bridie led the way into a massive hallway that had beautiful brightly-coloured mosaic floor tiles in geometric patterns. There was a large crystal chandelier hanging from the ceiling and a sweeping staircase up ahead.

"Well, what do you think of your new home," Bridie asked smiling at Vera, "will it do?"

"I can't believe it, Bridie, it's like I'm in a dream, it's beautiful."

"I'll show you to your room and then we'll have a nice cup of tea and talk about all the things we're going to do."

The bedroom that Bridie showed Vera into was huge, it was plushly carpeted in a pale green colour, had a double bed with pale pink bedlinen: a great big mahogany wardrobe with barley twist columns down the side. It was at the rear of the house which faced south and the walk-in bay window which had full-length pale green velvet curtains overlooked a large lawned garden, in the summer it would be absolutely wonderful to wake up with the sun streaming in and to be able to look out over the garden.

Vera was so happy she flung her arms around Bridie kissed her cheeks and thanked her for all her kindness and for liberating her from that horrible place that she likened to Dickens' 'Bleak House'.

"We are going to be such good friends my dear Bridie said, and I can't wait to tell you some of the things we are going to be doing over the next few months in preparation for your new baby's arrival."

They went back downstairs to a lovely kitchen that had a pine dresser with pretty crockery on it and a pine refectory table. Bridie made them a pot of tea which she put on a tray along with some assorted biscuits and she showed the way into a cosy lounge with a large marble fireplace, it was tastefully furnished in gold and beige shades with a three-piece suite, an onyx coffee table and a large bookcase filled with books.

"Well now, what do think of this young lady, Bridie said with a look of glee on her face, tomorrow after we've had breakfast we get ourselves ready to go out and into Birmingham for the day to do some shopping, we need to get you some maternity clothes, we need to order things for the nursery." As she said that Bridie realised that she hadn't shown Vera the room that was going to be the nursery which was next to Vera's bedroom.

"How silly of me, I forgot, I didn't show you the room next to yours that will be the nursery, I'll show you it after we've had our cup o tea, I'm sure you'll like it.

Vera suddenly blurted out, "You've already been so kind to me Bridie, I don't know, how I can ever repay you, I can only do a bit of shopping as Bill sent me ten pounds and that's all I've got."

"Aah Vera lass you don't need to be a frettin about money or how ya will repay me, it isn't necessary, just you humour a woman who wants to make sure you have the best of everything."

"I'm feeling a bit overwhelmed by all of this and everything that's happened today, I don't know what I've done to warrant such kindness from you."

"Aah I know it must have come as a bit of a shock ta ya lass t be sure, but all I ask is that ya humour a woman who for her own reasons felt she wanted ta help ya, when you've settled in, I'm going to tell you why I've chosen to do so, is that alright?"

"Yes, ok," Vera said submissively.

"Right c'mon then Bridie said, let me show you the nursery."

They went upstairs and into Vera's bedroom, and Bridie unlocked a door into an adjoining room. Vera had hardly noticed that there was a door or even thought about where it led to. The room was the same size as the bedroom with a large window, it was completely empty apart from an easy chair in a rosy pink 'Dralon' fabric and a single wooden chair. All of the paintwork was white, the walls had a pretty wallpaper with bunny rabbits all over it in pink and blue tones and the carpet was a creamy beige colour.

"I hope you like this Vera, Bridie said searchingly?"

"Like it, Vera almost squealed with delight, it's adorable."

"Aah, I'm so glad that ya like it, I thought it might be a bit too pink but we can add some blue touches later if needs be."

Later that day Bridie asked Vera to come and sit with her in the lounge and she began to tell her about her life in Ireland when she was growing up. It all sounded so idyllic, she had lived in Enniskillen, county Fermanagh, Northern Ireland, her father was a wealthy shipping magnate and she was an only child. Bridie's mother died when she was just sixteen and her father was left to look after her, sadly he died two years later. Her dear father, a staunch Catholic man had bequeathed her a substantial inheritance which included 'Chalfont' the family home, which was a large picturesque mansion set in several acres of grounds. He had been a good father to her, she had found his love to be unconditional; although shocked and disappointed, he did not judge her when as a young girl of seventeen, a year after the death of her mother she became pregnant. She had fallen in love with a young man that she had met at a society ball, he was ruggedly handsome with dark wavy hair, a cleft chin and a broad engaging smile. His name was Charles McCollum and he had charmed her from the moment he had asked her to dance. Unfortunately, when the young man in question discovered Bridie's plight he told her that he did not want to be trapped into marriage as he did not love her; he was embarking on an extensive tour of Europe with his fiancé and she was not to try to contact him as he was in no way responsible for her predicament. Before Bridie began to 'show' her father had provided her with a house in Ballymena, County Antrim which was far enough away to ensure that Bridie's secret remained just so. Through the family physician he recruited a nurse/companion to look after her until the child was born, he was the only person that her father had confided in and he was sworn to secrecy. Bridie's father had insisted that the child be adopted as he refused to allow his daughter's life to be blighted by a mistake that would mean she would have to bring up an illegitimate child on her own. The staff were told that Bridie was going to live with an Aunt in England and be her companion, she would accompany her on trips abroad and get to see something of the world. A lot of preparation and packing was done in readiness for Bridie's journey with staff fussing and enthusing about what a big adventure it was for a young girl and such a wonderful opportunity. There was a big show made of Bridie's departure when all of her trunks had been loaded onto the car that had been hired along with the chauffeur, all of the staff had lined up outside the house to say goodbye and wave her off. She felt terrible about all the lies and subterfuge but she knew it was a necessary evil in order to keep her secret safe and keep shame from the family. The house in Ballymena was absolutely perfect as well as all the arrangements that had been made for her.

Bridie's father had been meticulously generous in his provision for her, her nurse was kind, knowledgably experienced and efficient and she couldn't have wished for a better nurse companion to bring her baby into the world. Moira prepared Bridie for the emotions involved in giving her baby up for adoption and she explained that as soon as the child was delivered it would be kept apart from her so that she would not see it and not be able to form a bond with it. As soon as possible after that, the couple who had already been chosen to receive the child through an adoption agency would be given it. Despite the circumstances, Bridie said that her pregnancy was a pleasant one and the delivery was comparatively easy. She gave birth to a healthy baby and was not told if it was a boy or a girl or any other details concerning the child and she had been told previously that she was not to ask for any information, only to be glad that the experience was over and she could now get on with living the life she wanted. Bridie said that despite all the loving practical advice she was given it did not prepare her for the emotions and feelings she had, the sense of loss that she felt after she had given birth, it was as though her baby had died and she was grieving for it. Vera had tears running down her face listening to Bridie's story but she wiped them away and listened as Bridie continued. She said that as hard as her father's decision was at the time, on reflection later Bridie had seen the wisdom of it. She had eventually met a young man called Connor Maguire and they fell in love and married, they had lived at 'Chalfont' until he joined the army and unfortunately was killed at Dunkirk, they didn't have any children which was a deep regret for her. Bridie then decided because of its associated memories that she would sell the family home and move to England to start a new life. It was sold and the small staff that remained who had been employed by the family for years, which consisted of a cook, a housekeeper, a parlour maid and a gardener were all 'looked after' and given a generous sum of money for their loyal service along with glowing references to help them secure other employment.

This decision had been somewhat influenced by the fact that her father had been on trips to England on several occasions and he had told her how beautiful it was, especially the county of Warwickshire which he had loved. He said it was steeped in history and its Elizabethan buildings and Warwick Castle were magnificent. He had shown her photographs of Warwick, Stratford Upon Avon and Leamington Spa which she thought were lovely. When she came to England she had spent weeks sightseeing and had been drawn to Stratfords beauty and history so decided that this was where she wanted to buy a property. She looked at lots of houses and finally came to see this one, she knew instantly it was the one she wanted, although it was quite large with five bedrooms and surrounded by fairly extensive grounds.

After the pleasure of making all the decisions as to the interior design of the place, which involved choosing colour schemes, furniture, carpets and curtains that were to her liking and taste, she then felt that it wasn't enough to just have it for herself and rattle around in it. She thought of a way that she would be able to make it of use to the community. She felt that the best way for her to do that would be to join The Women's Institute and then she could open her house up for groups to use, it would also be a good way for her to socialise and make friends. This proved to be extremely interesting and rewarding as she became quite involved in the 'WI's different activities and began to take a real interest in cooking, she found that she really enjoyed following and adapting recipes and eventually felt that she could apply this knowledge to help others as she was quite a competent cook. Her first thoughts were of finding a volunteer opportunity somewhere, but these were few and far between, so then she started looking at local job opportunities and it wasn't long until she saw this one placed in the Warwick Advertiser:

Cook Wanted for small Nursing Home for Unmarried Mothers.
Must be able to cook basic nutritional meals for up to 26, kitchen help provided for vegetable preparation and cleaning.
Applications in writing to Mrs Folliett, Matron
The Sitwell -Derwent Nursing Home
19 Tiddington Road
Stratford Upon Avon

Bridie said she had applied and to her surprise was asked to go for an interview.

She had disliked the Folliett woman who was the 'Matron' almost immediately as her manner was arrogant and condescending but considering that she was told there would not be much contact between them unless there was a problem that Matron had to deal with, when she was offered the job, she took it.

"Aah n here we are lass, the rest is history, after working in the home for several months I had this flash of inspiration that told me I could give the same kind of help that I had received to a young girl in trouble. When I had worked with you for a while Vera me darlin, I knew that girl was you."

Vera and Bridie embraced and Bridie said.

"Now do you see why I brought you out of that place, we're kindred spirits Vera and I can give you and the baby a better chance in life!"

They were both crying now and Vera said.

"Oh Bridie love, you've been through some terrible times,"

"Aah that's true darlin t be sure, but these are better times for both of us now."

The rest of that day seemed to fly by until it was time to get ready for bed. Bridie kindly ran a bath for Vera; gave her a kiss goodnight and said:

"There's a nice fluffy towel, a dressing gown, some bath cubes and a bar of Yardleys lavender soap on the side for you, I'm just across the hallway if you need me at all, goodnight Vera, sleep well."

"Goodnight Bridie, thank you for everything."

Vera prepared her bath by crumbling a 'Morny' bath cube into it and swirling the water around so that it dissolved, there was a heady fragrance of lily of the valley, she stepped into the sweet-smelling water lowering herself down into it until the water was lapping gently under her chin; she lay soaking in its luxury, soaping and rinsing herself then stepping out and towelling her clean silky skin dry. Wrapping a towel around her head and slipping into the soft cotton dressing gown she cleaned the bath then walked into her new bedroom. She rubbed her hair dry and climbed into her sumptuously comfortable bed, thoughts were just whirling around in her head and for what must have been two hours or more she lay there trying to take stock of it all, until, worn out she finally succumbed to sleep.

She woke up the next morning feeling so rested after a really good nights sleep, the best nights sleep she'd had for a long time, a dormitory atmosphere wasn't always conducive to restful slumber, there was always something going on, talking, bickering, loud snoring, someone having a nightmare, Vera had seen all that and more. She gave a good lazy stretch and yawned wondering what today had in store. She remembered the things Bridie had told her the day before and she felt such love and gratitude for the woman, she had been through so much. She had said just before they went to bed that they were going shopping in Birmingham and that she was in for a lot more pleasant surprises. Vera had never been into the city before and was really excited about it.

"Aah good morning ta ya mi darlin, n how ar ya feelin," Bridie said when she saw her?

"Wonderful, Vera said, I've had the best sleep ever, but who wouldn't in a bed as comfortable as that."

"N what would ya like for ya breakfast lass, bacon, egg?"

"That would be lovely, thank you Bridie, but can I help I'm not used to being spoiled like this?"

"Aah no, a little spoiling won't hurt ya at the moment, t be sure, but I'll let you do the washing up, Bridie said with a chuckle.

When Bridie brought breakfast to the table it turned out to be Bacon, egg, beans and brown soda bread.

"Ther'yar you tuck into that lass, and we should be making a list of things you and the baby will need. As they ate, Vera was relishing every mouthful as she listened to Bridie's plans.

Vera had never eaten Irish soda bread before but she found it tasted delicious, she guessed it was some of Bridie's home baking.

"As soon as we've had our breakfast you can go n get ready, I've ordered a car for ten o'clock so that gives us plenty of time, I've made a little list of most of the things I think we need, if you think of anything else don't hesitate to tell me, ere yah, take a look, Bridie said as she passed the list to Vera?"

"A little list, I should think this will empty the shop, Vera said amazed, surely I won't need all this?"

"Aah ya will, ya will t be sure, and probably more besides."

She thanked Bridie for the lovely breakfast, and said, "I'll go and wash up, then I'll get ready."

Chapter 7

Vera came down looking very pretty in a navy blue wool dress.

"Aah very smart me darlin t be sure, the car will be here soon."

"Oh thank you, Vera said feeling excited, that's a lovely suit you're wearing.

"Thank you, Vera, aah now let me see, have I got everything," looking in her handbag she checked that everything was there, "that's fine, aah we'er going to have a grand day," she said sounding as excited as Vera.

Vera was fascinated by the city it was so crowded with people rushing about frantically here, there and everywhere, it made her feel quite dizzy watching them. The car journey had been very pleasant and comfortable and she and Bridie had talked about the shopping list and amazingly, somehow a few more items were added to it.

The chauffeur dropped them off outside the main entrance of Lewis's department store at the bottom of Corporation Street, Bridie had told him to pick them up at the same place in four hour's time which would give them time to do all their shopping and have a bite of lunch. They walked into the store and made their way up to the baby department on the second floor, the selection of goods was out of this world, everything you could possibly want from bootees and baby grows to lace frilled rocking cradles, cots and luxury prams. Bridie beckoned an assistant and told her that she would be making a large number of purchases on her store account and would welcome some help in bringing it all together on the shop floor so that it could be made ready for delivery to her address. She didn't want to be traipsing around the shops loaded with lots of shopping bags.

Together they had chosen a 'Silver Cross' coach pram in black with chrome fittings which the salesman said was *"The Rolls Royce of Prams"* They purchased a white wood cot a rocking cradle, a baby bath on a stand, they had baby grows and packets of cotton nappies, so much stuff in fact that Vera had completely lost track of what they had got.

Bridie gave the counter assistant all her details, the purchases were added to her account and would be delivered the day after tomorrow.

Bridie took Vera into a lovely little cafe for some lunch that she said she always used when she came to Birmingham and they were both glad of a sit down.

"Aah we did well didn't we, t be sure?"

"Yes we certainly did," Vera replied, "it felt marvellous choosing all those things, I've never bought so much in all my life, I can't thank you enough Bridie, I'm so grateful my love."

Aah, it's my pleasure darlin," Bridie said looking pleased.

Their lunch of leek and potato soup and buttered roll was very nice and sufficiently filling and set them up for continuing with more shopping. Bridie took Vera into ladies dress shop and bought her a couple of outfits, a cream linen suit and a day dress in a pretty floral pattern. They moved in and out of many other shops where they purchased numerous things, including a couple of maternity smocks.

They were both nearly dead on their feet by the time they had walked back to the car, which was already waiting to take them back home.

Vera's ankles were very swollen with all the walking she had done so Bridie said that she would need to put her feet up when they got home. The next day they were still as bad so she continued to rest and was able to write a long letter to Bill telling him everything that had been happening and how happy she was to be away from the home and living with Bridie. She told him that Bridie had said that this would be his home too when he came out of the navy until they decided what it was they wanted to do. Bill wrote back and said how worried he had been and was so pleased that Vera was out of that place. He said that he was so grateful to Bridie for taking care of her and what a kind, generous woman she was.

The days and weeks that followed leading up to Vera having her baby were pleasant and trouble free. Bridie couldn't do enough for her, the nursery was all set up and looked like something out of a womens magazine, it was wonderful. They had arranged with an agency for a nurse/midwife to look after Vera when her time came, her name was Ginny Parsons and she could not have been more highly recommended.

Vera's waters finally broke on Tuesday, December 23rd 1947, the midwife was called and Vera went into labour, Ginny arrived and took care of her assuring Vera that she was doing marvellously and that all was going well. She helped Vera deliver a healthy baby boy of eight pounds four ounces in weight, he was blessed with a full head of dark brown hair. Vera had already decided that if the baby was a boy she would call him Jake, if it had been a girl she would have called her Jacqueline. When Bridie saw the baby boy she was overjoyed; in tears she congratulated Vera on her fine healthy son. Vera joked that he was such a size because of Bridie feeding her such big meals. That first Christmas together with

Bridie had been such a wonderful time, Bridie and Vera had festooned the lounge with streamers and balloons and there was large tree in the corner that they had decorated with bright coloured baubles with a pink fairy on the top. Christmas Day itself had been magical although Jake wasn't really old enough to appreciate any of it apart from bits of chocolate delicacies everyone fed to him, which inevitably had resulted in him being sick. Bridie had bought him a little revolving musical carousel that played Brahms lullaby; she said to Vera that she hadn't known what on earth to buy them so she had presented them with an envelope which had contained forty pounds which Vera said was far too generous and she shouldn't have. Vera had also struggled to think what they could give Bridie for a present, but they eventually decided to get her a little silver photo frame and as soon as they had a photograph of Jake she could put that into it, she was absolutely delighted with it and said she would give it pride of place. Vera had bought Bill a pair of cufflinks shaped in the form of an anchor, she would give it to Bill after Christmas when he came home.

Jake was a very good baby he hardly ever cried. Bridie and Vera loved taking him for long walks in his pram; sitting on a bench on the village green having passers-by stop and admire him saying what a gorgeous baby he was. It was after one of these walks; on returning home, they turned into the driveway and Bridie looked toward the house and saw a man standing on the doorstep with a suitcase, she knew instantly who it was. Vera hadn't seen Bill standing there as she was leaning into the pram putting Jake's dummy back into his mouth.

"You're going to meet a dark-haired handsome stranger today, Bridie said to Vera's astonishment, she wondered what she was talking about. Then Bridie nodded toward the house and took hold of the pram rail and said:

"I'll wait in the garden."

Vera exclaimed, "Oooh it's Bill," and ran excitedly to meet him.

Bridie leaned into the pram and saw Jake's big eyes looking up at her, she said.

"Aah your daddy's home, yes he is den, yes he is," and Jake gave a little laugh.

Vera came and found Vera in the garden and said that she wanted to show Bill the baby and introduce her to Bill and Bridie said.

"Aah you go ahead n show Jake to his daddy; I'll wait in the garden for a while before I come in and meet him." So Vera took Jake out of his pram wrapped him in the crocheted cot blanket and took him in the house. Bill was over the moon to see his son and hold him in his arms. He said to Vera that he was such a healthy-looking baby and that she had done a great job in looking after him. Earlier when they had been alone in the house, he had showered her with passionate kisses and told her how much he had missed her and that he would never leave her again as he was now officially discharged from the navy.

When Bridie came in and was introduced to Bill she liked him instantly, he was a fine figure of a man and ruggedly handsome; the first thing he said to her was:

"Hello Bridie, I can't thank you enough for looking after Vera and letting me come and stay here for a while, you've been like a mother to her, and he leaned forward and kissed her on the cheek, there aren't many people in this world who would do what you've done!"

"Aah it's all been such a pleasure for me, t be sure, and I want to hear all about your adventures in the navy Bill and find out what you are planning to do now!"

Over the next few months after discussing his plans with Vera and Bridie Bill began searching the situations vacant columns in the local newspapers for a suitable position, he also bought a copy of Farmers Weekly as he had decided that he might have a good future for himself and his new family working on the land. It was in the March edition of this publication that he saw an advertisement that attracted his attention. It was for the position of farm labourer that could eventually lead to a farm managers job, but the thing that most caught Bill's attention was the fact that there was accommodation consisting of a two-bedroom cottage that went with it. The funny thing was that the farm was actually located in the same County. The advert said to apply in writing stating previous experience to a Mr Ned Trouch at Melford House Farm, Wood Lane, Grendore, Warwickshire. Bill wasn't put off by the fact that he had absolutely no experience of farming, he was strong, intelligent, hard-working and felt that he could easily learn on the job. He showed the advert to Vera and Bridie and they both said that he should apply for it so that very evening he wrote a letter of application stating his naval experience and saying that now he was out of the navy with a wife and baby to support he dreamed of making a future working on the land. He was positive in explaining that he had no experience but was extremely keen to learn and picked things up quickly as he had had to do in the navy. He gave Bridie's address stating that she was a family friend and also with her permission gave her telephone number. Much to his surprise, one evening a week later the telephone rang and Bridie answered it, it was Ned Trouch asking to speak to Bill. Bridie gave the phone to Bill and she and Vera listened intently to the one-sided conversation with occasional signs from Bill that indicated things were going well. They gathered from what Bill was saying that an interview or meeting was going to take place. When Bill replaced the receiver, Vera was so excited and said

"Well what did he say, what did he say,"

"Looking a bit shocked Bill sat down and said:

"It appears that there were a lot of people interested in the job, but he and his wife were impressed with my letter and the fact that I have been in the services. They want to meet both of us and show us the farm and the cottage, and then he said raising his voice and laughing with excitement:

"And he's coming here to pick us up tomorrow morning and take us there!"

"Ooooh I can't believe it Vera gushed, holding on to Bridie's arm, that's wonderful, isn't it Bridie?"

"It certainly is," Bridie said, "that's excellent Bill, you've done very well," she said it because she was genuinely pleased for them both but part of her already felt sadness at the possibility of losing the three of them.

Bridie offered the suggestion straightaway that she would be willing to look after baby Jake while they went to have a look at the farm and its accommodation.

"Aah ya don't want ta be having to look after the little one, I'll take care of him t be sure."

They both thanked her and said that they couldn't leave him in better hands.

The next day Ned Trouch arrived to take Bill and Vera to his farm, he was a very pleasant, amiable man and he made them feel at ease right away. As they drove away They waved to Bridie who stood at the doorstep to see them off. The journey through the Warwickshire countryside was very pleasant and as they got closer to their destination it seemed to get more remote and wilder. When they were nearly at the farm and going down 'Wood Lane' Ned pointed out the cottage to them and it looked very nice. Vera noticed that it was one of a row of four and that there was a wood on the opposite side of the lane. They pulled into the farmyard and Ned's wife Pauline came out to meet them with a black and white border collie running ahead of her that barked at them.

"Rover, she called out to him, heel," she assured them he was friendly and greeted them with.

"Hello there, I'm Pauline, shaking both their hands, I'll take Vera into the house and leave you men to get on with the business of the grand tour, we'll see you in a while for a cup of tea."

"Fine, Ned said, this way Bill, we'll start with the cowshed and the milking equipment."

For a small farm it was very well equipped with a newish red Massey-Fergusson tractor, a long flatbed trailer, a seed drill, a baling threshing machine and a grain store with bagging equipment, in fact, everything else that was needed for an arable dairy farm, there was also pasteurising equipment and a butter churn. Ned showed Bill his herd of 30 Friesian cows and the small herd of sheep and took him to the other side of the farm buildings to show him the open parkland that led down to the river. They spent a long time talking with both them asking each other questions; then they walked back toward the farmhouse.

"I know you haven't seen the cottage yet Bill, but I'd like to offer you the job, what do you say."

"Thank you, I'll take the job Ned," Bill said, "but I'll let Vera see the cottage and see what she thinks about it and then I'll tell her that the jobs mine and the cottage is ours if she wants it, that way she'll feel as though she's had her say in the matter."

"That's good news," Ned said smiling, "now if your wife does like the cottage, how do you feel about moving in and starting work in a week's time?"

"Gosh, there's a great deal to do, we need to get furniture, hire a vehicle to get the stuff moved in, but I'm sure we'll manage it, ok, yes."

"If it will help you, I can borrow a clean horsebox from a neighbouring farm, you could move your furniture in that if you like?"

"Marvellous, Bill replied, that would be a great help, thank you."

The two men joined Pauline and Vera in the farmhouse and had a cup of tea and a freshly baked scone before Ned walked Vera and Bill the short distance down Wood Lane to see the cottage. Vera and Bill couldn't believe how roomy it was and how massive both the front and back gardens were, the back garden looked out over a field towards a line of trees. The lounge had a fireplace with a wooden surround, there was a large kitchen with a lidded copper boiler in the corner for heating the water and a bathroom and w.c. off the kitchen. When they had seen the bedrooms Vera said.

"It's lovely Bill," Vera said enthusiastically, "I'm sure we could make this a nice home."

"Oh that's good," Bill said, "cos I've got the job."

"Really, oh that's smashing, Bill."

"Yeah, we'll be living here next week!"

"What," Vera exclaimed!

Ned and Bill laughed and Vera looked at them with a worried look on her face.

"It'll be alright Vera, you'll see," Bill said putting his arm around her reassuringly.

Chapter 8

They said their goodbyes to Pauline Trouch who was delighted that Bill was going to be their new labourer and the cottage was, at last, going to be occupied; Ned was finally going to get some much-needed help. Ned took them back to Stratford and dropped them off outside the house, he declined the offer to come inside as he said he had to get back to the farm to do some work and get the cows in for milking. He said cheerio and he would be in touch about the horsebox in a day or two.

Bridie was waiting to hear their news and was thrilled to hear that Bill had got the job, but she couldn't believe that they would be moving out within the next few days, they had such a lot to do. She told them that little Jake had been as good as gold all day, she had taken him out for a long walk and he had slept soundly most of the morning. That evening after they had eaten the meal of sausages & mash that Bridie had cooked, they sat and talked for ages about ....

The next couple of days were frantic, Vera and Bridie were busy packing while Bill had gone into Stratford with a shopping list, to buy furniture from a second-hand furniture warehouse. He managed to get a settee and an armchair, a table and four chairs, a brown carved oak sideboard, a large carpet, some rugs, and a double bed. He paid for them and arranged to collect them the next day as Ned had told him he had got the horsebox and could spare an hour or two.

The next day Ned and Bill collected the furniture then went back to Bridie's house to get all their belongings. Bill had said to Vera to get as much of it as possible down by the front door so they could just carry it out and load it into the horsebox, which to look at was very much like a removal van. Bridie, bless her had been her usual generous self, she had turned out her kitchen cupboards and found a spare set of saucepans that she said they could have as well as a patterned tea set that she never used, a frying pan, some cutlery, a glass vase all the bedlinen, tablecloths, tea towels and towels they could ever possibly use. She had even packed a box of groceries so that they wouldn't go hungry until they could get to the shops to buy food; given them a house brush, a mop with a bucket and cleaning stuff, the woman was an absolute saint!

Once it was all loaded up they said their goodbyes to Bridie; Vera promised that they would not lose touch, Bridie kissed Vera, Bill and Jake, wished them good luck and they climbed into the front of the wagon, although she had tried her hardest not to cry, the tears began rolling down Bridie's cheeks as she waved them goodbye. She thought to herself, the house just isn't going to be the same without them, I'm going to miss them so much, especially Jake the dear little sweet darlin, I won't be able to take him out in his pram no more.

Ned Trouch was a very nice man, he had really put them at their ease as they were going along, telling them all about the farm and how he hoped Vera would get involved with the different aspects of it throughout the year such as potato picking, turkey plucking and dressing, she could even help Pauline with the butter and cheesemaking if she wanted to, there was certainly plenty to do. Vera started to think about jobs she had to do that were a little more pressing, like cleaning the house as much as she could before they put all the furniture in place, she wouldn't allow a stick of furniture in the house until she had swept and mopped it. The journey seemed like it would take forever, Jake was irritable after being sick, he needed putting in his pram and rocking to sleep, perhaps he was already missing Bridie's soft lilting Irish songs that she always sang to him.

As they were getting closer to their new home Vera said.

"If you could both please leave everything outside until I can just give the place a 'spruce up', and Bill, if you could get Jake's pram out for me, I can put him in it and get him off to sleep."

"Ok, boss," Bill said, and they all laughed, which lightened their spirits a bit.

Ned brought the wagon to a stop so that the rear end was aligned with the gate and he jumped out, opened the gate and propped it open with a stone. Bill jumped down from the cab, told Vera to lay Jake on the seat for a moment while he helped her down. Then he and Ned opened up the back and started to take a few things off so they could get to the pram. Once they had lifted it out, Vera put Jake into it and wheeled him up the garden path, as she did so she thought about all the lovely flowers they would be able to grow.

She looked up and noticed that a woman was in the window of the house next door and she was waving a welcome, so Vera smiled and waved back. When she reached the front door she found that it was already open, she noticed that Jake was sound asleep so she put the brake on the pram and walked in. She could hear someone humming so she called.

"Hello."

"In here," a voice called back. Vera got to the kitchen door and was so surprised to see Pauline standing on a chair and leaning over the sink cleaning the windows.

"Couldn't have you moving into a dirty house, she said smiling and I know you haven't had the opportunity to do it yourself."

"Oh you're so kind, Pauline. I didn't expect that."

"I wanted to surprise you, all the floors have been swept and mopped, whatever ledges there are have all been dusted and polished, so apart from getting the furniture in and arranged as you want it, that's it. Oh and there's a chicken casserole cooking in the range that you and Bill can eat later when you're ready."

"I wondered what that delicious smell was," Vera said, "I can't thank you enough for all your handwork, you've done wonders, it looks so lovely, I'll put the kettle on and make you a nice cup of tea, you certainly deserve it."

Just as Vera said that she saw Bill and Ned bringing the carpet in for the living room, "I'm making a cup tea, if you want one," she said.

"That's right, keep the workers happy," Bill said as he walked to the far side of the room and dropped his end of the carpet down, Ned did the same up the other end and they began to roll it out across the room. Once it was in place its oriental pattern instantly cheered the room with its bright tones of red, brown and blue."

Vera called tea up from the kitchen, then went to have a look at the carpet.

"Oh that's lovely Bill, you chose that well, the patterns really nice."

"We'll soon have it ship shape and Bristol fashion," Bill said, stopping to drink some of his tea, we'll get this room sorted first, then we'll bring the bed in eh Ned."

"Fine Bill," Ned said.

"Have you noticed that woman in her window next door, I think she's making a list of what we're bringing in, Bill said laughing."

"Oh that's Mavis, Pauline said, nothing escapes her I'm afraid, I'm surprised that she hasn't been round to see you yet?"

"I'll have my inventory ready for her," Bill said, and they all laughed.

"Right, we'll go and get the bed then shall we," Bill said, and he and Ned went off to get it.

Once they'd got it through the door and started to lift it up the staircase it proved quite a struggle getting it upstairs as there was a sharp bend halfway up, but with a bit of pushing, pulling and heaving between the two men, they eventually managed it. When they had finally brought all the furniture and boxes in, Ned said that he and Pauline should be getting back to the farm as there were the cows to bring in for milking and Pauline had to get dinner. Bill and Vera thanked them for all their help and hard work and Bill said.

"I'll come with you, to see how it's done, and I can give you a hand as well, Bill said to Ned, Vera will be alright here sorting her kitchen out, won't you love?"

"You go ahead, Vera answered, delving down into a big cardboard box, I'll be alright."

"That's good of you Bill, It'll give you chance to say hello to the girls, he meant his cows, and I'm sure you'll pick things up in no time."

There was a chorus of goodbyes and Bill saying, "See you later, love."

Vera was getting really well with unpacking stuff and putting it away in drawers and cupboards and thought to herself, *I'll have it all done by the time Bill comes back for his tea.* She went out to check if Jake was alright and he was perfectly content lying gurgling and kicking in his pram.

Vera was just about to go upstairs and make the bed when she heard a tapping on the open front door, she went to see who it was and there was a man and woman standing there.

"Hello, you're the lady who waved to me earlier?"

"That's right, we're your next door neighbours, I'm Mavis Burridge she said, extending her hand to shake Vera's, and this is my husband Earnest,"

"I'm very pleased to meet you both, Vera said, shaking both their hands, as you can appreciate we're all at sixes and sevens at the moment?"

"Oh, of course, we're not stopping, we just thought we'd say hello and welcome you, didn't we Earnest?"

"Yes, dear," Earnest replied.

"We can all get acquainted some other time, we'll leave you to get on, and she wheeled round and said:

"Come on Earnest."

"Coming, dear."

Vera hoped she hadn't sounded unsociable and upset them because she wanted to get on and get things done, she was hoping she could finish unpacking and putting away before Bill came back, then she could dish up their dinner; they could eat it, she could feed Jake, get him bathed, off to sleep and laid in his cot so that they could have a bit of time together on the first night in their new home. She had a feeling they were going to be really happy here. She went to bring Jake and the pram inside in case it was getting a bit chilly for him, she thought to herself, *he really is a good little boy, he's no trouble at all.*

When Bill arrived home he was full of talk about the cows and the milking parlour and how he and Ned were getting along like a house on fire, he said.

"The job's going to be hard work, but I've never shied away from that, I think we made a good move here love."

"Well I certainly hope so after all this, Vera replied, I've nearly got everything put away. Oh by the way I had a visit from the next-door neighbours, their names are Mavis and Earnest, I may have irked her a bit as I was busy and I really didn't have time to spend chit-chatting, anyway we aren't straight yet."

"What were they like then?" "Alright I suppose as far as I could make out on first impressions, he didn't say a lot, I think she rules the roost there!"

Chapter 9

Vera and Bill had been living at Wood Lane for three months and Vera had been dreaming of this day for a long time. They had booked the registry office in Hanworth and were to be married at two o'clock today. They hadn't told anyone apart from their witnesses, Rosemary her old school friend, Bridie and Bill's employers Pauline and Ned as they didn't want people to know that they weren't already married. Pauline had kindly said that she would look after Jake. Bridie had wanted to send a car to collect them from the house, but they had thanked her and explained why they declined her offer. They were going to catch the bus from the top of the lane that would take them directly into Hanworth and they would meet them both there. They were both smartly dressed and they had previously arranged between them that if they met any neighbours who asked them where they were going, they would say to a friend's baby's christening. They walked up the lane and waited for the bus, when it arrived they boarded, Vera found a seat for them as Bill paid the fare. Once they were sat together Vera opened her handbag and took out a small corsage that she had made from carnations, rosebuds and gypsophila and asked Bill to pin it on with a safety pin. She had also done a buttonhole for him of a white carnation and gypsophila which she pinned onto his lapel. When they arrived at the registry office they went inside and found Rosemary and Bridie already there. They both looked lovely Rosemary was wearing a pink and blue print dress with a white blazer, Bridie had on a teal coloured two-piece suit. They all hugged each other and made their way into the Registry Office. They were greeted by the lady Registrar who was very pleasant and made them both feel at ease, the administration and paperwork was done with no fuss and then they all went into the room for the ceremony. When the Registrar was asking Vera and Bill to say their vows both Bridie and Rosemary became emotional and dabbed tears from their eyes with their handkerchiefs but especially so when Bill kissed his new bride. They then witnessed Vera and Bill signing the register and the Registrar, Bridie and Rosemary said their congratulations. When they came out onto the street in bright sunshine they threw confetti over the happy couple; Bridie said that she had a surprise for them and she told them that she had booked a table for afternoon tea at The Alexander Hotel which was the best hotel in Hanworth and quite posh. It was so warm that afternoon as they sat out on the hotel terrace overlooking the flower garden.

They were all enjoying delicious salmon and cucumber sandwiches and an assortment of scrumptious fresh cream cakes, it was all presented so prettily on a white china cake stand with paper doilies. Then the waiter came in with a bottle of champagne in an ice bucket, he made great ceremony of taking the bottle from the bucket, wiping the moisture off it with a cloth, and opening it with a loud pop, which elicited a loud, "Ooooohh," from all of them. As he was pouring the champagne and passing a glass to each of them Rosemary exclaimed.

"Speech," looking at Bill then Vera and Bridie joined in:

"Yes, speech."

Bill reluctantly stood up, coughed a couple of times to clear his throat and looking quite nervous began to speak.

"Oh crikey, I'm not used to this and I'm not really sure what to say, well, all I can say is I'm a very lucky man to have Vera as my wife and I've been waiting a long time for this day to arrive. She's the best thing that ever happened to me and she has made me the happiest man in the world. I know she has been through a lot, and I'm only sorry I wasn't able to be with her when it was all going on, if you know what I mean, but she couldn't have had a better soul looking after her than Bridie, so I thank you with all my heart for that my dear, but from now on I'll have the pleasure of looking after her as we spend the rest of our lives together, that's it, that's all I want to say."

The three women applauded him, all looking at him with admiration for saying such sincere and heartfelt words.

"This is so kind of you Bridie," Vera said, turning towards her, "it has made my wedding day even more memorable," and she gave her a kiss.

"Well, this should make it even better Bridie said, I'd like you to have this, handing her a half-moon shaped shagreen casket, it was my grandmother's and I would love for you to have it as I consider you as the only family I have now." Vera clasped Bridie's arm and said.

"What a sweet thing of you to say."

Vera took the case from Bridie wondering what was going to be inside, she pressed the little silver button on the front of the case and the lid sprung open to reveal a stunning emerald necklace and earring set.

Vera's eyes widened in astonishment as she gasped, "Oh Bridie these are absolutely beautiful, but you're too generous, I couldn't possibly accept these, they must be worth a small fortune."

"Aah, of course, you can, money doesn't come into it, they're yours, darlin, and I'll be offended if you don't take them."

Vera looked at Bill and Rosemary as if to say what shall I do; Rosemary smiled at her and gave a gentle little nod as if to say, take them, Bill said:

"If Bridie's sure she wants you to have them, love, you can't really say no." Vera looked at Bridie and said:

"You really are far too kind and generous, but I shall treasure them forever, thank you," she gave Bridie another loving kiss.

Bridie's car came to collect her about an hour later, the time had gone so quickly without them realising it as they had all been chatting away; enjoying the food and the lovely surroundings. Bridie insisted that she take them all home, as Vera, not being used to alcohol was quite squiffy and giggly as a result of the champagne she had drunk, she should perhaps have only had the one glass. Bridie paid the bill and left a tip for the waiter Vera unpinned her corsage and then Bill's buttonhole as she didn't want the neighbours to see them, they all got into the car, Bill in the front with the driver and the women in the back. The driver must have wished he had earplugs as the women were chattering away and laughing so noisily; he probably breathed a sigh of relief when they arrived back at Wood Lane and Vera and Bill left the car saying their goodbyes and giving kisses to Rosemary and Bridie, then the car drove away to take Rosemary home to Barton Village. Bill and Vera walked up the garden path and when they got to the door and opened it Bill couldn't resist adopting the traditional custom of lifting the bride over the threshold, as he did so Vera squealed with delight. When they got inside Bill put Vera back on her feet, kissed her then took hold of her hand and led her upstairs. They took off their shoes and he began to undress her eagerly, his kisses were hot and passionate, Vera murmured.

"Oh Bill, I love you," as she began undressing him, then they fell onto the bed in an embrace and made fervent love to one another. Bill was kissing Vera all over her body making her squirm and groan with delirious excitement and anticipation of him pushing his fully large and erect penis inside her, almost as she was thinking it she felt the bulbous helmet of his cock rubbing on the lips of her moist vagina as he entered her with sensuous passion. They must have fallen asleep after they had made love and when they woke up they went into a bit of a panic as they realised they needed to go and pick Jake up from Pauline and Ned at the farm. They would be thinking that his parents had forgotten him!

When they arrived at the farm to pick Jake up, Pauline opened the door with a big smile and said:

"Congratulations, come on in Mr and Mrs Wiggins we want to hear all about it?"

Vera apologised to Pauline and Ned for leaving him with them for so long but they both said it didn't matter as he had been a pleasure to look after and no trouble at all. Vera looked at little Jake fast asleep in his pram and tucked his arm under the cover.

"Come on, sit yourselves down," Ned said.

They congratulated them both asked how their day had been and listened intently as Vera recounted the day's events and said that everything had been so perfect. She told them about their surprise visit to The Alexander Hotel to have afternoon tea with champagne; she also told them about the gorgeous necklace and earrings that Bridie had given her. Pauline put her hand on Vera's arm and said:

"We can't compete with that but we do want you to have a little something, we had no idea what to get you, but felt it should be something you could both use and get pleasure from, as she was saying this Ned picked up large box wrapped in wedding gift-wrap; brought it over to them and placed it on Bill's lap.

"Oh it's heavy," Bill said questioningly, "I wonder what it is?"

"Only one way to find out Ned said."

Bill ripped off the paper that had lucky horseshoes and congratulations all over it and opened the lid of the box. He was delighted to see that inside was a radio:

"Oh marvellous look at this Vera, a radio, you'll be able to listen to 'Housewives Choice' and I can listen to the racing, thank you ever so much, you couldn't have bought anything better."

"It's all ready to use, I've put a plug on it for you," Ned said.

Yes, it's wonderful Vera said, and such a handsome looking thing, it will look good sat on top of the sideboard, I can listen to music while I do the housework, thank you both, now I suppose we ought to leave you folks in peace; I'll take Jake home, get him bathed and into his cot."

Bill stood up holding the box tightly and said:

"Yes, and I won't be late to bed, it's been a long day, and I need to be fresh for work in the morning."

Vera went over to Jake's pram took the brake off, turned it round and pushed it towards the door, Pauline and Ned rose and Pauline went over to open the door, as she said, Jake's such a good little baby he was absolutely no trouble, and we're so glad you both like the present, mind how you go down the lane, goodnight.

Bill and Vera left saying goodnight, thanks again.

"Wasn't that kind of them," Vera said, "you've got a really good boss there, Bill, haven't you?"

"Yes I have, he's a good bloke is Ned, a real gentleman, we made a good move when we came here."

They opened their front door and Bill helped Vera get the pram over the step and she pushed it round the side of the bannisters in the hall. She took off her coat and shoes and put her slippers on, then she walked into the kitchen to put the kettle on to fill Jake's little bath for him, once it had boiled and she had prepared his bath, putting some baby oil in it and testing the water with her elbow to make sure it was the correct temperature so it wouldn't scald the little cherub, she went into the hallway, pulled back the pram cover and blanket and lifted Jake out of his pram. Jake roused right away and stretched and yawned, Vera sat down and started to undress him, taking off his little matinee coat that she had crocheted for him when she was living at Bridie's house, then his bootees; mittens, his baby grow, changed and his little vest, then she changed his dirty nappy. Just then loud music suddenly blared out and the volume was instantly turned down to an acceptable level by Bill saying:

"Sorry love, didn't mean to do that, is that better now?"

"Yes that's fine," Vera said, having recovered from the surprise. Jake was wide awake now, he had jumped and looked very surprised but he was now looking up at his mother smiling as she gently lowered him into his bath talking to him in a baby-talk way as she was gently washing him, he was perfectly happy to be having all the attention and listening to his mother's voice. Vera laid a towel on her lap took Jake out of the water and laid him onto it, beginning to dry him off, then she powdered him all over with baby talcum, put a clean nappy on him and a clean babygrow. Vera put Jake's dummy into his mouth and began to gently rock him to sleep in her arms, it wasn't long before he was asleep, so she stood up, went upstairs and placed him in his cot.

Bill was doing well at his job, he liked the outdoor life and was on good terms with Ned, they had a good rapport together. They had settled in well at the cottage, it was very cosy and had a homely feel, Vera had made it look nice with pretty curtains and cushions, she was very happy that they now had their own place, she would be eternally grateful to Bridie for letting her live at her house and taking Bill in as well when he left the navy, but this was their own little home.

Vera had brought up the subject of having Jake christened several times in conversation with Bill but he didn't seem very keen on the idea, however, the last time she mentioned it he had conceded and said that if she wanted him christened that much, they had better do it and get it over with, but he couldn't understand it as neither of them were churchgoers. Vera just said to him that she felt it was the right thing do, and she would go to see the vicar and arrange the day and time; she thought, *there's no time like the present, I'd better sort it out before Bill changes his mind, I'll go to see the vicar tomorrow.*

Vera pushed the pram along toward the church and turned into the vicarage drive, the house was a solid built handsome victorian one, with ivy growing up the walls, the door had two glass panels in it so she could see inside along the hallway, she tugged the handle to ring the doorbell and could hear it clanging inside. Moments later the figure of a young woman wearing an apron appeared wiping her hands on a tea towel as she approached the front door. She opened the door and greeted Vera with a warm smile and an enquiring look, as if to say, *I don't know you do I?*

"Hello, can I help you, you'll have to excuse me, I'm in the middle baking scones for the WI?

"Oh I'm sorry to disturb you, I hope you can, Vera said smiling back, I'm Vera Wiggins and I live in Wood Lane, I'd like to see the vicar if I can, I want to have my little boy christened."

The woman immediately peered into the pram to see Jake happily waving his arms and kicking his legs; gurgling away quite contentedly, he saw the woman looking down at him and he smiled.

"Oh he's lovely isn't he, what's his name?

"It's Jake," Vera replied.

"I'm Theresa, Brian's wife, he's in his office, if you'd like to come in, I'll tell him you're here, how old is little Jake?

"He's eleven months," Vera replied, proudly as she went to lift him out of his pram.

"Oh lovely, you can wheel the pram inside if you like, if you don't want to disturb him." Theresa stood back and held the door open wide.

"Oh thank you, Vera said as she wheeled Jake through the door and into the hallway, where shall I leave him?"

"Oh just there by the side of the staircase will be fine, I'll just see if he's free."

Theresa tapped on a nearby door and walked in, seconds later she came out.

"He can see you now Vera," she said, as she held the office door open for her.

The Reverend Brian Soames stood up behind a large oak desk as she entered the wood-panelled office, he walked around the side of his desk and shook Vera's hand. He was a tall, good looking man, with dark wavy hair and he had a very kind face.

"Hello Mrs Wiggins, take a seat will you, Theresa tells me you want to arrange a christening for your little boy?"

"Please call me Vera, yes I do."

"Forgive me asking but you are of this parish aren't you, as I haven't seen you at church?"

"Yes I am, I live in Wood Lane my husband Bill works on the farm, sorry we're not really churchgoers. We were married at the Registry Office in Hanworth, taking her marriage certificate out of her handbag and handing it to him, but I went to Sunday school as a little girl and I know it's important for a child to be christened and brought up right."

"Yes it is, does that mean that when Jake is old enough you'll send him to Sunday school?"

"Yes definitely, Vera replied."

He looked at the marriage certificate; then at Vera, "Well, that's all in order, I think we should go ahead and arrange it for the little chap then, he said with a grin, looking in his diary, I could christen him on Thursday the 10th July at 2pm, that's three weeks away, would that be alright?"

"Yes, that would be wonderful, it gives me time to write and invite people."

"What names are you calling your child?" he asked her.

"Jake," Vera replied, "just the one Christian name, Jake Wiggins."

He wrote an entry in his diary for that day, *2pm Christening: Jake Wiggins.*

"There you are then, that's all arranged for you, I'll be happy to see yourself and your husband and Godparents on Thursday 10th July at 2pm," as he said this he jotted it down on a piece of paper and gave it to Vera.

"That's lovely, thank you," Vera said, "we will make a donation to the church on the day."

Bless you, Mrs Wiggins he said, coming from behind his desk and opening the door, it's been nice to meet you, goodbye then."

Vera went to the pram and looked in at Jake who was fast asleep, she took the brake off and started to go down the hall when the Vicars wife came out and spoke from behind her.

"Oh you're off then, I'll get the door for you, he's fitted you in then?"

"Yes, Vera said, the 10th of July."

"That's lovely, so nice to have met you, you're welcome to come to the WI meetings on Tuesday afternoons here at the vicarage if you like."

"Oh thank you that's very kind, I'll bear that in mind, Cheerio, nice to have met you too."

On the walk back home Vera began to formulate in her own mind her plans for Jake's Christening day, she wanted the day to be really special and she wanted to be surrounded by friends who were going to want the very best for Jake's future.

So that evening she planned to write three letters, one to Bridie, one to Ivy and another to Rosemary, inviting them all to be Jake's Godparents and giving them the date and time of his christening, she hoped they would all be able to accept the role of Godparents, which she appreciated was a big responsibility to undertake, but she certainly couldn't wish for three more eligible people to pick for the task.

She was thinking she had three weeks to get herself organised, she needed to go into Hanworth on the bus and visit the wool shop as she wanted to buy a pattern and some white 4ply wool, so that she could knit Jake a christening robe. She must write a list of things that she had to be doing nearer the time, such as baking cakes, making sandwiches, deciding which of her clothes she could wear that wouldn't look shabby, she couldn't afford anything new. When Bill came home that evening Vera told him that she had been to see the vicar and the date had been arranged for Thursday 10th July at 2pm.

"Crikey, you didn't waste any time, did you?

"I just wanted get proceedings started Bill, I shall write to Bridie, Ivy and Rosemary tonight asking them if they will consent to being Jake's Godparents, I hope they all will, it's going to be so nice."

"Bloody hell, three Godparents, couldn't you decide which of em to ask?

"No silly, it's just that Bridie and Ivy have both been so good to us, without them I'm not really sure if Jake would be here at all; Rosemary, she's my oldest school friend so I couldn't not ask her, could I?"

"I don't suppose so, I didn't know she was that old though," he said chuckling.

"Oh stop it, be serious, do you think Ned will mind you taking the afternoon off?"

"He hadn't better, I work my guts out for him every day, he'll have to cover for me."

"I'll ask Pauline to come, she loves Jake, so I would think that will prompt him to cover for you."

"How much is all this business going to cost us," he asked warily?

"Oh it shouldn't be much, I'll have to make a couple of sponge cakes, a trifle and enough sandwiches for everybody; then we'll have to give the vicar a donation for the church, a fiver should be enough."

"A fiver, streuth, I was thinking more like half a crown."

"Bill, really, you skinflint, I'll manage with what clothes I've already got in my wardrobe and you can wear your blazer and flannels, to spare us any extra expense, is that ok?"

"Oh I forgot, I'll have to go into Hanworth to buy some wool to knit a christening robe, bootees and bonnet for Jake, but that won't cost much."

"Waste of money if you ask me, he could wear a set of rompers."

"No he couldn't Bill, it's his special day, he needs to look nice, he'll be the centre of attention."

"Yeah, he always is," Bill said.

Vera didn't know what Bill meant by that but she ignored the remark.

"Are you going to get yourself washed for tea, it should be ready and on the table in about half an hour."

"What av we got," Bill enquired.

"Your favourite, liver and onions."

"Oh good, c'mere and give us a kiss, Bill said grabbing hold of Vera round the waist and pulling her close to him?"

"Only a little one Bill, geroff you smell like a farmyard."

"Charming, mooooo, Bill mimicked, letting her go, I'll get cleaned up, I'll see you later."

"Promises, promises," Vera taunted.

Chapter 10

The first reply letter to arrive was from Ivy who said that she would be absolutely delighted to be Jake's Godmother along with Bridie and Rosemary. She was so looking forward to seeing Vera again and to meeting Bridie for the first time, she asked if there was anything she could bring to help on the day. Bridie also sent a letter saying more or less the same things that Ivy had, apart from the fact that she had been feeling rather under the weather lately, but she was now feeling better and would be pleased to see Vera, Bill and little Jake and have a change of scene for a while, as she hadn't been getting out a lot. Rosemary cycled from Barton to visit the day after she received Vera's letter, she said she was so excited about Jake's christening and they happily chatted away to each other about all Vera's plans and arrangements; Rosemary offered to come early on the day to help prepare and make sandwiches which Vera was very grateful for. She told Rosemary that she wanted to get some wool in Hanworth and get started on Jake's christening robe; Rosemary said that she would like to go with her to keep her company and help with managing Jake, so they arranged to go into town tomorrow as it was market day; they might be able to grab some bargains.

Vera saw Bill off to work after she had given him his breakfast then she had a good strip wash, got Jake bathed dressed and fed, put him in his carrycot and walked up the lane to catch the eight-thirty bus into town, which went via Barton where Rosemary got on and they continued the rest of the journey together. They talked about just about everything and caught up on all the village gossip. Vera sadly learned that old Mrs Truelove who kept the village sweet shop had died of bronchial pneumonia last week after apparently having had a short illness, her funeral was next Thursday. Rosemary thought there would be a few villagers going, but she didn't know if there would be any family, her husband died years ago and they had never had any children. She was a lovely lady and always used to have a cheery word to say when you met her, *so sad,* Vera thought.

Hanworth was always busy on market day as there were lots of different stalls trading their various wares, there was always one selling wet fish, one fresh vegetables, another hardware and household goods as well as the wool stall that didn't only sell balls of wool, but baby clothes, ribbons, buttons and knitting and crochet patterns as well. They bought what food items they wanted first then went to look on the wool stall to see if the lady had a suitable pattern.

"Hello, love," the stallholder greeted, recognising Vera.

"Hello do you have any christening robe patterns to either knit or crochet', Vera asked?

"Yes, I think so the woman said, handing Vera a folder of patterns as another customer arrived to browse, have a look through these Darlin while I serve this lady, what can I do for you, love?"

Vera began thumbing through the various patterns which were a very good assortment, there were actually two christening robe patterns in the book, but one of them was really pretty with a knitted bodice and crocheted scalloped shell motifs making up the skirt. Both Vera and Rosemary liked this one the best.

Vera waited as the woman finished serving her other customer.

"I'll take this one if you have the right wool for it in white." Vera enquired.

"Let me see, she said checking the pattern, 'Valdisere' 4ply, 6 balls, I should have it; she ducked beneath the counter top, there was a lot of rustling of cellophane packets for a while, then she said.

"Ah yes, here we are, it's lovely wool this, have you got a number two crochet hook and number 10 needles?"

"Yes I've got those, but I've just noticed, I'll need a pack of four white buttons for the back of the bodice, then she spotted a box of assorted buttons and picked out the very ones she wanted, these will do nicely, how much is that?"

"Let me see now, thirteen and six for the wool, one and threepence for the pattern, that's a gorgeous one isn't it, and ten pence for the buttons, that's 15 shillings and ninepence please love?

Vera paid the woman, said thank you and she and Rosemary walked on to have a look in the Co-op.

"Thank you, dear, see you again, happy crocheting."

Vera and Rosemary laughed and walked off toward the Co-op, as they entered the main doors into the drapery department which sold furnishing fabrics and dress materials they saw signs telling them that there was a sale on throughout the store. Rosemary wanted to go to the womenswear department to have a look around she needed a new blouse to wear at the christening. She found that they had a good selection; she was a bit spoilt for choice, but after trying several on and listening to Vera's comments on each of them, she decided to have one that had a little collar with embroidered flowers on it as they both thought it was very pretty, Rosemary knew exactly what she would wear it with.

The trip back home was pleasant, the conductress was quite chatty with everyone she wasn't having to take any fares as she had a full bus, she was quite a character and had people talking and interacting with each other as though they were on a trip going to the seaside, it made the journey go so quickly; as Vera and Rosemary reached their stop and got off it was as if she was saying goodbye to old friends. They started to walk down Wood Lane and Vera said:

"That conductress is as good as a tonic to everyone travelling on that bus, she made everyone so cheerful, didn't she?"

"She certainly did, she was the life and soul of the party, you couldn't be glum with her around, could you?"

"Absolutely not, bless her, what time is it Rosemary?

"It's a quarter to twelve."

"I'll get some lunch on as soon as we get back, Bill will be home for his lunch soon, soup and a sandwich do you?"

"That will be lovely, thanks, Vera."

When they reached the garden gate, who should be in her garden next door but Mavis Burridge, she was talking to another neighbour Mrs Castle, they both looked over when they saw them, but Vera didn't want to be held up talking and listening to their gossip for ages so she just shouted:

"Good morning, lovely day, can't stop to talk, I've got to get Bill's lunch on and Jake needs changing; she and Rosemary just carried on walking to the front door and went inside.

"Phew, that was a narrow escape," Vera said, and they both laughed.

"Are they that bad," Rosemary asked.

"Once you let Mavis get started you can never get away from her; she knows everything that's going on for miles around."

"Oh dear, you did very well there then."

Just at that moment Jake woke up and started crying, Vera put his dummy in his mouth but he promptly spat that out with disgust. Vera thought he was probably hungry so he would have to be fed first. While Vera was preparing his bottle Rosemary said:

"What soup shall we have?" as she looked at the tins in the pantry.

"Bill likes chicken, so open two tins of that will you love, we can have some of that lovely boiled ham we bought in a sandwich."

Bill came home shortly afterwards so they all had lunch together and Rosemary made her way home to Barton.

Over the weeks leading up to the christening ceremony Vera spent every spare moment she could knitting and crocheting to finish Jake's christening robe, it was absolutely gorgeous when it was done; she couldn't wait to see him wearing it on the day, he would look a picture. Bill didn't enthuse over it though, one comment he made rankled with Vera, he had said.

"I think you should have had a little girl, putting him in a dress."

She let it pass in order to keep the peace but she thought to herself, *Sometimes you can be a right Phillistine, Bill Wiggins.*

On the day of the christening, Rosemary was true to her word she arrived on her bicycle at ten o'clock and had brought her outfit to change into later. Vera had made the trifle and baked two sponge cakes the day before and filled them with strawberry jam and buttercream. So all they needed to do today was open a tin of salmon and make the salmon and cucumber sandwiches, make cheese sandwiches, there was a nice big pork pie and they agreed that should be plenty of food.

Rosemary and Vera started to butter the sliced bread and between them had soon made up all the sandwiches, Vera covered them all with very damp tea towels so that the bread wouldn't go hard and curl up at the edges. She put her best tablecloth, the one that Bridie had given her on the table; together they laid the table, arranging all the plates of food, the trifle and the sponge cakes ready for when they came back from the church. Vera had impressed upon Bill that he shouldn't be late as they didn't want to keep the vicar waiting.

Rosemary had just suggested that they should have a cup of tea, so she went to put the kettle on just as there was a knock at the door. Vera went to see who it was and was thrilled to see her friend Ivy standing there.

"Ooh Ivy, how lovely to see you," she said, throwing her arms around her and giving her a big kiss, "it's been far too long, come on in, Rosemary's here."

"You look really well Vera, Ivy replied, you're right it has been too long; I can't wait to see Jake, I'll bet he's really grown."

"Let me take your coat," Vera said, "Oh you do look smashing, what a pretty outfit, come on through."

"I've bought Jake a little present, I shall give it to him at the party later," Ivy said putting the bag she was carrying on the floor under the coat stand.

"Hello Ivy, Rosemary said as Vera brought her into the kitchen, you look lovely."

"Thank you, Rosemary, it's good to see you, I haven't seen you in ages."

"I was hoping I'd be able to help prepare the food, but it looks as if you've done it all, I must say, it looks absolutely splendid."

"Thank you," Vera said.

They all sat and drank a cup of tea, talking about all the different things that had happened, Vera gave Jake to Ivy to hold and she sat there gently rocking him in her arms.

"He is such beautiful boy, look at his mass of hair, those big brown eyes and long eyelashes, who's a beautiful boy then, Ivy said to Jake, tickling him under the chin and making him laugh."

Bill came home from work and walked into the kitchen:

"Hello ladies he said smiling a broad grin, what a lovely happy sight for a man to come home to, who's first to give the homecoming worker a big kiss."

"Bill, don't frighten them away, Vera said, anyway I'm first in line I'll have you know."

"Of course you are my sweetheart, clasping his hands on both sides of Vera's head and giving her a big smacker, then looking at Jake, hello little un, moving toward Rosemary he gave her a kiss on the cheek, then did the same to Ivy, a man could get used to this," he said.

"Afraid you won't be able to, it's just for today, Rosemary said, and they all laughed.

Vera said, "If anyone is hungry now and unable to wait until we get back, I can make you a sandwich, I don't want to hear growling tummies during the christening, so please say."

Bill said, "I'd better have one then love, or you won't be able to hear what the vicars saying over mine."

Ivy also said, "Yes please Vera, I will."

"I'll do them," Rosemary said willingly, jumping to her feet and moving to the countertop to make a start.

"Thank you, Rosemary, Vera said, I'll just see to Jake in the other room."

Vera was just pinning Jake's nappy back on when there was a gentle knock at the door, so she lay Jake down, shouted:

"I'll get it," as she opened the door to see Bridie there, "hello Bridie my love, wonderful to see you," giving her a kiss, "how are you?"

"Aah I'm fine so I am, how are you, and how's my lovely little darlin Jake on his special day?"

"Come and see for yourself love, he's in here."

Vera thought, *thank goodness I'd just changed him,* as she took Bridie into the living room.

"Aah there he is, the little man, then she started talking to Jake in a baby-talk voice, helloooo den ya little darlin, ya aunty Bridie's come ta see ya, Jake wriggled with laughter; kicking his legs and waving his arms in delight as Bridie picked him up and cuddled him and sat down.

Vera saw how she looked at him with such love in her eyes and it made her well up with emotion and she started to cry.

"Aah Vera, whatever's the matter, Bridie asked, looking really concerned?

"Nothing Vera replied, I'm just so happy and so pleased to see you, love, I'm being silly, hope I'm not going to be like this later on at the ceremony."

"Aah, you're not being silly at all and if ya are people will understand, but you're sure that's what this is about, nothing else?

Bridie was a very intuitive woman and she sensed there was more to it than what Vera was telling her but she didn't want to force her into talking, so she just let it go.

What Vera hadn't told her was that the night before Bill and her had a row. It had started when Bill said that he didn't particularly want to go to the christening as there was so much that needed doing on the farm. The remark really hurt Vera, for why wouldn't you want to go to your child's christening; she couldn't remember hardly anything else of what was said, except at the end of the spat she said to him.

"I'm beginning to think that you don't love Jake; perhaps you don't love me anymore either?

Bill's reaction was, "Don't be so bloody stupid," and he'd pulled his arm back with a clenched fist as though he was going to strike her.

Thankfully he had realised in time and hadn't hit her but it had seriously alarmed and troubled Vera as to why he would behave in such a way. The thing that troubled her most was that she remembered his clenched fist, if he had hit her, it would not just have been a slap of the hand, not that any violence was justified, but a vicious punch, and what would that have done to her. She was brought back to the present by Bridie saying.

"My word, you were deep in thought then, a penny for them love."

"They're not really worth a penny, Vera said, forcing a smile."

"I don't believe that for one moment mi darlin, now let me show you what I have bought for Jake, I hope you'll like it, Bridie took a little box from her smart astrakhan coat pocket, go on you can open it now."

"Bridie you shouldn't have, what can it be, she asked as she opened the gift box?"

To Vera's delight it was a square silver photo frame with a heart-shaped aperture and beneath the heart-shaped opening there was a raised nameplate which had Jake's name engraved on it.

"There yah, ya can put his little picture in it, so ya can."

"Oh Bridie, it's so beautiful, what a thoughtful present, it's adorable."

"It will be a memory to look back on, you could take a photograph of him today when he's dressed in his finery and it will be something for you to treasure and keep as a family heirloom."

"Yes it certainly will be, Oh you're so good Bridie; such a wonderful, kind friend."

"Well how could anyone be anything other than kind to you mi darlin, you only deserve kindness."

Hearing what Bridie had said, Vera replied, "Don't worry Bridie, I'm just feeling a bit under the weather, that's all."

Vera realised that she hadn't fooled her friend for one minute, Bridie knew that something was deeply troubling her; she so wanted to confide in her and unburden herself of the confusion and doubt she was feeling but her conflicted feelings were stopping her. After all, Bill hadn't actually hit her had he, although it had certainly looked as though he wanted to, she would be being disloyal to him, she needed to be strong and forget that it had ever happened. No, whatever problems Bill and Vera had in their marriage they should remain private, they were for them to sort out and deal with between themselves, no-one else.

"What a sweet thing for you to say, Vera replied with a lump in her throat, she was determined not to cry again in front of Bridie, we're going to have such a lovely day, come into the kitchen and say hello to everyone."

She took Jake from Bridie so that she would be able to greet everyone freely and not be hampered by holding Jake. They walked through into the kitchen and everyone looked towards them as Bill greeted Bridie:

"Hello Bridie, good to see you, love, he said planting a kiss on her cheek, are you well?"

"Aah Yes, I'm fine so I am, you're looking well, the outdoor farming life agrees with you."

"Yes, I love it he replied."

"Bridie you haven't met Ivy," Vera said, gently catching hold of Ivy's arm and pulling her towards Bridie.

"No, I haven't, so pleased to meet you, my dear, I've heard so much about you, and I have you to thank for bringing Vera and I together," she gave Ivy a kiss on the cheek and said, "we must have a little chat later, t be sure."

Then Vera ushered Bridie to Rosemary, "Rosemary you met at our wedding."

"Ah yes, hello again my dear, it's going to be a lovely day I'm sure."

"Hello Bridie dear, it's so nice to see you again."

"Right, introductions over with, if anyone is hungry please help yourself to a sandwich now, there'll be plenty of food to eat when we get back, Rosemary do you want to get yourself changed and ready, you can use the box room; I'll get little Jake dressed and ready. Bill, your blazer and flannels and a clean shirt are hanging on the front of the wardrobe if you'd like to get washed, shaved and dressed. Vera saw Bill give her a funny look. Sorry to sound a bossy boots, I'm just trying to get us organised as we only have an hour before we need to leave for the church. Bill, did Pauline and Ned say they would see us at the church or are they coming here?"

"Ned said they would see us there, then they'll come back here afterwards."

"Oh thanks, lovely," Vera said looking suddenly flustered as she took Jake upstairs to wash his face and dress him.

Rosemary and Bill duly went to get ready and Ivy and Bridie sat together in the kitchen and started chatting. Bridie loved meeting and talking to people, listening to their stories, finding out what kind of person they were, this is one of the reasons she had embraced the WI, she loved company. Bridie could read people well and she had already formed the opinion that no wonder Vera and Ivy were friends, they were alike in so many ways, but she felt that Ivy was more independent and sure of who she was than Vera, and Bridie was somehow able to draw people out to talk about themselves, as though they had known her for ages. They had been chatting away for some time when Bridie asked Ivy what she did for a living; Ivy told her that she was a factory worker at the moment but she didn't really like it, she hoped one day that she could work in a shop, she would love to sell ladies dresses as she was crazy about clothes, but there weren't many opportunities available. Bridie could see by just looking at Ivy that she had good dress sense, a natural flair if you like. She really liked her for who she was, and how she had helped Vera when she needed it most.

Bridie rested her hand on Ivy's and softly said, "Aah don't think I'm being rude now Ivy with what I'm going to say to ya, but opportunities don't always come knocking on your door mi darlin, sometimes you have to go out and find them, it's good to have a dream, but turning that dream into a reality is something else."

Bridie's pearls of wisdom were not lost on Ivy they hit home in a very positive way, it was as if what she'd said was something she had needed to hear for a long time, she put her other hand on top of Bridie's; squeezed it affirmingly and smiled, Bridie thought she looked as if she'd had a revelation and she obviously had because she said.

"You know you are absolutely right, I've been dreaming about it for far too long, it's about time I tried to bring it about, Thank you Bridie.

"There's no need to thank me Ivy, but you could do something for me, keep your eye out for Vera from time to time, I'm a bit worried about her."

"In what way," Ivy asked curiously.

"Well, I don't want to sound too dramatic, and please don't tell anyone I said this to you, but I think things aren't as they should be with Vera and Bill, if you know what I mean."

"No Bridie, I'm not sure what you mean?"

"I think Bill may have a dreadful temper on him, and he may lose it sometimes, especially if he's had a drink, then things can get dangerous, do you know what I mean?"

"Oh no, poor Vera, yes I do."

"I know we can't be with her all the time, but we can be there for her if and when she needs us."

"Definitely, she knows she can always count on me Bridie."

"Please remind her of that would you, when you get the opportunity?"

"Yes, of course, I will."

"Aah your a darlin girl so ya are, t be sure, but let it be our little secret eh?"

"Of course, I won't tell a living soul."

Vera had finished dressing Jake, she had shown him to Bill and Rosemary who had said how marvellous he looked, now she so wanted Bridie and Ivy to see him.

They could hear someone coming down the stairs so Bridie quickly changed the subject and for the benefit of whoever it was said."

"Well we couldn't have wished for a better day to give our little Jake for God's blessing, could we now!"

"No we couldn't," Ivy said in agreement.

Vera overheard, "Here he is all dressed up, what do you think?"

Bridie and Ivy looked at Jake dressed in the beautiful white christening robe that Vera had knitted and crocheted for him, she had also crocheted him a bonnet and booties to match.

"Oooh, they both exclaimed.

Bridie said, "Doesn't our little man look a picture, so he does?"

"Vera you're so clever, he looks absolutely beautiful, it must have taken you ages?"

"It did, but it was a labour of love, of course, the pattern wasn't a difficult one though, thankfully."

"Aah he looks like royalty, so he does."

Bill and Rosemary came into the room then, Rosemary also started enthusing over Vera's handiwork.

"She's always been a fantastic knitter, far better than me, she was always the best in class at school, well done Vera."

"Thank you, Rosemary, I think we should get going don't you Bill, we don't want to have to rush there and get ourselves all hot and bothered."

"No, you're quite right dear, we can take a gentle stroll and be there in plenty of time."

"Is everyone ready, oh, who's going to take some photographs, I've just thought, it might be a good idea to take one of Jake now in case he's sick over himself later, or starts crying, take one with ours, Bill?"

Vera sat holding Jake and each person there took at least one snap of them.

"I'm not carrying him all the way, Vera said, it'll be easier to take the pram, let's see now, I've got his dummy, I've made up a bottle in case he gets hungry and I have to feed him before we go inside the church. that's in the bottom the pram, there's a towel to put over him if he does want a feed, now have I forgotten anything?"

"Yes the blooming baby, Bill said, now let's get going."

Bill took the pram outside, deftly manoeuvring it over the doorstep and everyone filed out behind him and followed him down the garden path, when they reached the gate with the high step beyond it, Rosemary inched past the pram, opened the gate and helped Bill lift it over the step. Vera placed Jake in the pram and they all set off up 'Wood Lane'.

They arrived at the church in plenty of time to see Pauline and Ned standing at the entrance to the porch, they all greeted each other. Vera lifted Jake out of the pram and Bill found a place to leave it by the side of the porch.

"He looks gorgeous Vera, Pauline said, doesn't he Ned?"

"He does that," Ned agreed.

They walked into the church, the Reverend Soames was standing by the font, he smiled and said hello then he did his preliminary checks to make sure all the details Vera had given him were correct before he proceeded with the christening ceremony. It was a very simple, pleasant and uncomplicated ritual, the bible verse was read by the vicar which had been chosen by Vera when she first went to arrange the christening, it was Mathew Chapter 19, Verse 14. Which reads: Jesus said:

Suffer little children to come unto me: and forbid them not: for such is the kingdom of heaven. Verily I say unto you, Whosoever shall not receive the kingdom of God as a little child shall in no wise enter therein.

Jake didn't so much as murmur when he was actually christened; the water was splashed on his head and the vicar made the sign of the cross on his forehead, in fact, he had been as good as gold all through the whole ceremony.

They thanked the vicar and Bill gave him a donation for the church, they walked out into bright sunshine and stood chattering amongst themselves. Theresa the vicar's wife came out of the vicarage gate, she walked over to congratulate them and have a look at Jake.

"Doesn't he look lovely, she said, you must be very proud, is he always as well behaved as this?"

"Yes, most of the time he is, he very rarely cries," Vera replied, then Theresa said:

"You're very lucky then," and she carried on into the church.

Bridie commented to Vera what a very nice simple ceremony it was and how she was honoured and privileged to have been asked to be his Godmother. Vera told her that if it wasn't for her, they might not even be here today, she was so grateful to her for everything she had done; if anyone should feel privileged it was her and Bill, Jake couldn't have a better Godmother. Bridie welled up at this and began to cry.

"Aah silly me, so I am to be crying, this is a happy occasion, as she dabbed at her eyes with her handkerchief."

Vera said, "Yes it is, one I shall remember for a long time and you're not silly at all." The moment was suddenly lightened as Bill asked:

"Shall we take some photographs?"

No sooner he'd said it than most everyone took their cameras out and started snapping, some wanted Bill and Vera holding Jake, then Bridie, Rosemary and Ivy wanted to hold him and be photographed, there was a lot of juxtapositioning and posing to get the desired results, providing no one shook their camera while they were taking the snap, put their finger in front of the lens, forgot to wind on the film after the last shot or managed to simply cut someones head off because they were rushing, It would be interesting to see what the results were like when they were developed and collected from the chemist. Having told Theresa that Jake hardly ever cried, he suddenly started wailing with a vengeance, he was probably fed up of being passed from pillar to post, or most likely he was hungry. Vera took him over to the pram; she put the towel she'd brought over his front to protect his christening robe, reached under the coverlet for his bottle and put it to his little lips. He began to gulp at it as though he'd never been fed before.

"I think it's time we made our way home, Bill said, I'm hungry, I don't know about anyone else?"

There were a few murmurs of approval at Bill's remark, so as soon as Jake had finished his bottle, Vera wiped his mouth, burped him, laid him in his pram and they all set off home.

Everyone was sat around the table tucking into the food that Vera and Rosemary had prepared, they all said how delicious it was and what a lovely occasion it had turned out to be. Vera thanked Rosemary for all her help in getting everything ready and she mentally gave herself a big pat on the back as well, it truly had been a day to remember.

Over the next nine years, Jake grew to be a healthy boy physically, but he was emotionally troubled due to his domestic situation and the constant fear of being beaten up by his father, often for no apparent reason. This naturally impacted on his schooldays, the work that he did and his interactions with other children. He was always being told that children should be seen and not heard, therefore he was never as confident as he should have been, his self-esteem was low. He appeared different to the other children and it was this that made him a target for bullies. Indeed, Jake himself felt different in terms of his sexuality, he wasn't interested in girls in a romantic way, but found the other boys and men immensely attractive, of course outwardly he suppressed these feelings for fear of abuse, because the accepted norm was the boy-girl template.

Jake had one real friend called John Smedley who he cycled to and from school with and who he sat next to him in class. They were both from similar backgrounds, John's dad worked at a nearby farm as a labourer and the family also lived in a tied cottage, the only difference between their backgrounds was that John had brothers and sisters, so he didn't feel as alone as Jake did. They often used to get into mischief on the way home from school, they delighted in doing one particular thing on a regular basis until one day it backfired on them. There was a steep hill on part of their journey; at the bottom of the hill on a corner was a petrol garage with a large forecourt, it had rubber cables running across the ground which when a vehicle ran over them sounded a signal to the garage owner that he had a customer waiting. Jake and John would cycle down the hill at speed and if there were no cars on the forecourt they would cut the corner and cycle across the cables setting off the signal, when the owner came out he found that there was nobody there. This must have made him quite angry because one particular afternoon the lads did their usual trick and the owner was lying in wait for them, as they came past he drenched them with water by turning the hosepipe on them, they had to go home soaked, they never did it again. One day the lads who were about fourteen years old stopped by some shrubbery as Jake needed to have a piss, he left his bike with John and went into the bushes and was having a piss when John said:

"I've got to have one as well now." So he wheeled the bikes out of sight into the bushes, to join Jake, he really didn't want a piss at all he wanted to have a look at Jake's cock. Jake was quite surprised when John said he had a nice cock and could see that John had a big hard-on. John reached out and held Jake's cock which had sprung into life and instantly became stiff. They both unfastened their trousers and let them fall to the ground and they were fondling each other's balls and admiring each other's cocks as they wanked them, Jake's being only slightly larger in length than Johns as well as a little thicker. They suddenly found themselves kissing and then John stooped down and put his mouth around Jake's cock and began sucking it, Jake was squirming with pleasure, it was all so heady and unexpected he hadn't realised his friend was interested in him that way at all. Jake wanted to do the same to him so he whispered:

"Let me suck yours," John stood up and Jake dropped to the ground, eagerly taking his smooth knob end into his mouth and gently sliding his lips up and down the length of its shaft, after a few blissful seconds he could hear John murmuring groans of ecstasy as he shot his thick warm cum into Jake's mouth. Jake stood up and spat the spunk onto the ground as John got down and started to suck him again, he could feel sensations welling up from deep inside his balls; his cum wildly exploding into John's deep throat as he gulped and swallowed it down. Jake was shaking with the reverberations of his climax feeling a mixture of elation and lightheadedness. John got up and smiled at Jake as they both began to get dressed.

"Phwoarr that was good," John said, "you didn't half cum a lot!"

"Yeah, so did you, it was all the excitement, I can't think why we haven't done this before?"

"I've wanted to Jake, but I never had the nerve until today, I don't think it will be the last time, do you?"

"No I'm sure it won't," Jake replied as they embraced and kissed each other again before peering out and checking to see if the coast was clear before emerging from the bushes with their bikes.

They mounted their bikes and rode towards their homes two abreast, holding hands in their pleasure and satisfaction of the new secret discovery of each other. When they reached the crossroads where John usually turned off to cycle the last half mile to his home alone, they stopped their bikes for a moment, looked all about them to see if anyone was about; when they felt they couldn't be seen they kissed goodbye saying they would see each other and ride to school together tomorrow. Jake felt as though he was on top of the world, he didn't know if John was feeling the same but he hoped he was. The two boys became each other's confidantes and their friendship developed into a dangerous closeness that they had to control in the company of anyone else in case people suspected or detected it was not an ordinary everyday friendship. After that first occasion on the way home when they had found out about each other, they had many other similar encounters, they also spent a lot of time together in the school holidays and found special secret places where they could strip off naked and make love. Their favourite place was the barn where the hay bales were stacked, Jake had climbed to the top at the back of the bales; lifted and rearranged some of the heavy bales so that once they were inside they were completely enclosed and safe from any prying eyes, their passion was often fulfilled here.

Towards the end of their school days when they were doing exams and preparing to leave school there seemed to be a natural cooling down between them and though they remained good friends the sexual activity stopped. After they left school and both started work they just never found time to see each other anymore.

One day Jake arrived home from work in Hanworth and his mam said she had some bad news to tell him, she went on to say that his friend John Smedley had been killed in Addlestone, he had been driving a van and there had been a crash with another car.

Jake was obviously upset and went up to his room and cried, remembering what they had been to each other and grieving for the life of his friend that had not been half lived, the following weekend he visited his family and took a wreath giving his condolences and his apologies for not attending the funeral.

Chapter 11

The man sat at the kitchen table, and stared at the photograph with tears rolling down his cheeks, then he just leaned forward with his head resting on his arms emitting low growling sobs that came from somewhere deep inside him and racked his whole being, It was four months since the accident, but it only seemed like yesterday. He had been meaning to fix the wall at the end of the old barn on his smallholding for a while, but he had never got around to doing it, it was crumbling and the wall was severely bowed. It would have cost a lot of money to pay bricklayers to come and do it, money he just didn't have. So he had just let it ride, knowing that one day it would probably just fall down, then he could just clear the rubble away and use the bricks for something else. He had told his son to steer clear of it but maybe he hadn't fully understood the danger. He didn't know to this day what he was doing to be so close to it when it fell down on top of him and crushed the life out of his little body, he was eleven years old. Arthur had discovered the accident on his return from fixing the wire on the far side of the field where they kept the pigs. "He was screaming Danny, Danny, Oh God no Danny," as he scrabbled at the pile of bricks to try to get his son out from under them, hoping that he would still be alive. He could see the sole of one of Danny's wellingtons poking out from under the rubble. "Oh God, Danny no," Arthur cried as he grabbed bricks from the pile and threw them to one side desperately trying to get to him. It wasn't until he had cleared quite a few of the bricks that he realised that a heavy roof beam had fallen and was on top of the boy. He knew for certain then that he was dead. Since that terrible day his whole life had changed, it was as though the bottom had fallen out of his world and he was just going through the motions of living, there was no pleasure in life for him anymore. he missed Danny so much, he had been his whole life as he had raised him since he was four when his bitch of a mother went off with her fancy man and left him to look after him and manage the smallholding all on his own. It certainly hadn't been easy for him, but Danny had given him so much joy and it had been a privilege to watch him growing up and enjoying his life on the farm. He loved the pigs; the chickens and the ducks, from a very early age, had taken on the task of feeding them and he would help his dad in all sorts of ways. His mother had missed all that, wherever she was he certainly didn't wish her well. He blamed himself of course, if only he'd done something about the barn wall, Danny would still be here now. He could still picture his little smiling face and his curly light brown hair and could still see him sitting on his dad's lap talking. He had cleared all the rubble from on top of Danny and he had broken down and anguished over his little broken form, then he had lifted the body and carried it to what he knew was one of Danny's favourite places on the bank of the small pond at the far side of the pig field. He used to sit on the bank and watch the ducks swimming and he was able to see what was going on all over the smallholding, Arthur buried him there along with the secret of his life. He knew that there would be no-one to ask where he had gone, or why he had never been to school because they had never registered his birth, his mother had brought him into the world in their little cottage and he was raised with love. His school was the farm, the animals and the neighbouring countryside, his mam and dad were his teachers. He never ventured far away from the land that the cottage was on and they never saw a soul apart from Roy who occasionally came to help Arthur about the place. Arthur was the only one who would mourn him, and he would do that every day for the rest of his life.

Chapter 12

Jake loved the long summer holiday break it was a great time and sunny days gave scope for venturing further away from home and the wood to other favourite places that he knew, or find new ones to go to. Today he was off to the other side of a different wood about a mile and a half away from his home and the nearby farm where his dad worked, to visit the local municipal tip to see what he could find there. He had to be careful though as sometimes a workman was there with a mechanical digger spreading and levelling off the refuse that the council rubbish wagon delivered and tipped more waste on the site. If he or the lorry driver saw Jake there they would shout at him to clear off as it wasn't really a suitable place for a young boy to be. Jake loved it here though and was prepared to take the risk of being caught as he could find some really great stuff, the only thing he didn't really like were the bad smells that pervaded the place or that he sometimes unearthed when he was poking around with his bare hands or a stick. He had found a gas mask here once and a brass telescope, he never knew what he might find. There were dangers at the tip that Jake was well aware of as he'd had a nasty accident one day when he cut a flap of skin off the top of his thumb on a tin can when he was scratting about with his bare hand. It poured with blood and was really sore, he had wrapped his handkerchief around it as it wouldn't stop bleeding and then run off back home. He had been greeted by his concerned mother who bathed it with warm water and iodine which stung like hell and caused him to scream out and cry. His mother soothed him and told him it was hurting because the iodine was cleaning it so that it would heal.

"You don't want it to go sceptic do you?" She then put a strong-smelling pink ointment on it and bandaged it up with a clean white cotton strip that she tore from an old pillowcase, it looked very dramatic. She had asked him how he had done it and before he knew what he was saying he'd lied and told her that he had cut it on a piece of metal when he'd climbed over a fence, because he didn't think she would approve of him scratting on the dump! Jake was relieved that she had accepted what he had told her.

However, it was a different story when dad returned home from work at dinner time and saw the heavily bandaged dramatic thumb.

"What the bloody hell have you been up to lad?" Jake sheepishly repeated the same account he had told his mother but his father didn't believe him, for one thing he had not met his dad's eyes when he was re-telling him the lie, and the other thing was that his dad had known for a while that he was going to the dump.

"You look me straight in the eye and tell me the truth, you didn't do that climbing a fence, you did it scraping on the dump didn't you?" He didn't wait for an answer as he knew he was right and he brought his hand up and clouted him hard round the ear.

"An that's for telling your mother lies an'all, now get up to bed." With the pain of the clout still stinging him Jake ran out of the door and up the stairs to his room flinging himself on the bed he sobbed into his pillow.

About half an hour or so later his bedroom door creaked open and his mother came in carrying a mug of hot cocoa and a sandwich made from the remainder of the dinner he hadn't eaten, which consisted of a sausage, egg and some chips.

"Here y'are milad, I've brought you the rest of your dinner, sit up and eat it, there's a cup of cocoa as well." She placed the plate and mug on the bedside table as Jake was sitting up. She sat on the edge of his bed and he saw the sympathetic look in his mother's eyes and he flung his arms round her neck and cried. She gave him a kiss and said, "Now, now, come on, no more tears, drink up some of your cocoa."

Jake still sniffling said, "I'm sorry, mam."

"Yes, I know you are said his mother, but you mustn't go telling us any more lies, you promise me you won't?"

"I won't mam."

"That's a good boy, now you finish that, then get yourself undressed and go to sleep."

"Alright, Mam," Jake said.

Jake had never forgotten that experience, he was always careful when he was digging on the tip as well as being clever about not letting his dad know where he'd been or else he'd get a good hiding. He often seemed to be in trouble with his dad, he was always hitting him for no reason and shouting at him, he couldn't understand why. He often lay in his bed at night frightened and couldn't get off to sleep because his mam and dad were rowing downstairs or having a fight. He once heard his mam shout at his dad:

"He's always with me, you never take him anywhere or spend any time with him!"

Great, it's Saturday morning Jake thought as he woke up! He could hear his mother moving around downstairs and the smell of porridge was wafting under the bottom of his bedroom door, by the time he had been to the bathroom, washed and dressed his mother was calling out to him that his breakfast was ready.

He was just thinking to himself how glad he was that he didn't have to go to school, he hated it as the other boys bullied him all the time and made his life miserable, even some of the teachers were bullies. Often in class Mr Gray the geography teacher would throw a piece of chalk or even the blackboard rubber at someone who was talking or larking about. Mr Brodle was the worst though, he was the P.E. instructor and he could be really vicious, he would smack you around the head, or grab your ear and twist it until it really throbbed and burned, if you weren't one of his favourites he would regularly pick on you. Then, of course, there was always the possibility of the cane if you upset one of the teachers and they sent you to see the headmaster Mr Roberts. The only teacher he really liked was Miss Dowling the English mistress as she was really kind, he enjoyed her lessons, especially composition.

Break times and going home time were fraught with danger as fights would often break out and all the children would crowd around the ones who were fighting, they would jeer and goad them on, pushing and shoving and sometimes kicking at the one they wanted to lose! Jake was a gentle, sensitive lad and he hated the idea of fighting. His dad had tried several times to teach him to fight and stand up for himself, but he was a bit too rough with his son and it usually ended up with him losing patience, and Jake crying. Alarmingly none of the teachers ever seemed to be around to see anything going on at break times to put a stop to it! When the home bell rang Jake was often chased and spat at or punched and kicked for absolutely no reason, he was always relieved when he had escaped the school grounds and was well away from the area and safely on his way home. Well, he wasn't going to worry about any of that until after the weekend was over and he had to go to school on Monday morning, he still had the rest of today and Sunday to have fun. What was far more important was where he was going to go today after he had finished his breakfast. He had told himself that he must never go back to the refuse tip in case his dad found out and walloped him, but now he found himself thinking about it more and more and he knew that he would have to go there again if only for one last time. After he'd finished his breakfast he put on his warm jacket and two pairs of socks inside his wellingtons as it looked cold outside, he said goodbye to his mam.

"Now you watch what you get up to today, mi lad, don't go getting into any mischief." "I won't Mam." The quickest and easiest way to get to the dump would have been to leave the cottage by the back door from the kitchen, but Jake thought that by him using that way out of the house his mam might realise where he was going, so he decided that he would leave by the front door which would take him onto the lane leading to the farm, and make it look as if he was heading in completely the opposite direction. He could then double back further up the lane, cut across a couple of fields and get to the dump that way.

When he got there Jake was glad to see that there was no sign of any workmen so he had a good look around and could see where new stuff had been dumped. He didn't think there would be anybody about on a Saturday morning. He made sure he was on reasonably firm ground and started to poke around and dig with a piece of wood he had found. After about twenty minutes he saw something glinting in the sunlight so he reached into the refuse and pulled it out. He cleaned the dirt of it and could see it was a chunky piece of glass with markings and strange writing on it. Jake looked at it for a while, he couldn't make any sense of the writing at all but he thought it was pretty so he took the bag that he had brought from out of his pocket and placed it in it. He thought to himself that it would look nice as an ornament on top of the upturned crate in his camp.

Chapter 13

Jake had spent all morning at the dump and had found a few more interesting things for his collection, a set of dominoes in a wooden box and a canvas bound book that had lots of pictures in it. He decided that he would take them back to his camp. He would enjoy reading his book later after he'd been home for a sandwich and a warm cup of tea, as the chill November wind had made him quite cold. When he had taken the book from his bag later, on closer inspection it turned out to be an encyclopaedia and it had lots of interesting things in it, although some of the pages were a little stained and marked from the dirt and muck at the dump, but he didn't mind that, and he was right about the piece of glass, it looked splendid sat on top of the crate in the corner.

He had come back to the wood after lunch, it was looking so beautiful in the pale midday sun, it was brightening the leaves with sparkles of light and speckles were dancing on the woodland floor as he walked towards his camp. He was always careful to look around him everywhere to make sure that no one was about, he didn't want anyone to find his hidden sanctuary. He hadn't encountered anyone on the way through the wood, but he had one last quick look around before parting back the leafy branch that concealed the entrance to his camp before he quickly went in. He was dying to read his encyclopaedia so he settled himself down on the large cushion on the floor that he had made from an old potato sack which he had stuffed with dry leaves. Jake had asked his dad to get it for him from the farm. Dad had asked why he wanted such a thing, but when Jake simply said it's for my camp he agreed to ask his boss if he could have one. He didn't ask Jake where his camp was, he just presumed it was somewhere in the wood.

Jake was delighted the next day when his dad had come home from work and presented him with the rolled-up hessian sack. When he had finished filling it with leaves he made some holes along the open end with a pointed stick he had whittled with his penknife, then he threaded a long piece of supple green willow backwards and forwards through the holes along the sack to seal it shut. He found it was really comfortable to lie on and he could rest his shoulders up against the trunk of the ash tree that filled one corner of his camp. He decided that he would take them back to his camp. He would enjoy reading his book later after he'd been home for a sandwich and a warm cup of tea, as the chill November wind had made him quite cold.

What could be more pleasant of an afternoon he thought, than lying here in his camp reading his new book, he was reading about native American Indians, how they tracked and hunted animals, killing them skilfully with bows and arrows to provide food for the tribe. They then cured the hides and made them into moccasins, which was the name for the shoes they wore. Totally absorbed, he just read and read and didn't really notice himself yawning and becoming sleepy.

He must have fallen asleep he thought as he awoke stretching and yawning, surprised to realise that it was beginning to get dark. Mum would have his tea ready for him and she would be worried if he didn't get home soon! As he began to get up he heard a rustling noise nearby and thought that it was probably an animal of some kind but then there was a heavy snap sound and Jake knew that someone was out there close by and they had just stepped on a stick. He didn't know who it was or what to do, whether he should just make a run for it or stay here and hide, he was all of a tremble, but as scared as he was he thought it best to lie low and keep quiet until whoever it was had passed by as no one had any idea that his camp was here! He was breathing so heavily that he felt sure whoever it was would be able to hear him, so he put his hand over his mouth as if to make it more quiet.

Then suddenly there was another rustle as a man threw aside the leafy branch that concealed the entrance to his camp, and stepped inside.

"Aaaagh," Jake screamed out in shock and tried to scoot past this intruder to run back home. He was a great big hulk of a man who looked a bit scruffy, he was wearing a tattered old gaberdine raincoat which was tied around with binder twine, the stuff dad used to tie bales of hay together.

"Hold on there young un," the man said brusquely as he caught hold of Jake by the collar of his coat, "I ain't gonna hurt ya. I just want to talk to ya."

"What about?" Jake asked puzzled and still frightened, he hadn't done anything wrong that he was aware of! "I'm not supposed to talk to strangers, mam said.

"Well, I'm not really a stranger lad I've been a watching you for a while, I saw yo building this camp and bringing things to put in it. I knows your dad works for Ned Trouch up at the farm. I just want to be your friend, I know yo haven't got many friends as you'n always playing alone like, an I know yo like collecting things so I brought yo this."

The man reached into his pocket and took out a small metal object that had a glass face with a moving hand in it, similar to a clock, "Bet you aint never seen one o these before, it's called a compass," and he held it out for Jake to take.

"I have," Jake said, "but I ain't never had one of mi own, is it for me to keep." The man took hold of Jake's hand as he held the compass.

"Yes, he replied seeing the joy on the boy's face, look how the arra spins round when you move in a different direction, he said, holding Jake's shoulders and turning him around, d'ya know why it does that?"

"No," Jake replied.

"It's looking to find magnetic north pole all the time," the man said, "it'll always show where north is."

"Cor," Jake gasped absolutely forgetting that the man was a complete stranger and that he could be in great danger.

"What's your name," the man asked.

"Jake, he said still engrossed with the compass, then looking up at the man, he asked, n what's your name mister?"

"I'm Arthur, he said, I hope we're going to be great friends Jake?"

"Yeah, n where do you live mister?"

"I only live a short ways away, on a farm, wud you like to come and see it and help mi feed mi pigs, an then I'll bring you back home to your mam and dad?"

"Yeah please mister!"

"Call me Arthur."

"Ok, Arthur."

"Cum wi mi then an we'll be there afore yo know it?"

Jake liked his new friend, he was kind and he wanted him to like him, he slipped his hand into Arthur's hand and they left Jake's camp, walking to the far side of the wood away from Jake's home. Jake felt excited to have found a new friend, he wondered if Arthur was going to be like his other friend Mike that lived further down the lane, and his Uncle Tim. Would he do nice things with him too, like they did!

Arthur's farm was further away than Jake thought, his legs were getting tired from the long walk. Arthur must have sensed this, he looked down at Jake who's still holding his hand and said."

"A'yo alright Jake, a'ya getting tired, d'ya wanna piggy back?"

"Yes please, Arthur, it's a long way ain't it!"

"It seems a long way cos yo ain't bin ere afore," Arthur said as he bent down and helped Jake onto his back.

"S'that better lad he said as he set off walking again, t'aint far now."

Jake liked the closeness of having his arms around Arthur's neck and the warmth coming from his head and back, Arthur's big hands were reaching backwards cupping the cheeks of Jake's bottom to keep him from slipping off his back; the motion of the walking was causing Jake's cock to stiffen and he put his face next to the side of Arthur's face and nuzzled into it, he wondered how long it would be before Arthur might kiss him. Jake was fast asleep when they reached his cottage, Arthur didn't undress him as he didn't feel right about doing that, it didn't seem proper, he just took off his wellingtons; pulled the eiderdown over him, stroked his hair and kissed him lightly on the cheek. He would tell him in the morning that he loved him and was glad he was back at the farm with him, they were together now.

Chapter 14

"Where on earth can he be?" Jake's mother sobbed into the shoulder of her husband William. "Something must have happened to him Bill, he knows better than to stay out this late."

"Now, now love, don't worry, perhaps he's met up with one of his school mates and they're having such a good time, he doesn't want to come home," Bill said, not really believing it and trying to convince himself as well.

"No Bill, Jake wouldn't do that, it's nine o'clock and it's pitch dark, somethings happened to him, he's been gone since lunchtime, I think we should get Ned Trouch to telephone the police."

Ned Trouch was the farmer Bill worked for up at Melford House Farm further up the lane, and he owned the cottage that Vera & Bill Wiggins rented from him. Bill felt that his wife's feelings were right, their Jake wouldn't stay out this late as he knew his dad would probably give him a good hiding when he got home.

"I think you're right Vera, you stay here a minute and I'll nip next door and get Mavis to come and keep you company while I go up the farm.

"Ok, Bill," Vera said tearfully. Mavis could be a bit of a busy body, she thought, but she would rather have her company than be left on her own tonight.

Bill was soon back with Mavis Burridge coming in quickly behind him, he had grabbed his cap and jacket from off the hall stand and was putting his cap on as he said

"Here's Mavis to keep you company love, I'm just off up the farm," and with that he was off like a shot!

"Oooh Vera you poor love, you must be worried sick Mavis said as she held her arms out to put round Vera's shoulder, Bill's told us young Jake's gone missing, but don't fret, he'll soon be back home, I'll put the kettle on and make you a nice cup of tea," she said sympathetically as she walked into the kitchen. Mavis was a tall thin wisp of a woman with sharp features, she always wore a scarf on her head tied so that there was a bow at the front and Vera had never seen her not wearing a floral printed wrap-around pinny. She was in her late fifties but looked at least ten years older.

"Thank you, Mavis," Vera said, "it's very kind of you to come round, I'm sure Bill won't be long."

"Think nothing of it mi dear, if a neighbour can't help at a time like this, well…"

Vera sat in the armchair by the roaring coal fire with her head bowed down and wringing her hands tensely in her lap, desperately trying to think where Jake could be. Earlier about eight she had been out with Bill searching the length of the lane, calling out Jake's name and shining their torches in every nook and cranny in the hope of finding him. They even went into the wood calling for him but they couldn't see or hear any sign of the lad.

What if he is lying seriously hurt somewhere she thought, she didn't dare think of anything worse than that.

"Ere yar mi dear, you drink this nice sweet cup of tea, I'm sure everything will be alright, ee ya look plumb wore out you poor thing."

"Thank you, Mavis," Vera said taking the cup and saucer from her.

They had sat together not really saying very much for what seemed like an eternity, though it couldn't, in reality, have been much longer than forty minutes or so. Vera had begun to wonder what could be keeping Bill so long when she heard the front door open and Bill calling:

"I'm back love."

Bill walked into the living room and straight up to the fire, rubbing his hands together in front of the flames to warm them. He sat on the arm of Vera's chair and put his arm around her.

"The police are on their way love, they should be here very soon, Ned and Pauline send their best wishes and said that if there is anything at all they can do, or if we need anything to let them know. Vera began crying again, taking her handkerchief from up the sleeve of her cardigan and blowing her nose.

"Come on love, bear up, I'm sure they'll find him."

"I think I can hear the police car, Mavis said, looking very excited, and then almost mentally told herself that she should temper her enthusiasm as it wasn't appropriate under the circumstances.

A few minutes later they could all hear the clanging klaxon bell of the Ford Zephyr Mark II police patrol car as it came down the lane and screeched to a halt at the bottom of the front garden path. Bill got up and went into the hallway to open the door for them. There were three policemen walking up the path, two were in plain clothes and the other in uniform.

"Good evening sir," the older one in plain clothes said, "are you Mr

Wiggins?"

"Yes I am, come in," Bill said as he ushered them into the living room. Bill stood next to Vera who had now risen from her chair. "This is my wife, Vera, and this is our neighbour Mrs Burridge, please sit down won't you?"

The older man introduced himself as Detective Inspector Melgrove and indicating the man next to him said:

"This is my assistant Detective Sergeant Baxter, thank you," and they both sat on the settee opposite the armchair where Vera had seated herself down again next to Bill, but the constable remained standing by the living room door looking as if he was on guard at Buckingham Palace.

Detective Inspector Ian Melgrove was a tall good looking man in his late forties, he wasn't a local man. He had moved here six months ago from the South London suburb of

Morley Cross with his wife Patricia and their two children Sam aged seven and little Alice aged five. They had moved to the country as they thought it would give them all a better quality of life because they needed a bigger house and prices were cheaper up here. He looked at the two anxious faces of Vera and Bill and he really felt for them, he couldn't begin to imagine how he would feel in their situation if one of his children went missing.

The Inspector took a notebook and pen from his overcoat pocket, and looked towards Vera and Bill. "Now, I know this is a very distressing time for you both but I just need to ask you a few questions, how old is your boy, Jake isn't it, he said looking up and giving a concerned smile, when did you last see him?

"He's eleven, he came home for a sandwich at about half-past twelve," Vera said, dabbing her eyes with her hanky.

"And what time did he leave the house?" the Inspector asked, writing in his notebook.

"I think it must have been about one o'clock, he never stays in the house for long."

"Did he tell you where he was going?"

"No, he didn't, he could have gone anywhere!

"It was around that time I happened to be looking out of my window, and I saw him going into the wood," Mavis interjected, "he plays in there a lot."

"Thank you Mrs er…"

"Burridge," Mavis reminded him.

Are you absolutely sure about that?" D.I. Melgrove asked.

"Oh yes, Mavis said, I have a wonderful view from my front window."

"And you live just next door do you?" "That's right, I do yes."

"Are there any other places that he likes to go to?"

Frowning, Bill said, "Yes, the local dump, although we've told him not to!"

Turning to Vera he asked, "Can you give me a description of Jake, how tall is he, is his hair dark or fair?

"He isn't very tall for his age, about four foot six inches I think, an his hairs dark brown."

"Can you tell me what he was wearing Mrs Wiggins?"

"Yes he had on a pair of grey flannel trousers, an old white school shirt, a green jersey I knitted for him and his brown jacket."

"What shoes was he wearing?" Melgrove asked.

"His wellingtons, I'm always telling him not to wear them all the time as they draw his feet terrible," and with that, she burst into a flood of tears.

Bill leaned his head against his wife's and held her close, "Ssshhh," he said soothingly.

We've nearly finished for the moment Melgrove said, "but the other thing is, have you seen anyone suspicious, any strangers about in the area?"

"No we haven't," Bill said.

"He won't be in any of your neighbours' houses do you think?" "No, Vera said, Bill's been round them all, an they havn't seen im."

"Does he have any friends that he would go and visit?" D.S. Baxter asked. "There's only John Smedley, but he lives a couple of miles away at Horton, they ride to school together.

"What's his address?" he asked.

"Well, I don't know the number but it's a cottage down Spinney Lane near Blakes Farm.

"Ok, thank you we'll pay them a visit."

"Oh and do you know if he had any money on him?"

"No he wouldn't have," Bill said.

D.I. Melgrove then told them that they would be mounting a thorough search of the local area initially covering a five mile radius at first light tomorrow morning and that if Bill felt up to it he could join them as he was more familiar with the surrounding countryside than his officers. Bill had said that he would certainly go with them and he was sure that Ned Trouch and some of the other workers would go with them as well. Melgrove also informed them that they were bringing in a large number of officers from surrounding forces to help them with the search, he said that he was optimistic that they would find Jake.

"Should I make everyone a cup of tea?" Mavis asked.

"That's very kind, Melgrove said but we must be going as we have a lot to do before the morning."

Melgrove walked towards the front door with Baxter and the constable following him, "Rest assured that we will do everything we possibly can, try to get a good nights sleep, and if you think of anything you've forgotten to tell us, ring the police station and ask the desk sergeant to give me the message. We will obviously keep you informed as to how things are going, we will just pay a visit to the Smedleys this evening, just in case Jake might have gone there and we'll start our search at the farm at six am in the morning, goodnight."

"Goodnight Inspector," Bill said and showed them out, he never mentioned as he came back inside that the night sky was clear and starry and how cold it was, a sure sign that there would be a frost overnight. he was sorely afraid for Jake out on a night like this. He hoped to God that he was somewhere safe and warm.

Chapter 15

Jake woke up and for a while couldn't think where he was, this wasn't his bedroom and why had he slept in his clothes, then he suddenly remembered that Arthur had brought him to show him the farm. He must have fallen asleep and he hadn't woke him up. He got up to see where Arthur was and as he lifted the latch on the door and stepped into the corridor, he could smell the lovely aroma of bacon and eggs and looking down the corridor could see Arthur in the kitchen, yawning and stretching his arms above his head he walked along the corridor and into the kitchen. Arthur looked up and smiled at Jake.

"Mornin sun, yo slep well, are yo ungry?"

"Yes, I am," Jake replied, I didn't go home for mi tea, mi mam n dad'll be really mad at me."

"Yo sit yer down sun cos I got sumthin ta tell yer afore yo as yer brekfast, Arthur drew a chair up close to Jake and continued, yo see it's like this sun, he said putting his arm around Jake's shoulder, yo ain't in no trouble cos yer mam and dad knows where yo are, n they asked me to look after you for a while cos they had to go away on urgent business. They said sorry for not telling yer, but it were sudden like. They said you'd be happy to stay ere wi mi an be ararnd the farm, it'll be like an oliday and yo can elp mi wi the animals. So as soon as yove ad yer brekfast we'll go for a walk rarnd farm, alright sun?"

Jake was surprised at what Arthur had told him but he was excited about the prospect of a holiday with his new friend and said to Arthur eagerly:

"Does that mean I won't have to go to school while I'm on holiday!"

"That's rite sun," Arthur replied.

"Yippee Jake shouted with delight, can I ave mi brekfast now?

Arthur breathed a sigh of relief that the boy was happy and wanted to stay here, he wasn't sure how long it would be before he started asking questions and getting homesick, but this was his home now, he'd cross that bridge when he came to it. He watched his boy tucking into his breakfast and he felt a contentment that he hadn't done for a long time. Although his farm was out of the way and he never had visitors there was always the off chance that someone might suddenly come onto his property, he was going to have to be extra careful and vigilant in protecting Danny from being seen, he wasn't going to lose him again.

As soon as Jake had finished his breakfast, Arthur said:

"Ere yar sun go an have a wash and clean yer teeth, ere's a tarl and a new tuthbrush, yer'll find tuthpaste in the bathroom darn the all, when yove dun that I'll show ya rarnd the farm."

Jake looked up at Arthur and gave a great big smile, "Oo smashin," he gushed.

Jake was so excited as Arthur took him around the farm, he saw the chickens, the little ducks on the pond; the three goats, but his favourites were the pigs, Arthur had five of them, one boar which was the male; three sows and one gilt, he explained that a gilt was a pig that hadn't had piglets yet. He also told him they were a breed called Tamworth. Jake absolutely loved watching them they were covered with ginger hair. Jake thought that Arthur was lovely as he kept putting his arm around him and explaining all about the animals, his dad never did that he was always too busy.

Jake was pleased that Arthur had said he could help look after the animals, especially that he could feed the pigs, and he told him that in late spring when it was a bit warmer, the gilt that was being kept separate from the boar would most likely have baby piglets, he couldn't wait for that. After Arthur had shown him the animals he took him a bit further away from the house and they climbed up a small hillock that bordered a cluster of trees where the pigs were able to come and root about. Jake could hear the faint peeling of church bells in the far distance. From here Arthur pointed out to him the adjoining fields that circled the farm and the boundary of his land, beyond that was dense woodland for miles; then more open countryside beyond. Arthur had his hand on Jake's back and looking down at him, said something strange to Jake.

"One day all this'll be yourn Danny, if I teaches yer well n wi work hard this'll provide evrythin wi need to keep us goin." Jake didn't know why Arthur had called him Danny but he didn't mind what he called him, it was so lovely here, he thought. He put his arms around Arthur's girth;

his head against his side, and said, I love you Arthur, you're my best friend in all the world. Then Arthur bent down put both his hands on either side of his head and kissed his mouth.

"I love you too sun, mor an yer'll eva know." They then began walking back towards the farm.

"There's jobs to do," he said.

Jake felt so happy, he felt in his pocket and took out the compass that Arthur had given him.

"Look, Arthur, we're goin towards the east, that's good init."

Arthur smiled, and said, "That's real good sun, cmon, when we've done some work, ah'll show yo har ta catch a rabbit."

"Phoarr, really, I've never done that before Arthur."

"Ah'll teach yer," he said.

For several hours Arthur got on with things he had to do on the farm like feeding the animals and Jake was there trying to help him, watching how he did things so that he would be able to do it on his own soon. There was a piece of fencing that needed reinforcing over by the hillock, Arthur had noticed it when they were there earlier, the pigs were always trying to find a way through it. He knew he'd better do it straight away or else the pigs would be through it like a shot, and then they'd have a hell of a job trying to get them back in again. So both of them went back over there, Arthur carried a roll of metal netting some pliers and clips and Jake carried the hammer and a bag of nails. Arthur got on with the job occasionally asking Jake to pass him something he needed. The rest of the time Jake sat on a tuft of grass watching him work, but more interesting watching the contours of Arthur's buttocks when he was bending over and once when he straightened up and stretched leaning back as he did so Jake saw the glorious form of his cock protruding under the cloth of his trousers and he began to feel his own cock was getting aroused. He longed to reach out and unbutton Arthur's flies and take it out of his pants and hold it, but he didn't dare. Then it was time for Jake stand up as they were ready to go back to the farm and he still had a great big full hard-on, Jake thought he had seen Arthur notice it and then look away and he was thrilled to think that Arthur now knew he was a big lad for his age, his other friends often said this to him.

Later, they left the farm to go and set some snares to catch rabbits as Arthur had promised, and Arthur took his gun along as well. He'd warned Jake never to touch the gun as it was very dangerous. Arthur showed Jake some rabbit runs on the edge of the wood and he took a piece of wire; made it into a running loop like a noose then fastened one end to the base of a small sapling and positioned the loop so that it rested in the channel of the run.

"Ther yar sun that's har yo set a snare, Arthur said, nar yo can do the next un, move along a bit farther n see if yer can spot another run like this un."

Jake walked a bit further intent on finding one and was quite surprised to find several in a patch of taller grass about three feet from the first one.

"Ere, I've found some Jake exclaimed with glee, can I have a piece of wire?" Jake was trying to remember how he'd seen Arthur make the loop; as he was doing it Arthur said:

"That's it sun, yove got it, yome a natral at it, well dun, nah lay it s'os the rabbit'll run and put is yed thru it, there yove dun it. I'll jus do a few more n we'll cum back termorra n see if we's caught us one for the pot."

They made their way back to the farm; just as they turned the corner of the field Arthur put his outstretched arm in front of Jake's chest to halt him, whispering he said:

"Keep still a minit sun, and lifting his shotgun to his shoulder he let off a shot at a cock pheasant that he had seen feeding about a hundred yards away, got ya." The gunshot had made Jake startle as he'd never been close to one being fired before.

"Oooh that made me jump, Arthur." he said laughing.

"Yo'll get use to it sun, yo mite evn be shooting yerself afore long!"

"Dya mean it Jake said all excited!"

"A corse I do, cmon, let's pick im up."

When they reached the dead bird Jake was in wonder at the beauty of its feathers, all the many speckled colours and its bright red head, he'd seen them from a distance in the fields but never close up.

"It's beautiful," Jake said.

"Yeah an it'll make gud eatin anall, dya wanna carry im ome, Arthur saw Danny's reluctance, goarn, ee can't urt ya," he said holding the pheasants claws out for him to take hold of.

Reluctantly Jake grasped the birds feet and they walked on homeward.

Arthur said, "We won't able to eat I'm til next week though."

"Why?" Jake asked.

"Ee needs ta be kep angin for abart five days, it meks um taste berrer, then ah'll pluck im; draw his innards art n we'll av im in't frypan for us suppa."

"Can I av sum ov its feathers, please," Jake asked.

"Cors ya can."

When they got back Arthur hung the pheasant on a hook high up by the door, they were both hungry so Arthur cut them both a couple of thick chunks of bread and butter with a piece of cheddar cheese on to last them until Arthur made their dinner for about six o'clock.

Arthur said, "Yo can go art n play a bit safternoon if ya want to."

"Ok," Jake said.

"But yer musn't goo too far from t'harse."

"I won't," Jake said.

The afternoon turned out to be great for Jake he spent his time getting to know the animals, he found some wild herbs growing under a hedge so he fed the goats with it. He then walked up to the hillock and climbed up a tree and had a good look around. He thought about his mam and thought she would be pleased to know he was enjoying his holiday.

When he finally ambled his way back to the cottage after a few hours and ran in to tell Arthur what a smashing time he'd had he found him busy in the kitchen and there was a delicious smell coming from the oven in the range, he sniffed the air, he hadn't realised how hungry he was.

"What ya cooking Arthur, it really smells good?"

"A nice cheese, bacon and taetar pie, that suit ya?"

"Yeah," said Jake eagerly.

"Twont be ready for an har or so tho, want some bred n jam, tide yer over?"

"Yes please," Jake replied.

While Arthur cut a noggin from the loaf, buttered it; spread it with strawberry jam he asked Jake what he'd been doing and Jake told him what he'd been up to. Arthur didn't say anything to Jake but he had kept an eye on him from time to time by looking out of his bedroom window, in case he wandered off too far away.

Later after they had eaten dinner, Arthur did the washing up as Jake stood beside him drying the dishes:

"I really like it ere Arthur," Jake said.

Arthur teased him saying, "Yo jus larkes mi cookin."

"No I do, n I like you anall."

Arthur leaned over and kissed the top of Jake's head, when they had finished the dishes and put them away Arthur went over to the old brown threadbare couch and sat down. Jake sat right next to him snuggling close and Arthur put his arm around his shoulders. He began to tell Jake tales of when he was a young lad and the jobs he had to do around the farm. Jake was listening intently and occasionally casting loving glances up at Arthur. When Arthur had finished speaking, Jake said.

"Why don't mi dad cuddle me like you do stead of hitting me all the time?"

"Ahm sure ee only clips ya rarnt ear if yose bin nordy."

"No ee don't he thumps mi one wi is fists n he won't stop sumtimes, mi mam sharts at im, but then ee its er anall, ere, look at me bruises."

Jake pulls his jumper over his head and opens his shirt, revealing the colourful expanse of old and new bruises on the front of his body, then he turns around to show Arthur the ones on his back.

"Whart, he shudn't it yer lark that, I'd like ta get mi ands on im, n eed av more n a few bruises. I dunno why ee shud treat ya like that, yohm such a gud lad, tell yer what yo can call me dad if yer like, arl never it yer!"

"Can I really?" Jake asked disbelieving.

"Yes yer can n arhl luk arter ya if yole let mi call yo Danny?"

"Yeah that's alright, I know you called me that before, n can I stay ere wi you forever?"

"A corse yer can lad, this'll be yer ome ahll look arter yer."

"N ya won't mek mi go ta school, cos I get it an spat at when I go there?"

"Narsty crule liddle buggers, ner ah won't mek yer g ta school sun," Arthur said holding him close and kissing his head again, the farm'll be yer school n ahll be dad n teacher to yer?

"Ah'll miss mi mam though, but she's got mi dad to luv er aint she?"

"Thats rart lad, but won't yer get lonely wi jus mi ta talk to?"

"No I won't Arth… mm dad, cos I know yole luk after mi?"

Chapter 16

Enid Miles wasn't what anyone would call a raving beauty by any means but she knew how to make the most of herself in terms of her make-up and the dyeing of her hair, she was really a mousy brunette but her idol was the Hollywood film actress Marilyn Monroe and ever since she had seen her in the film Niagara at The Rialto cinema in Addlestone she had modelled herself on the star and gone blonde, even though the overall effect tended to make her look bit brassy, especially if she wore her 'Scarlet Rose' lipstick. Not long after she first went blonde she met Roy and thought she had found her soulmate, he was ten years younger than her, tall and handsome with a good physique. Edna didn't ever think she would have a love affair at all, let alone with a younger man and be tempted to leave her husband, but she had been swept off her feet and everything had happened so quickly. She had been married to Arthur for six years and she knew when she married him that he wasn't going to set her world on fire, but he was steady, gentle and kind and she knew he loved her and would look after her, she didn't love him though. Now here she was running back to him with her tail between her legs because Roy had found himself a younger piece of stuff, he'd brought her back to live with him and had kicked her out on to the street. She didn't leave quietly though, there had been an almighty row that had ended up with her getting a black eye, but she'd left him with a souvenir too, in the kerfuffle she had brought her knee up into his groin with a vengeance so he would have a pair of sore bollocks for a couple of days.

She had managed to pack her case with what few clothes she had and unbeknown to him she had taken the money he had saved that he kept hidden in the bottom of the wardrobe in his best shoes, Didn't know I knew about this, did you, she thought as she put the money, all fifty pounds of it into her purse smiling to herself, it's only what you held back from me for housekeeping money anyway you lousy bastard.

Enid walked to the bus stop, put her case down on the grass and waited. She took her compact out of her handbag and looked at her eye in its mirror, taking her powder puff she loaded it with powder and dabbed it gently around her sore eye to try to hide the purple bruise. When she had finished it didn't look as bad as it had done, but there was no way she could hide the swelling.

The bus arrived just as it had started to rain quite heavily so she was relieved to get on board before she got soaked, as she climbed up the steps the conductor took her case from her with a cheery hello and lifted it up onto the luggage rack. Fortunately, there weren't many people on board to gawp at her and notice her eye, she moved down the aisle to a seat behind them and settled down to begin the journey back to the farm which was about twenty miles in all. The conductor came to take her fare, "Where to Mrs?" he asked. "Addlestone please," Enid replied. "That'll be Two and Six then please, the conductor said, turning the handle on the ticket machine and holding it out for her while she searched for a half-crown in her purse. "Thank you," Enid said taking the ticket and putting it in her purse. She began to think about what she would say to Arthur when she explained why she had come back. What would his reaction be, she would say how she had made a big mistake and knew she had hurt him, she pictured and rehearsed in her mind how she would beg his forgiveness in the hope that he would take her back. He always was a bit soft she thought, I'm sure that will work, and how would Jake react to her, a mother who'd abandoned him and that he hadn't seen since he was four years old, would he even remember her?

Gosh she thought as she looked out of the bus window, she hadn't realised how close it was to Addlestone, another couple of miles and she would be there. She had been so engrossed in her thoughts about meeting Arthur again and thought that she may have nodded off for a while as well, probably as a result of taking a couple of aspirin that she had in her bag, to relieve the pain in her face.

She got off the bus in the centre of Addlestone, thankfully it had stopped raining and it was just beginning to get dark. The place looked the same, the old tin shack cafe was still there, she remembered the times that she used to come here on market day to get whatever bargains were on offer, it was a welcome break from the farm and she always had a cup of tea there, as well as a sausage and tomato batch. She would get a taxi from here to take her the rest of the way to the farm, she wasn't worried about the cost now, she was loaded.

She found it strange as the taxi approached the farm, she never ever thought she would be back here, she got out, the driver opened the boot and lifted out her case, she paid him and generously tipped him two bob, "Oo, thank you Mrs," he said, surprised, then he got back in the cab turned it around and she watched him moving away back towards the main road. Whilst she was in the taxi she had decided that she would wipe some of the powder from around her eye so that Arthur would instantly be able to see her bruised shiner glowing black and red, she thought it might shock him and make him more sympathetic toward her. She knew coming back here wasn't going to be a long term thing she just wanted to get her head together and figure out what she wanted to do next.

She picked up her case and walked towards the kitchen door, she could see there was a light shining through the window as she knocked nervously.

She could hear a bit of a commotion and talking going on, as well as an inner door closing and then Arthur said, "Who's there?" the door was opened about six inches or so to allow Arthur to see who it was?

"It's Enid," she said feebly!

"What, go away," Arthur said gruffly, "you got a bloody cheek coming back here woman, I don't want you here!" His reaction was a surprise to Enid so before he had time to close the door in her face, she put her weight against it a little and said, "I need help Arthur I'm hurt!" "I can't help that he said, it's no concern a mine you don't belong here no more."

"I know I don't deserve any consideration but please let me in Arthur, I'm in a bad way, Roy's beaten me up and chucked me out, I don't have anywhere else to go!"

Arthur opened the door and stood looking at Enid as if still trying to decide whether to let her in or not.

"He's given you a right shiner there, I s'pose you'd better come in for a bit, but you ain't a stayin, mind you."

"Thanks, Arthur, I'm fair worn out."

Arthur took her case and let Enid come in, putting the case down by the side of the kitchen table, Enid sat down.

"You look dreadful," Arthur said as he sat down at the table opposite her.

"I should've left him before now Arthur, he's been knocking me about for months!"

"Well I knew it wouldn't last," he said, giving her a cold look.

Enid put her hand up to her eye and gave a deep sigh, "Ooh, make us a cuppa tea duck, I could really do with one."

Arthur automatically rose and began to make a cup of tea, from her chair Enid looked around the kitchen, it hadn't changed at all except that it needed a darn good clean and the curtains needed washing, or better still, throwing out and replacing with some bright new ones. Well, not my problem she thought, *I aint come here to do no skivvying, this is just a stop-gap for me, then I'm off.*

Arthur put a cup of tea down in front of Enid and she began to drink it.

"Ere yar, drink that he said, then putting his own cup down on the table said, "I'm off to the lav, we'll sort summit out when I get back," and he walked over to the back door and went outside to go to the lavatory. Enid was curious to look in Danny's bedroom just to see how he had grown up, she had often wondered how he had turned out. She quickly picked up the candle, went down the corridor to his box bedroom door, gently lifted the latch and pushing open the door she peered in to take a quick look before Arthur came back. She moved quietly toward the bed and held the candle so that she could see Danny's face, but she was surprised to see that the face she was looking at was not Danny's, it couldn't be, his hair was curly and light brown, this boy had straight lank black hair, so who was this, and where was Danny!

By the time Arthur came back inside, Enid was sat back at the kitchen table drinking her tea pretending as though she hadn't moved from the spot. She was really puzzled and very suspicious, her instincts were telling her that something extremely odd was going on, and before she could stop herself she just came straight out with it.

"Where's Danny, she said pointedly?

"He's in his bed asleep a'course."

"The boy that's in his bed aint Danny," Enid challenged.

Arthur jumped up suddenly knocking his chair backwards, "Av yo bin a snooping woman," he shouted angrily a'course it's Danny?

"No, it's not Arthur, who is he!"

She knew from his reaction that she was right, that was proof enough, the boy wasn't Danny, but now she was worried about what Arthur might do as he was looking at her very strangely.

"Oh no, oh God no, it had suddenly dawned on her, it's that young boy I read about in the papers that's gone missing, the one everybody has been searching for, but what on earth's he doing here Arthur and where's our Danny, we'll have to tell the police!" Arthur didn't answer her question as to where Danny might be, he just began to rant at her in a very menacing way, and she was now scared, very scared indeed.

"Well he ain't your Danny, see, yo gave up any rights to im when yo walked out on us years ago, what yo wanna come back ere for anyway yo nosey bitch, if yo thinks yo's gunna take im away from me yer slag yo ain't see, an yo aint telling no police either.

It was now quite obvious to Enid that Arthur had gone off his rocker, he really believed this missing boy was Danny, she was now in a state of panic and wondering what she could do to get help. She had to get out of here and run for it, run for miles if she had to. Enid pulled her wits together sufficiently to try to calm Arthur down.

"I didn't come ere to do anything like that, Arthur, honest," her voice quivered as she saw him coming towards her with a murderous look in his eyes.

"No, no Arthur she pleaded as she backed away, we can sort something out, I won't tell no one." She tried to run past him to get to the door but he sidestepped and blocked her escape. The next thing she knew was that his rough horny hands were around her throat and he was choking her. She had no time to scream or do anything, she just felt a searing pain in her throat and the only sound she was making was a gurgling noise as her feet lifted from the floor. She began to drift away into a deep dark black void of nothingness, there was no escaping.

Jake half woke from a deep sleep and sat bolt upright in his bed, he thought that he'd heard raised voices but then felt maybe it was his imagination as it was still the middle of the night and he couldn't hear anything now. must ave been one of mi nightmares he reasoned, he snuggled back down under the bedclothes and went fast asleep.

Arthur looked down at the crumpled body of his estranged wife lying on the floor, his mind was in turmoil, what was he going to do now, how was he going to get rid of the body, why the hell did she have to come back here, did *Danny* hear anything, all these thoughts were going round and round in his brain! He tiptoed along the corridor to the bedroom where Jake was asleep and stood for a moment listening at the door, then he gently lifted the latch and poked his head around the door and looked towards his bed, he was fast asleep. As he walked back to the kitchen he thought thank God I didn't stab her, there's no blood to clean up. He leaned over Enid's body caught her up with one of her arms and heaved her over his shoulder, then opening the back door with one hand he walked out with her into the night. Keeping to the side of the cottage he skirted round to the back, down the garden path and then out through the wooden gate onto the field, where, if he kept to the hedge he could get to the old ice house about a half-mile away in the middle of Pilworth spinney. Years ago the deer hunters used this to store and preserve their kills, he intended to leave her there covered over with leaves, he doubted that anyone would ever find her as no one ever came to this inaccessible spot, and he was fairly sure that nobody would report her missing or bother to look for her either. When he reached the wood he was so tired from carrying Enid that he stopped for a rest, placing her down on the grassy bank beside him. After about five minutes he got up and with renewed vigour picked up the body and carried on. He still had to cross a ditch and fight his way through a bramble thicket as well as get over a fallen tree before he was finally able to clamber up the slope of the igloo-shaped mound of the ice house to get to the hole at the top. By this time he was near exhaustion with the dead weight of Enid's body on his back, but he managed to position himself above the hole and let her just slip off his shoulder down through the opening, where she landed with a hollow echoing thud on the floor twelve feet below. Good riddance, he thought, Danny and me don't need you no more. He made his way back to the cottage feeling quite exhausted and hoped that Danny hadn't woken up and missed him. When he got back to his cottage he was careful not to make a noise in case he woke Danny up, he went to his room to check on him and thankfully found that he was sound asleep. He was so exhausted he just lay fully clothed on the settee and tried to get to sleep, but what little sleep he managed was troubled and fitful. His thoughts were whirling around his head and he kept re-living the nightmare of the last few hours since Enid had turned up and what he had ended up doing to her, but he couldn't have her spoiling everything could he, *silly bloody woman, she shudda stayed wi er fancy man that she ran off wi,* he thought. He was absolutely certain that no-one would find her body, and he knew that foxes would probably have had a go at her already, they could enter the 'icehouse' along the passageway and easily jump down the three-foot drop and spring back up again.

He lay there and watched the daylight filter through the windows, he got up once to go to the lav; it wasn't long after that when he heard the sounds of Danny noisily waking up and yawning and then making his way to the lav. Arthur started to make Danny some breakfast.

Chapter 17

Arthur sorted out a pair of Danny's pyjamas and gave them to Jake:

"Ere'yar Danny yo can ware these ternite when yove ad yer wash if yo loik, ah think they'll fit yer."

"Ooh, thanks Art…mm dad, I'm feelin tired, I think I'll go ta bed nah, will ya come and tuck me in when I'm ready?"

"Yeah ah'll cum n say gunnite."

Arthur gave Danny time to get washed; undressed and into his pyjamas and went to say goodnight. Danny was sat up in bed smiling:

"See they'm a perfect fit Dad, an nice n warm."

Arthur sat down on the bed, "Av yo enjoyed taday Danny," he said?

"Yeah it's bin great, Jake said, giving a big yawn."

"We'll avta go n see if we cawt us a rabbit or two in the sners termorra, ok!"

"Yeah, bet we did," Jake said.

"If we av ah'll show ya ow ta skin im an get im ready fort pot, nah ile say gunnite, he leaned forward and kissed Danny goodnight on the cheek, nah snuggle dahn an gu ta sleep, ahl wake yer int mornin, gunnite."

"Gunnite, Dad."

Shortly afterwards, Arthur went to the bathroom to have a wash and get himself ready for bed, it had been a long day and he was tired himself, as he went past Danny's door he could hear the sounds of heavy breathing and he thought at first it was snoring, then he heard moans and groans and faster heavy breathing with a soft slapping sound. Arthur guessed what he was doing then and thought to himself, *it's only natural for a lad his age.*

However, I'm sure Arthur would have been very surprised to find out that he was the object of Jake's fantasies while he was wanking himself off and cumming his load.

The next morning Jake woke up and chuckled to himself when he realised it was Monday and he didn't have to go to school, then he almost whooped with joy remembering his conversation with Arthur who'd told him he didn't have to go to school ever again. Jake was so happy, he was singing a popular song he and his mam had sung together by Doris Day; it had a catchy chorus, and Jake really liked it. "Que sera sera, whatever will be will be, the future's not ours to see, que sera sera."

Arthur heard him singing and shouted down the hallway from the kitchen

"Yome an appy chap this morning sun," remembering last night and smiling to himself.

"Yeah said Jake, "Cos I ain't gotta go to school n do horrible lessons like maths an get into no trubble with the other kids."

"No yo aint sun, Arthur said, an when yome ready n ad yer brekfast we'll go an see if we cawt any rabbits in our snares yesterday."

"Ok, dad," Jake said cheerily.

After they'd both eaten breakfast they set off back to the edge of Pitry wood where they had set the snares, they found that they had caught two. Jake was thrilled to bits that one of the snares he'd laid had trapped one of them.

"I cawt one, I cawt one, he said gleefully giving a little triumphant dance."

"Yeah yo did gud sun, when we get back ome yo cn tek is innards art n skin im, ah'll show ya ow."

"Eerrgh, Jake said grimacing, do I av to."

"Yes ya do Danny, yo cawt im, ees yourn, so yo'll get im reddy fort stew pot."

"Ok, dad," Jake said.

Arthur took the rabbits out of the snares and shoved them into the hessian sack he'd brought with him, and they set off back home. On the way Arthur laid the sack down on the ground and said:

"I gotta av a piss," and went to go behind a nearby bush.

"An me," Jake said quickly following behind him.

They were standing together about three feet apart both with their cocks out. Arthur was urinating a gushing flow of piss and Jake was pretending to pee and watching Authur's cock, he began to get an erection, then he noticed Arthur had stopped pissing and was shaking his cock before going to put it back in his trousers. Jake momentarily forgot himself and reached out and touched Arthur's cock."

'That's a big un," Jake said with rasping breath.

"Wot d ya think yer doin lad, Arthur said rather taken aback and stepping away from Jake buttoning his flies, ya don't do things like that!"

"Sorry Dad, don't it me!"

"I ain't gonna it ya sun, but don't ever do owt like that agen."

"I won't dad," Jake said with a sniffle of both regret and disappointment.

They walked briskly in silence the rest of the way home, Arthur was some distance ahead of Jake who was dragging his feet and brooding about what he'd just done and how it hadn't worked out the way he wanted.

Arthur couldn't believe what had happened, why would Jake do a thing like that, must be boyish curiosity he thought, but he'd have to have a good talk to him when they got back home.

Arthur got back home, put the sack down by the door and went inside, he had been deep in thought all the way home about what he would say to Danny, he didn't want to get it all out of proportion and make a great big thing of it and frighten the lad, he'd been through enough, he just wanted to set him right so that nothing like that would ever happen again, the lad obviously didn't understand personal boundaries. When Jake sauntered into the house about ten minutes after Arthur had got back, he was looking very sorry for himself and looked sheepishly at Arthur who was sitting at the kitchen table waiting for him.

"Come and sit down here Danny, Arthur said, trying not to sound too stern and indicating the chair opposite him, I wanna tork ta ya."

Jake pulled the chair out from the table and sat down, hardly daring to look at Arthur and wondering what he was going to say to him.

"Nah luk ere sun, wot yer did ter mi wen wi woz avin a piss back theer woz rong see, lads doont tuch ther dads darn theer, n dads doont tuch them theer neether, d'ya understand?"

"Yes Dad, Jake said as he started to cry, ahm really sorry an I won't do it. agen, please don't send me back home."

"I aint gunna send yer bak ome sun, so thes no need for ya ta cry."

"An ya still luv me?"

"Caus I still luvs ya, yer silly lad, nah stop ya cryin an I'll show ya har ta gut yer rabbit n skin im, fetch mi the sack from artside."

Jake wiped his face on the sleeve of his jacket, sniffled and stopped crying as he got up to fetch the rabbits, he brought them in and gave them to Arthur, "Ere'yar dad, he said.

"Gud lad sun, Arthur said reaching out to tousle Jake's hair, nah let that be an end ta wot happened earlier, yo wotch mi cos yo'll av tu doot same ta yourn in a minit."

Arthur took the two rabbits out of the bag and put them on a small table that had a thick block of wood on it he opened the drawer at the end of the kitchen table and took out a sharp knife and a big meat cleaver, then he proceeded to show Jake what to do.

"Fust, yo lay it on the block then ya chops the feet off im lark this, he said, raising the cleaver and bringing it down to sever the rabbits feet, wen yove cut the four on em off, yo cut im ere like this, then yo can start peeling skin off im." The rabbits innards started to spill out of its body, so Arthur pulled them out and put them to one side, he then continued with his demonstration.

"Yo av ta be cerful not ta bust the stumak open cos that poisons the meat wi wanna eat. Wen yove peeled it right back to its ed, yo cut is ed off, like this. Then yo teks it ta sink ta gi im a wash, when yove washed im gud yo cn chop im up in pieces, an ya put im int pot wi sum carrats, an unyan, a chopped tater, cuver it wi water and put sum salt in. Yo should av yourself a gud droppa stew then arter abart three ars."

After watching all this Jake was beginning to feel a bit queasy he looked at Arthur and said pleadingly, "I don't really av ta do that, do I dad?"

"Nah sun, nod if yer dunt wanna," Arthur said noticing Jake had gone a bit pale and smiling to himself, yer cn do it sum other time."

Over the next few days, Jake tried to stop thinking about Arthur the way he'd done before, telling himself he wouldn't have done anything like that with his real dad as he didn't fancy him; anyway, he'd have got a bloody good belting, so he shouldn't want to do it with his pretend dad either. He knew Arthur loved him as a son and would never raise a hand to hurt him. He wanted him to stay on the farm and live with him; that's what Jake wanted to do too more than anything. As several weeks went by Jake got more used to life on the farm and had organised himself into a good daily routine. Arthur had told him that he was doing well with the animals and his chores and that had really pleased Jake. He didn't even miss going to scrap on the dump anymore or spend time in his camp. He had a good life here, Arthur was good to him he sat and talked to him, cuddled him, told him he loved him and what a good boy he was, he'd even started to get some of the things that Jake liked to eat when he went to collect his pension, things like rice crispies, sweets and his favourite comic 'The Dandy'. He wasn't frightened of being beaten anymore, either by his dad or the other kids at school, he did miss seeing his friend John Smedley as they used to have a great time playing together, Oh and he missed his mam sometimes.

There were a couple of days last week when Jake had thought he was sickening for something as he was very quiet and subdued, he never even laughed when Jake told him the funny story of how he'd climbed a tree one day and found that he couldn't get back down and his dad had climbed up to help him and get him down by lowering him to the ground, but had then fallen out of the tree into some overgrown stinging nettles.

That same week Jake had got up one morning and found a ladies handbag by the side of the couch and when he'd shown it to Arthur, he had snatched it from his hands saying that it was his ex-wife's and that he had been looking through it to try to find some papers. Jake suddenly remembered that during the previous night he'd dreamt he had heard raised voices, but he never mentioned that to Arthur because he looked so worried. He wondered if he had done anything to upset him, but he didn't think that he had. Anyway, he had been alright since then and seemed to be back to normal.

Chapter 18

It was a cold and frosty morning, alarmingly there had been a hoar frost overnight, the ground was white over, almost as if there had been a light fall of snow. The trees and hedgerows were covered with what looked like white feathery moss. The whole length of the lane saw people and cars coming and going with police and civilians congregating in clusters, white-hot clouds of their steamy breath floating up into the air. Everyone looked frozen already before the search had even got underway. Police cars and vans had parked at the top of the lane where it broadened into the perimeter of the farm. There were four dog handlers with sniffer dogs, one would be assigned to each team. Thankfully Pauline Trouch had been well organised and generously provided much-needed refreshments. She and about six other women helpers, probably her fellow WI members had placed a couple of large tables at the rear of one of the farms small barns, and placed a big catering size urn on top full of hot steaming tea, and there were sandwiches and cakes galore for everyone. as keeping their stamina up for the search was really important. Last night Pauline had contacted her friends and told them what she intended to do and each of them had immediately volunteered to do something. They sorted out between them who was to do what, some made cakes, others sandwiches, there was even a pile of blankets in the event of someone getting really cold to their bones. They must have worked well into the night and then been up again at the crack of dawn, bless them.

Melgrove called to everyone through a loud haler, marshalling them into readiness for action, mobilising four different groups to cover different areas and issuing walkie-talkies to the four leaders of them as well as giving instructions as to the direction they were to move in. He stressed to them that they were to look everywhere, to leave no stone unturned so to speak and report back to him immediately if there was any development. He spoke to Bill and gave him the option of going with whichever group he preferred or he could stay back at the farm if he wanted, so as to be closer to Vera at home. Bill had told him earlier that she was not in a good way when he left her this morning and she hadn't hardly had a wink of sleep and the doctor was calling to see her.

It was now 7am and the search was now underway, Ian Melgrove was secretly praying that they find the boy soon, but he felt sure that the boy would not have survived the night, if he was out in the open but for some miracle, and judging by Bill's demeanour, he must have been thinking the same thing too. The group moving north were the ones who would have the unpleasant task of searching the council tip, and although there wasn't usually anyone working there on a Saturday, two council representatives were on site to oversee matters there as safety was their primary concern and it was their job to ensure that there were no accidents. Melgrove and six constables along with Ned Trouch would search the farm and all its outbuildings, that way he could control operations and be on hand if he was contacted by any of the search teams. The group moving south would cover 'Wood Lane' and the spinney; as well as the large deer park area that bordered the river, which if the land-based search proved unfruitful would have to be searched by a dedicated diving team. The group moving East would be searching open farmland leading to the neighbouring village of Crowsworth which would involve door to door interviews and information gathering. The group moving towards the west would encounter a stream and a railway line. The group working east would have open fields surrounded by hedges. They would all work until 4pm when it was deemed visibility was too poor to enable them to conduct an effective operation.

When that deadline was reached they would all assemble back at Melford House Farm for a briefing from D.I. Melgrove as to what would be the next course of action to take.

The people on the searches were meticulously thorough in their efforts to find clues or any trace of the boy. The dog handler in the team that was searching the wood near Jake's home had a good result. The dog led him to a hidden camp in the wood, that he thought might possibly have been built by Jake, he immediately blew three long hard blows on his whistle and waited there until the constable who responded went to inform Melgrove. The constable got to the farm and kept blowing his whistle until Melgrove came to him they immediately went back to the scene. He had a good look around inside the camp and felt certain that this was Jake's secret hide-out, he made one interesting discovery, he had moved a wooden crate and behind it in a plastic bag was a collection of magazines, they all had pictures of semi-naked and naked men in them and had titles like 'Demi-God' and 'Physique'. He wondered what an eleven-year-old boy was doing with these and how he had come by them. He quickly put these inside his coat so no-one else would see them. He also considered the idea that the discovery of the magazines could be linked to the boy going missing, what the link might be he dreaded to think, obvious abduction crossed his mind. He didn't think that the boy had been here overnight as he would surely not have survived the freezing temperature. He thanked the dog handler and made his way back to the farm. All the teams found it cold tiring work and it took their toll on a few of them. One woman fainted apparently due to the fact that she hadn't eaten anything that morning, so she was taken home. A man searching on a ploughed field broke his ankle when he twisted it on the rough hard ground, he had to be carried quite a distance to where an ambulance was waiting to take him hospital. Apart from those two, there were no other casualties, people were just frozen and physically exhausted.

Melgrove greeted everyone and thanked them for their hard work and perseverance in doing such a difficult job. He told them that sadly despite their utmost efforts the search of each group had not revealed the whereabouts of the boy. There was a groan of disappointment from the search parties. Melgrove indicated that in some respects it could be said that this was a hopeful sign that Jake might still be alive and well somewhere but that the search was obviously ongoing and tomorrow an underwater diving team would be searching the river as they could not rule out any possibility. He also mentioned that he would be meeting with the press later in the evening to give them a statement.

Ian Melgrove didn't much like this aspect of his job, meeting the press and media put him a little too much in the limelight for his liking, but it was nonetheless an essential part of the job and it could help the police in their exhaustive enquiries as to the whereabouts of the missing boy. But before his meeting with the press Melgrove wanted to brief his team colleagues that were working on the case.

Addlestone Memorial Hall was the venue the Inspector had chosen for the press conference as it was centrally situated and offered good car parking.

Melgrove and Baxter were sat behind a desk covered with a green baize tablecloth that had a jug of water and two glasses on it, they were facing a barrage of reporters who were ready with their notebooks and pens and cameramen who were continuously clicking off shots with their noisy flashbulbs popping everywhere. Neither of them could believe how many of them there were but the numbers indicated that it wasn't just local press it was the nationals as well. Melgrove didn't know how the nationals had gotten hold of the information unless a local journalist had possibly passed it on as it was deemed sufficiently newsworthy to warrant the country's interest.

Looking tired, Melgrove stood up to address them with a prepared short statement.

"As I think you all know, a young local boy, Jake Wiggins has gone missing. He has been missing since Friday, sometime around 1pm when he was last seen going into Wood Lane spinney close to his home. He was wearing a white school shirt, a green hand-knitted jersey, a brown jacket and black wellingtons. We have strenuously searched the local area and conducted house to house calls to no avail. We would urge the whole community to be vigilant and pro-active in trying to find Jake, we would ask you to search your own backyards, outbuildings property and land just in case the boy has sought shelter somewhere. If anyone knows of his whereabouts we would ask them to come forward and tell us where he is. A dedicated diving team will be undertaking a search of the river Uder tomorrow morning to ascertain whether the boy could unfortunately have fallen in. We would ask you to respect the feelings and privacy of Jake's parents and the Wiggins family at this difficult time. Thank you all for coming. That's all I have to say at this moment." More camera bulbs flashed and popped as a young spotty faced reporter wearing a raincoat and brown derby hat stood up and shouted:

"Do you think Jake has been abducted, Inspector!"

"That's pure speculation, as I said, I have no further information to give you at this time, thank you, goodnight."

Chapter 19

D.S. Baxter pulled up outside the four terraced cottages in 'Wood Lane', he surveyed them admiringly as he walked the long garden path up to number three where The Burridges lived, this was the first time he had seen them in good light, he thought that they had probably been built sometime in the mid-thirties and he found them quite charming little properties with their large front canted bay windows and shared tiled porches. He could see Mavis Burridge peering out of her front room window watching him approach. He had called to see her as a result of the newspaper report he had read on the coverage of the search for Jake. The 'Addlestone Herald' had been particularly sensational in their coverage of the boy's disappearance although they appeared to be sympathetic towards his and his parents' plight, their approach and overzealous delving for background information and there subsequent publishing of hearsay and gossip had been quite irresponsible to say the least. Their reporting had stirred up quite a hornets' nest and caused considerable upset and stress for Jake's parents.

He knocked on the door of number three and almost as he had done so the door was opened by Mrs Burridge who, after he had said good morning invited him in eagerly.

He was taken into the front room, he saw it was pleasantly decorated, the wallpaper had an embossed floral pattern in mid-green and brown tones, the carpet was a darker beige and brown combination and it looked as though the room had recently been re-decorated. There was a brown sideboard with four drawers and bowed cupboard doors either side all of which had gold brass handles. A large oak table with large bulbous legs occupied the centre of the room with a 'Mother in Laws Tongue' in a large green pot sat in the centre of it on a chenille table runner. There were several pictures hanging from copper hooks on the picture rail around the walls and the heavy curtains at the window were in a tapestry design, there was a cuckoo clock too which suddenly began noisily cuckooing the hour, it was 10am. The cottage was spotlessly clean, the furniture highly polished and smelling of lavender and beeswax. It was obvious that Mavis Burridge was a bit house proud and liked things just so. He sat on one of the leather chairs and looked at Mavis who was seated on another one in the corner of the room opposite him. He noticed that she seemed a bit on edge and her eyes were red as though she had been crying.

"I've come to ask you a few questions Mrs Burridge regarding a statement you made to a reporter of the 'Addlestone Herald' and which appeared in yesterday's edition."

"Yes," she queried?

"Well, it appears you said that you had often heard domestic disturbances in the Wiggins house, arguments, raised voices and the young boy crying, is this true?"

"Yes, of course, it's true," she said, obviously offended.

"Can you tell me exactly what you have overheard please?"

"They're always rowing you know, kicking up a terrible racket sometimes, you wonder what on earth's going on and how it's all going to end!" She looked at him for his reaction.

"Go on," he said.

"Well, it's obvious he knocks them both about, I often hear the boy shouting no dad, don't hit me and then him running up the stairs sobbing, these walls are thick and solidly built so you can imagine the noise, can't you!"

"So in your opinion, this sort of thing is a regular occurrence then?"

"I'm afraid so, she said, I get so worried for them both."

"Have you ever seen any bruises or marks on the boy or his mother?"

"No, can't say that I have, no."

Baxter finished writing his report and stood to go, he thanked Mrs Burridge for her help with his enquiries, however, he did say that he thought it would have been more helpful if she had thought to tell the police this information before mentioning it to the newspaper reporter.

"What's going to happen now then officer," Mavis said?

"We will be interviewing Mr Wiggins in due course," Baxter said, "in the meantime I would appreciate it if you didn't have any contact with the Wiggins at all, and if you have any more information, to come to the police station."

"Oh Don't you worry on that score, I've no intention of having any more to do with them, I can assure you, and I'll let you know if I hear anything else, Mavis replied as she was showing him to the door, thank you, officer."

Baxter got in the car and drove off heading along the Hinton road towards the river. He needed to report to Ian Melgrove and get some back-up before he came back to the farm to see Bill Wiggins.

D.I. Melgrove stood gazing at the river where the underwater diving team were searching, he greeted his Sergeant and asked him how the interview with Mavis Burridge went. He listened intently to what his detective sergeant was telling him and he didn't like what he was hearing. Bill Wiggins had seemed a reasonably amiable sort of chap on the face of it and had shown what looked like genuine concern for his missing son but in his experience, the impression that people gave to the police and what was really going on was often quite different. Families were renowned for concealing all sorts of things, often what happened behind closed doors belied what appeared to be on the surface. The private view was different to the one that was presented to the world for public scrutiny!

"Take a couple of constables with you sergeant and go and bring him in for questioning, for all we know he could know more about his boy's disappearance than he's letting on."

"That's what I thought, sir," Baxter said.

"He obviously has a very short fuse where his anger is concerned, perhaps he lost control in a fit of temper, things got out of hand, and he ended up killing Jake. He knows this area better than any of us, it would be easy for him to find a place to conceal a body. I'm not saying he has harmed him, but we'll soon find out once we get him here. Don't take any chances with him, sergeant, be ready for him if he has a go."

"Righto, sir, I'll get back there straight away, no doubt he'll be at work on the farm somewhere but I'll find him, I just hope he hasn't got wind that we may be on to him!"

"I'll get back to the station and wait for you to bring him in, I'll sit in on the interview."

"Ok, sir."

The police car containing D.S. Baxter and two police constables arrived at Melford House Farm pulling into a large open quadrangle surrounded by the Trouch's house and the various adjacent outbuildings. There was an inner wall bordering the quadrangle which presumably provided a protected walkway from animals or mechanical activity that took place there, but apart from a new green-coloured Austin A35 Countryman car, the yard was empty. Baxter gave a long envious look at the car and thought how much he would like to own one, as he and the officers walked up the sloped walkway towards the house, passing what was obviously the farmer's office. He wanted to speak to Ned Trouch or his wife first in order to find out exactly where Bill Wiggins could be found, and to let them know that he would be taking Bill in for questioning with regard to helping them with their enquiries. Their knock on the door brought a response from Pauline Trouch who was quite surprised to see the three of them standing there.

"Good Morning Mrs Trouch is Mr Trouch in?"

"Yes he is Sergeant, come on in, he's in the kitchen, I was just about to get some lunch ready for him." Baxter told the officers to wait outside for him, she led the way along a flagstone tiled hall into the kitchen. Ned Trouch looked up from reading his morning paper.

"Oh, good morning, Sergeant."

"Good Morning, sir, I'm sorry to trouble you but I need to ask you where I'm likely to find Bill, I need to have a word with him; he paused. Actually, sir as you are his employer, I'll be candid with you, I need to take him in for questioning." Ned looked at him astounded.

"Never not Bill, why what's he done?"

"I'm afraid I can't discuss that with you, sir, if you could just tell me where he is and take me to him, I'd be grateful."

"Yes, of course, I'll get my coat, I should think he'll either be mucking out the cows in the cowshed or down in the root cellar getting some Mangels up.

Turned out it was the latter, Ned led them to a stone-built outbuilding with a corrugated tin roof in an adjoining yard, he stood at the top of a flight of stone steps and called to Bill to come up. Bill came up the steps, he was very concerned when he saw the police there.

'What's the matter, have you found our Jake?" he said.

"No I'm afraid not Mr Wiggins, we need you to come with us to the police station and help us with our enquiries."

"I don't know any more than I've told you already," Bill queried.

"We can talk about that down at the station, D.S. Baxter said.

"I can't just leave my work here, there's a lot to do," Bill said looking at Ned.

"I can deal with all of that Bill," Ned said, "you had better go with them."

"Will you let Vera know what's going on then, she'll be worried if I don't pop in at lunchtime?"

"I'll get Pauline to go and see her Bill, don't worry."

One of the constables took hold of Bill's arm and began to steer him back towards the car. Bill was confused but went along with them, wondering what the hell was going on! The car ride to the station was uncomfortably frosty Bill felt as though they were treating him like a criminal who had done something seriously wrong; every time he asked a question it was answered by.

"We'll talk when we get to the station."

Bill expected to be taken to a room and interviewed but to his anger and surprise he was put in a cell and told that he would be interviewed shortly. When he was finally taken from the cell about an hour later he wasn't in a very cooperative mood to say the least, he was taken to a room with a table and four chairs in it, and it had a small window with bars, He was gruffly told to sit down by a constable and as he did Detective Inspector Mulgrove and D.I. Baxter came in and sat at the table opposite him.

"What's all this about, why have you brought me here?" Bill asked!

Mulgrove was the first to speak.

"We'll ask the questions, Mr Wiggins. Now, you haven't been arrested, you've just been brought here to help us with our enquiries regarding your missing boy."

"Huh, it bloody well feels as though I have," Bill said angrily.

Mulgrove ignored him and went on, speaking in a louder tone, "What have you done with your son, Jake, Mr Wiggins!"

"What, I haven't done anything with him, you can't possibly think that I would harm my own boy!"

"Oh but that's exactly what we do think Mr Wiggins, you're always hitting him aren't you, and from all accounts, you don't pull your punches either?"

Bill was dumbfounded at his remark but nervously replied, "I only do what's needed to correct the boy."

"Why don't you admit that during one of your so-called 'corrections', something went wrong, you hit him too hard and killed him, then you hid his body somewhere where he wouldn't be found and pretended that he'd gone missing?"

"What, yer off yer bloody rockers, if yer think that's what's happened, I haven't done anything to Jake," Bill said rising to his feet.

"Sit down, the constable that was standing behind him said sharply, pushing him back on to his seat by his shoulder. Bill thought he was going mad this was a bloody nightmare, how could he convince them that he was telling the truth.

D.S. Baxter joined in with, "We've had it on good authority from your neighbours that there are always arguments and fights in your house and that you regularly beat the boy, got quite a temper on you they say."

"I'm telling you the truth, Vera and me do have the occasional argument and I do sometimes hit the boy, but only when I think he deserves it, as for killing him, that's too much to think about."

"That's just it, you didn't think about it did you, you let fly with your fists and then it was too late."

Melgrove leaned forward over the table putting his face closer to Bill; pretending to sound friendly, "If you tell us what happened Bill and where he is it will be so much easier for you, cmon, you don't want this to go on for hours do you now?"

"I've told you, I don't know where Jake is, I only wish I did then maybe you'd let me go home to my wife, she'll be worried sick."

"We've given you every opportunity to tell us the truth, perhaps a night in the cells will jog your memory, take him back to his cell, constable," Melgrove said.

Chapter 20

Dr Carlston had given Vera a strong sedative to calm her down and help her to sleep. He felt deep compassion for her, he had been Vera's doctor for years, he'd looked after her all her life, Bill after they were married, then Jake shortly after he was born. Not only was she having to cope with the fact that her only child had gone missing and there were search parties out combing every bit of the surrounding countryside looking for him, but the poor woman had been relentlessly pestered by persistent newspaper reporters intent on finding out all they could about the family. Some of this was mainly due to Mavis Burridge gossiping to them and anyone else who would listen about how she had heard them arguing, that Bill was cruel to Vera and the boy and that the poor little mite was allowed to just wander the woods and fields all day long without them having any idea where he was; what he was doing, or who he was with. She thought it was scandalous and such people shouldn't be allowed to have children. Earlier that morning just after Bill had gone off to work Vera had gone round to see Mavis and confronted her, she'd given her a piece of her mind, telling her well and truly what she thought of her and making it absolutely clear that she would never speak to her again as she wanted nothing more to do with her, she was trembling with rage and she could see that her words had gone home, Mavis was so stunned she didn't say a word. She didn't threaten her or lay a finger on her, but she could have cheerfully strangled her.

While Dr Carlston was tending to Vera, her friend Rosemary Wiseman came to visit, she was also one of Dr Carlston's patients. Vera and Rosemary had gone to school together and had always been very close, Jake called her Auntie, though she was not a relative at all.

"Hello Rosemary," the doctor said.

"Hello Dr Carlston," Rosemary replied, her pulse racing as she had always found him very attractive.

"How is she?"

"Well she'll sleep now, I've given her a strong sedative, are you able to stay with her until Bill gets home. She'll be a bit groggy when she wakes up and will need looking after?"

"What a terrible thing to happen, doctor, I'll stay for as long as I'm needed, I think I'll be more help here than walking the fields looking for Jake, Rosemary said, smiling at him.

"Oh good, I know she'll be in safe hands then he said, smiling back, I'll see myself out, tell Bill I'll come back and check on Vera in the morning."

"Yes, I will," said Rosemary, "thank you, doctor."

Rosemary looked at her friend lying sound asleep and her heart went out to her, she lifted Vera's bare arm that was lying on top of the candlewick bedspread and tucked it under the bedclothes to keep her warm, she sat beside the bed and silently said a prayer that they would find dear little Jake safe and well.

Rosemary must have dozed off, she could hear a banging sound then she realised it was someone knocking at the front door, she went down to open it and saw Pauline Trouch standing there.

"Oh hello Mrs Trouch, I hope you haven't been knocking long, I'm afraid I dozed off."

"No not long, she lowered her voice, "Can I come in, I don't want the neighbours to hear what 'm going to tell you," she'd seen Mavis Burridge watch her come up the front path so she wasn't about to let the village gossip hear what she had to say.

"Yes, of course, come in Rosemary said, looking very worried; she took her into the kitchen where it was warmer, and she pulled out a chair from the kitchen table for Pauline to sit down; she sat on the other side, and hardly daring to ask said what's happened!"

Pauline tried to break the news as gently as she could:

"Bill's been arrested and taken to the police station for questioning, they came and took him from the farm about half an hour ago. Ned and I think they might suspect that he knows something about Jake's disappearance, but we know that's ridiculous, he's been at his wits end over all this."

"That's terrible, what on earth can they be thinking, it's absolutely preposterous, this will kill Vera when she finds out, poor Bill!"

"Well, I certainly don't think we should tell her at the moment, Ned's contacted his solicitor and he'll be going to the police station to sort it out. How is Vera?"

"She's fast asleep bless her, Dr Caulston gave her a sedative, he's going to look in on her again tomorrow morning."

"The longer she sleeps the better, we'll try to get Bill back here as quickly as we can. Ned said his solicitor told him that they can only question Bill for so long before they have to bring a charge against him or let him go. Let's hope they come to their senses soon and realise Bill's completely innocent, I can't believe that that woman next door would have the gall to say those things to the newspapers?"

"No, neither can I, just let her ever speak to me, she'll wish she hadn't!"

"Well, I had better be going, Ned will want his lunch, as soon as we hear anything, we'll let you know, look after Vera and if you need anything, don't hesitate to ask."

"I will, thank you Mrs Trouch, Rosemary said showing her down the hall and out of the front door. Pauline was stunned she just couldn't believe it, as if Bill and Vera weren't going through enough, the police had to make stupid mistakes and put them through even more hell. She wouldn't let on to Vera what had happened, ignorance was bliss as far as this was concerned. She went back upstairs to see if Vera was alright and still asleep.

Chapter 21

Martin Trubshawe walked into Addlestone police station stepped towards the counter said, "Good Afternoon to the desk sergeant and told him that he wanted to see Detective Inspector Melgrove concerning his client Bill Wiggins who they were questioning over the disappearance of the boy Jake Wiggins.

"Good Afternoon sir, can I have your name please?"

"Martin Trubshawe," the solicitor said in an upper-class voice. The desk sergeant wrote the name down on a piece of paper, ripped it from his pad, folded it and said:

"I'll see if Detective Melgrove is available, take a seat would you, I won't be a moment," and he went through a frosted glass panelled door into a private area.

Martin Trubshawe remained standing, he was a tall distinguished-looking man with silver-grey hair, he was wearing a camel overcoat with a brown suede collar and he had a definite military bearing. He was determined to get Bill Wiggins released from custody, Ned Trouch was an old friend and he trusted his judgement implicitly regarding the character of his employee.

The glazed door behind the counter opened again and the desk sergeant appeared, "D.I. Melgrove will see you in his office sir if you'd like to come through," he said, lifting the counter flap up to allow the solicitor to get behind the counter. The sergeant led him down a corridor with offices leading off it until he reached a brown door with a nameplate on it saying D.I.Melgrove. The sergeant tapped on the door and Melgrove's voice said, "Come in," Melgrove rose; still standing behind his desk he reached over it extending his arm to shake hands with the solicitor, "Good afternoon," he said, "I understand you are representing the suspect Bill Wiggins we are holding in custody."

"Yes I am Trubshawe said, and my client should not be being held in custody at all!"

"Oh and why not," Melgrove said indignantly?

"Well, firstly, he's an innocent man, secondly, he has been through enough trauma over the disappearance of his son and thirdly, you have absolutely no evidence whatsoever to keep him here!"

"We have a witness who has said she's often heard arguments and fights going on in his house and she has heard the boy begging not to be beaten by him."

"Is your witness the woman who has been talking to the newspapers?"

"Yes, that's right, Mrs Burridge."

"She isn't a credible witness man, the woman is the village gossip, a storyteller, everything she has told you is just hearsay and could for all we know just be malicious slander, you can't possibly hold my client on those grounds!"

"I'll decide on what grounds I can hold a suspect Mr Trubshawe, until I'm satisfied he is not responsible for his son's disappearance he stays here locked up."

Trubshawe was losing patience with Melgroves attitude, "Can I see my client," he said?

"Yes, I'll have a constable take you to his cell," he said curtly.

"Thank you," Trubshawe said.

Trubshawe was shown into Bill's cell and he introduced himself, shook his hand and told him that it was as a result of Ned Trouchs instigation that he was here to represent him. The solicitor thought that Bill Wiggins looked all in, he spoke with him at great length as well as listening to Bill's protestations about his innocence. He assured him that he would do all he could to get him released, it was obvious to anyone with an ounce of sense that he was an innocent man.

Trubshawe went back to see D.I. Melgrove and laid the law down to him, "My client has told me that he has helped you all he can. He has told you the truth, protesting his innocence repeatedly. You have no viable grounds to hold him any longer so I am telling you now that if you do not release this man immediately on my cognisance and allow him to leave the police station with me, I will obtain a writ from the high court to do so and you will have a lawsuit on your hands sir, do I make myself clear!"

Melgrove blanched white, he felt that the only sensible course of action open to him now was to comply with the solicitor's demand, the last thing he wanted was Trubshawe going over his head and him ending up with a lawsuit that would make him look incompetent to his senior officers. He kept his dignity by saying, "I will release him on police bail into your custody, you will sign a release paper to that effect and you will ensure that he does not leave the village, he is your responsibility now, if you wait in the reception area I will have the papers sorted out and get him brought up from the cells.

Bill emerged from a doorway on the other side of reception and was greeted again by a smiling Mr Trubshawe who shook him roundly by the hand, went over to the desk took out a gold Schaeffer pen and signed Bill's release papers. He turned around placing his hand on Bill's shoulder and said, "Come on sir, you're going home."

"I can't thank you enough," Bill said with a look of complete relief on his face. When they came out of the police station there were press reporters and photographers outside, their bulbs were flashing and a reporter asked them they would like to give them a statement. The Solicitor said that Inspector Melgrove would be issuing a statement later and got Bill in his car and away from them. By the time Bill arrived home, it was beginning to get dark, he walked up the garden path looked towards the house and it had never looked so beautiful. He couldn't wait to see Vera and wondered how she was, he had been so worried about her. As he walked through the front door and into the hallway, to his surprise Rosemary opened the living room door.

"Bill, she exclaimed, so pleased to see him, and she threw her arms around him and hugged him, those fools let you go then!"

"It's good to be home Bill said wearily, they put me through hell, but how's Vera doing."

"She's slept a lot since the doctor gave her the sedative, she woke up once and I made her a cup of tea but when I took it up to her she was fast asleep again."

"I'll go up and see her now, he said, thank you for looking after her Rosemary."

"It's nothing Bill, what are friends for eh!"

Bill stood by the side of the bed and looked down at his wife, even though she was sedated and had slept for most of the day her face looked troubled and careworn with all the worry of what had happened. Her arm lay outside of the bedclothes so he took hold of her hand and what with the ordeal he had gone through in the hands of the police and seeing Vera lying here so helpless everything that was flooding his mind suddenly became too much and he broke down and sobbed. He had only ever cried once before as an adult and that was at his mother's funeral, just like then this was such a release emotions. He thought about Jake and though he was not religious in any way, he called on God to please bring him back home. Vera woke up about an hour later and he and Rosemary had agreed not to tell her anything about Bill having been taken to the police station for questioning. The first thing she asked Bill was if they had heard anything about Jake and Bill just shook his head and said:

"Not yet love but I'm sure we will soon," trying to sound hopeful, "Rosemary's making some chicken soup for you, if you'd like some?"

"I don't think I could eat a thing," Vera said, screwing her nose up in disinterest.

"Well, you can have a try and see how you go, you haven't had anything all day, I'll go and tell her shall I, do you want it up here or do you think you can get up."

"I'll come downstairs, she said, I'm not an invalid yet."

Rosemary saw that Vera was attempting to eat the soup that she had made and she said:

"I'll get on my way home now Vera, I'll come back and see you as soon as I can, I hope you have good news about Jake soon," and she blew Vera and Bill a kiss and left.

The next morning Bill and Vera were woken by knocking at the door, Bill slipped his trousers on over his nightshirt and rushed downstairs to open the door, thinking that it might be the police with news about Jake. Still bleary-eyed from being woken from his sleep he opened the door and before he could really see who was outside, a flashbulb exploded in his face and a reporter started bombarding him with questions.

"What the hell, Bill said surprised as he shielded his eyes from the camera flashes and heard a reporter saying.

"Would you like to tell us why the police arrested you, Mr Wiggins?"

Bill immediately slammed the door shut on them and went back upstairs to Vera who had heard everything that had gone on and was sobbing her heart out. Bill was shaking with rage and had closed the door in order to stop himself laying into the bastards who were trying to get a sensational story out of people who needed to be left alone. He put his arms around Vera and said:

"It's alright love, don't let them upset you."

"You didn't tell me that you'd been arrested, Bill."

"I didn't want to worry you any more than you already were sweetheart, it dosn't matter now anyway, it happened and that's it, we've been through enough to let those buggers get to us, we can just forget about it now." Unfortunately, Vera and Bill found that it wasn't to be like that as the morning newspapers were anxious to let all and sundry know the facts as they saw them, all in the public interest of course.

Chapter 22

MISSING BOY: FATHER ARRESTED

The story went on to say that Bill Wiggins the father of the missing eleven-year-old boy Jake Wiggins was arrested and taken from his place of work to Addlestone police station for questioning, he was later released without charge. It was also mentioned that Detective Inspector Melgrove who was heading the investigations had issued a statement stating that Mr Wiggins had not been arrested but was merely helping the police with their enquiries. He also said that there had been no further developments in the case to date; that the police were now concentrating their efforts in a broader search with neighbouring forces and they were looking into the possibility that Jake may have been abducted and taken out of the area. He again urged the public to continue to be vigilant and report anything that could be of interest to the enquiry, no matter how insignificant it might seem. It said that Mr Wiggins had declined to give any statement to the press but along with the headline was the picture that had been taken the previous morning.

When Vera and Bill saw what had been written in the newspaper they were absolutely distraught.

"Oh why can't they leave us alone?" Vera said, crying on Bill's shoulder.

"Cos they're like bloody vultures," Bill said angrily, you just let any more of the buggers come round here and they'd wish they hadn't."

"No, you mustn't do anything silly Bill, you'll only get yourself into trouble, then where'd we be."

"That madam next door hadn't better come within shouting distance of me either or she'd better look out," Bill said, "I'll bet she gloated when she saw the papers!"

"You don't think he's really been taken by someone do you Bill?"

"I don't know love, why would anyone take our Jake, it's not as though they can ask for a ransom, we don't have any money!"

"It don't bear thinking about Bill, I dread to think why, she said dabbing her eyes with a handkerchief!"

They were keeping the living room curtains shut because reporters had been looking through the window and flashing their cameras in the hope of getting a photo of them so they didn't see that a posh car had pulled up in the lane and a woman had got out and was coming up the garden path, it was their friend Bridie Maguire.

There was knock at the door and because their nerves were on edge it startled them, they didn't want to answer it in case it was reporters, but the knock came again so Bill went to the front door and said in a very officious voice.

"Who is it, what do you want?"

"It's Bridie, Bill."

Bill opened the door and said:

"Oh Bridie, come in, love, am I pleased to see you. Vera will be glad to see you too."

Bill led her into the darkened living room and as soon as Vera saw Bridie she burst into tears, putting her head down and sobbing into her hands. Bridie's initial thoughts at seeing the curtains drawn were to think the worst had happened and that Jake was dead. She went over to her and said:

"Aah there now my love, I couldn't believe it when I read about it in the newspaper, I just had to come and see you, you must be going through hell!"

"I don't know what we're going to do, if they don't find him soon, I'm at my wit's end and I don't know how much more I can take!"

"I hope to God they do find him soon and bring him home safe to you, love, Bridie said trying to comfort her." Bill had gone into the kitchen and had put the kettle on to make Bridie a cup of tea. Bridie had her arm around Vera; they just sat not speaking until Bill came in with a tray of cups and saucers and a pot of tea.

"Here you are, I've made us a cup of tea," he said, as if it were panacea for all ills.

"Oh thank you, Bill, that's very kind of you."

He poured a cup and gave it to Bridie who said:

"Here you are Vera love, Bill's made you a cup of tea," she passed it to her and Vera thanked her and began to sip it.

"I'm only able to stay an hour or so as I have a very important meeting with my solicitor later this afternoon, but I just had to come to see you both and let you know that I am thinking of you and saying prayers for you all."

"We're very pleased to see you Bridie, Vera said, and we certainly need all the prayers we can get."

Chapter 23

Throughout the coming weeks, the newspaper reports sounded less and less hopeful and their coverage had drastically diminished to just a small piece like this in the Addlestone Herald that read:

The search for the missing boy Jake Wiggins continues but the police say that they have no new leads as to where he might be, they do say that they have done everything that they can think of that might reveal any clues as to his whereabouts. Their public appeals, door to door interviews even house searches have all failed to turn up anything new. A police spokesman said that they have not given up hope of finding the boy.

However, the day after this appeared in the paper there was a major development in the case.

"Bloody hell! I think we've found him, sir," sergeant Baxter exclaimed excitedly as he pushed open the door to the detective Inspector's office and put his head round the door. "He's at a small farm near Ambleside on the Horton Road, the local postman spotted him as he was on his rounds and recognised him from his description. Apparently, the place is owned by a bit of an odd bod who lives on his own there, he very rarely goes into the village except to collect his pension and the postmaster reckons he never hardly speaks to anyone at all. He generally buys a few meagre groceries and that's it, except we've checked and it seems he's been buying a lot more provisions lately, including a lot of sweets. The postman a Mr Ralph Bardon being quite a community-conscious chap thought he ought to check if the old boy was okay. so he had a look through the kitchen window and to his surprise, there was a young boy sitting having breakfast at the table with the old bloke. He didn't bother to put the letter through the door as they hadn't seen him and he didn't want to alert them, he came straight here sir, he's in the interview room now giving a statement. He said the boy looked well looked after!"

Melgrove, jumped up from behind his desk, scattering a load of papers as he did so and came towards the door. "Thank God, good work sergeant. Right, now I want a squad car with two constables to follow us there."

"I know the place where the boy is, sir, but what I can't understand is how on earth we missed him when we visited the farm and interviewed The owner back about two weeks ago. His name's Arthur Miles sir, there didn't seem to be anything suspicious that warranted bringing him in for questioning, he was just a sad old man leading a solitary existence, his wife had deserted him years ago, ran off with the hired help apparently!"

The two detectives jumped into the patrol car and their driver sped away in the direction of Ambleside which was approximately five miles away, they were followed closely by the two constables who were talking very animatedly to each other and were no doubt wondering what they would encounter when they got there. There was a fairly good B road that would take them about two miles from the farm but the rest of the way would be down winding country lanes and a rough cart track up to the farm. The place was situated between two hills, 'High Tor' & 'Mull Cragg' lying in a small shallow valley it was quite a remote but beautiful spot.

The police cars alarms were ringing all the way until about a mile away from the farm, when they switched them off so as not to warn the man, the two cars trundled their way up the bumpy cart track towards the house and Melgrove was hoping they wouldn't be spotted and they would have the element of surprise. However, that sadly was not going to be the case. In the distance, they could see a man carrying a shotgun in one hand and two rabbits in the other, what's more, he had seen them and he was running towards the house as fast as he could. He was in the house doing God knows what for at least five minutes before they reached the house and got out of the cars. "Just keep down, I don't want any heroics, we know he's armed and we don't know what he might do to the boy," They were all a bit fidgety not really knowing what to do and awaiting instructions. Melgrove used the loud hailer to tell the man to be sensible and come out unarmed and to let the boy go. They seemed to be waiting for a response for ages when one of the constables who was crouching near to the ground began making his way round the side of the house and disappearing out of sight.

"I said no heroics, he'll go and get himself killed," said an angry Melgrove.

Seconds later constable Pierce came back from the other side of the house and shouted, "They've left the house, sir, I saw them going up a path to High Tor!"

"Does he still have his rifle constable," D.S. Baxter Shouted

"Yes, sir he does," came the reply.

"Detective, radio H.Q. and get them to send us two officers trained in the use of firearms out here, meanwhile we'll follow cautiously behind so that we won't rattle him into harming the lad, but we can't just wait here and do nothing until they get here."

They followed the path up the hill until they were about two hundred yards from the top. They could see the man Miles up ahead and he had a firm hold on Jake. At this point D.I.Melgrove who was leading the party stopped, turning around he addressed them saying that he intended to go on alone. "Are you sure about that, sir?" D.S. Baxter said as he had now caught them up, "the firearms chaps should be here in another half hour or so."

"Yes, it's alright sergeant, but I can't wait that long. I hope it doesn't come to it, but in case there should end up being a struggle, I'd welcome your assistance quickly as he's a big bloke and I'm not sure I can handle him on my own!"

"Sure, sir, I'll be ready."

Melgrove walked slowly, gradually approaching Miles and Jake and talking gently as he went, "It's alright Arthur, I'm only coming closer so that I can talk to you without having to shout." Inching forward another couple of steps caused a reaction that Melrose didn't want. Miles picked the boy up, holding him under one arm like he was a rag doll and took a step back. "Ok, it's ok Arthur, I won't come any closer, you really don't want to hurt 'Danny' do you, you love him. Why not put him down and let him come to us, we just want to check that he is alright as we think he might need a doctor."

Arthur looked confused and bewildered as he looked down at young Jake, for a moment no-one knew what the man would do. Then he said something inaudible to the boy, stroked his head and put his feet down on the grass, Jake looked up at him, Arthur kissed his forehead. Jake turned away from Arthur, faced Melrose and began to walk towards him. The air was fraught with tension but a few more steps and he would be safe. Once he had the boy safe with him he beckoned two constables to step forward and carry Jake to the waiting ambulance that would take him to hospital for checkups. Moments later the ambulance clanged its way towards Addlestone hospital 15 miles away.

Arthur Miles looking like a crumbling broken shell of a man put his fist to his mouth and bit a finger as if tormented and struggling to think what to do, he looked towards the ambulance and saw that Jake was going to be taken away, then he staggered back lost his footing and disappeared over the precipice with a piercing scream as the onlookers gasped in horror.

There was a stunned, eerie silence and the seven of them including the two officers with guns seemed rooted to the spot in frozen animation. Melgrove cautiously went to the edge and looked over to see the broken body of Arthur Miles lying on the rocks below. Thankfully he didn't think that Jake had seen or heard what went on as he was already in the ambulance and the siren was blaring, he was spared that. Gradually they all collected themselves and began to climb into the patrol cars and move away back to the station. After a few hours Melgrove went to the hospital and asked if he was permitted to talk to Jake, he was told not to tax him too much. One of the questions Melgrove asked the boy was:

"What did Arthur say to you when he let you walk towards me, Jake?"

Jake looked at the policeman and said," He told me, *Yo be a gud lad n go wi them, they won't hurt ya, n orlwaze remember I luv ya."*

Later that same day the Almoner led Vera and Bill into Silas Ward of Addlestone Hospital to be re-united with their son. It had been five weeks to the day since he had gone missing and it had seemed like a nightmarish lifetime to them. Jake had been told that they were coming to see him he was feeling a mixture of excitement, nervousness and concern about it as he didn't know if he would be in trouble or not for causing them to worry about him. The medical examinations that the doctors had conducted on Jake had not revealed any signs of him having been interfered with sexually and apart from the psychological trauma of his recent experience, he was a normal healthy boy. He would be referred to a Child Psychologist and Psychiatrist for mental health assessments.

Vera and Bill noticed that the ward was filled with beautiful bunches of flowers that well-wishers from all over the country had sent; they could see Jake sitting up in bed with a worried frown on his face, they smiled at him and moved to the bedside. Vera was the first to hug and kiss him, it was a great long lingering hug as she said, "Oohh my lovely boy, we're so glad you're safe and sound. Then Bill said how everyone had missed him and would be glad to see him back home soon.

The local paper The Addlestone Herald which had been covering the whole story of Jake's disappearance for weeks, had blazoned a photo of Jake on its front page and printed the news of his dramatic rescue and the accidental demise of Arthur Miles who had abducted and held the boy captive for five weeks. Where and how they had acquired the photo of him Vera hadn't a clue, she certainly hadn't given it to them. The police had searched the farm and land thoroughly with sniffer dogs as a Mr Roy Finmore had reported that Mr Miles estranged wife Edna, with whom he had had an affair, had robbed him of a considerable amount of money when she had left his flat after a fight, it was fifty pounds to be exact. He'd said that he'd met her when he did some work on the farm and that she and Miles had a son called Danny who was eleven years old, and lived on the farm with them. The police had found evidence of an accident where a barn wall and part of the roof had collapsed and there were some bloodstains on the underside of a wooden beam. It was whilst they were searching near some trees on the perimeter of a small pond near a field with pigs in it, that they saw a piece of disturbed ground, which on investigation turned out to be a shallow grave containing the body of the young boy, Danny Miles. On searching the house they discovered a red handbag which Roy Finmore identified as belonging to Vera Miles, inside they found money to the value of fifty-two pounds ten shillings. This meant that the police would now have to try to find out what had happened to Enid Miles, D.I. Melgrove felt certain that it meant searching for her dead body. It was a case of her being in the wrong place at the wrong time, it was obvious to him that she had unwittingly returned to her old home and discovered that her son Danny wasn't there, yet there was another boy who she didn't know sleeping in his bed. It must have dawned on her that it was the missing boy Jake who everyone was looking for, her discovery and possible accusations resulted in Arthur Miles murdering her.

An autopsy report was conducted on Arthur Miles and Danny Miles and the Coroner gave a verdict of Accidental Death on both of them. What the papers or the general public never got to know was that the autopsy had also revealed that Arthur's body was riddled with cancer and that he would have been dead within months if he hadn't fallen to his death. As for the 'bodybuilding' magazines that D.I. Melgrove had found in Jake's camp, well, he did not pursue this matter as he presumed that Jake had found them on the dump and was innocently intrigued by them. He did not want grubby minds misconstruing anything and stigmatising the boy; he certainly didn't want the press getting hold of that sort of material, they would have a field day.

Nine years later people would read in the newspaper that Enid Miles body, or rather her skeletal remains were discovered as a result of a second more extensive police search of the area, due to the cold case being re-opened after a human bone was found in a farmers field. Forensic examination of the remains found that the hyoid bone in her neck had been fractured probably as a result of strangulation.

Vera, and Jake climbed the steep hill until they reached the spot on 'High Tor' where the drama was played out a year earlier. They stood motionless alongside one another for a few minutes then Jake stepped forward and laid a small bunch of flowers on the ground in memory of his lost friend. When he first came back to live at home with his mam and dad it hadn't been an easy time for Jake, he grieved for his friend Arthur who he had become so close to, Arthur had never hurt him in any way or done him any harm, he had only been a kind, gentle soul to him and although Jake had wanted him sexually Arthur had lovingly told him that was never going to happen; he continued to love and care for him until the day the police found him. Yes he knew now that Arthur had lied to him when he first met him, his parents had not gone on holiday and allowed him to stay with him, but he didn't care about that, he understood why he had done what he did, he also appreciated his willingness to be lured away and the impact it had had on his parents, but he was more sorry for what he had put his mother through, than any thought for his dad. He would always remember Arthur's last words to him, *I luv ya.*

Chapter 24

It seemed to Vera that they were all just getting back to a sense of normality after the shock of all that had happened when another bombshell hit them, they received a letter from a Mrs Vincent who was chairwoman of the Women's Institute in Stratford Upon Avon to say that sadly her friend Bridie Maguire had died a week ago and that she was sorry to be the bearer of bad news. She gave details of the date and place of the funeral, it stated she was to be buried on Wednesday 5th of September at eleven o'clock at St Bartholomews Catholic Church if Vera wished to attend. There was to be a wake at Bridie's house after the funeral ceremony.

One of Vera and Bill's neighbours and a friend of Bill's who helped out on the farm sometimes, Ted Beavis, kindly offered to drive them to Stratford on the day of the funeral so they could pay their last respects to Bridie. He said he would be perfectly happy to spend the day in the town sightseeing as he had never been before. Vera had managed to borrow a black coat and skirt off Rosemary, luckily she had a pair of black shoes and a handbag already. They had to go into Hanworth to John Colliers men's clothing retailers to buy a black suit for Bill on the never-never for three shillings and sixpence a week as they couldn't afford to pay cash for one.

Thankfully the weather was fine on the day of the funeral, Ted picked them up in his very fine Ford Prefect Saloon car at 9,30 am as he said he wanted to make sure he got them there within plenty of time, better to hang around a bit than be late, he said. He commented on how smart they both looked and joked that he knew where to come when he needed to borrow a suit, which lightened the tension a little. The journey proved to be a very sad one for Vera although the views of the countryside they went through were lovely, she was preoccupied thinking about Bridie and feeling guilty because she hadn't been in touch and had no idea she had been ill, if she had known she would have gone to see her, but perhaps for some reason Bridie didn't want that. She was remembering what a good friend Bridie had been to her, how she had saved her from God knows what fate in the nursing home, it certainly was a sad day, there weren't many people in the world like Bridie, she had been like a mother to her. She had tears in her eyes already and was dreading the emotions that the funeral service was going to arouse in her, she hoped she would be able to hold herself in check. They had arrived and had made excellent time, they were about three-quarters of an hour early, but that didn't matter as they could have a wander around to fill in time before the service.

"Here we are then, Ted said Betsys done really well today, she's had a good run, it'll do her good," referring to the car, what time do you want me to pick you up folks?"

"Shall we say three o'clock?" Bill queried, looking at Vera.

"Yes that should be fine if that's alright with you Ted, it's only about a mile to Bridie's house from here, it'll be a nice walk for us."

"That's ok by me, hope all goes well, see you at three o'clock then, cheerio." Ted had been admiring Vera without making it obvious and thought, *Bill's a lucky so and so to have a lovely lass like Vera.*

"Thank you. Bye, Ted," Vera said.

Bill said, "See you, pal."

As he drove away Bill said:

"We'll have to give him some money for petrol, it was good of him to bring us,"

"Yes, of course, we must," Vera replied.

They walked through the lychgate and along the path through the churchyard with its carefully manicured grass and looked toward the church.

"It's a beautiful old church Bill, I'll bet it's lovely inside."

"Can't say I'm especially fond of churches," Bill said, they tend to give me the creeps!"

They could see a man and a woman both dressed in black standing by the church porch and as they reached them the woman smiled at Vera and said:

"Hello, my dear, are you Vera?"

"Yes I am, Vera said, are you, Mrs Vincent?"

Yes, that's right, but please call me Pru, I'm so pleased to meet you, Bridie spoke so much about you, I feel I know you already, she said that she looked upon you as a daughter."

"Vera welled up with emotion and said, Yes she was like a mother to me, and dabbed at her eyes with her handkerchief, sniffling."

"We became very good friends, we met at the Women's Institute meetings that she allowed to be held at her house," Oh sorry, this is my husband John," she said slightly gesturing towards him. John shook Vera's hand and said poignantly, looking at Vera and then lowering his head down.

"Sad day."

Vera said to them both:

"This is my husband, Bill."

They both shook Bill's hand and Mr Vincent said:

"Pleased to meet you, but sorry it's under these circumstances."

"Oh, by the way, I've arranged for you to come with us in the first car on the drive back to Bridie's house."

"Oh thank you, you're very kind," Vera said.

"We must make our way down to the gate and wait for the hearse to arrive," Mrs Vincent said.

So they proceeded to make their way there.

A lot of other people were starting to arrive and congregate together outside the churchyard, after fifteen minutes or so it looked as if there was going to be quite a crowd that would be saying a fond farewell to Bridie Maguire. Shortly afterwards the hearse transporting Bridie's coffin arrived to bring her to her final resting place, it stopped by the gate and the pallbearers all wearing mourning dress in grey and black and wearing black top hats with grey ribbon bands, got out of the hearse. The coffin which was strewn with a large spray of pink carnations and white chrysanthemums was drawn out and lifted gracefully onto a trolley, an officiate walked upright and dignified to the front of the coffin and began to walk slowly toward the church leading the cortege through the churchyard.

Vera and Bill walked behind the Vincents at the front of the procession and as the coffin was taken into the church followed them inside and they were ushered to sit along the front pew which had orders of service on the seats for each person. It was the most beautiful Requiem Mass during which Pru Vincent gave the eulogy and spoke glowingly of Bridie's life and good works. Those in the church who were Catholics took Holy Communion whilst the other people reflected or prayed during this time. Two hymns were sung, All Things Bright and Beautiful and Abide With Me; there was a young female soloist with an angelic voice who sang Ave Maria. Vera had cried on and off throughout the whole service, comforted by Bill's strong arm, but Vera couldn't help but notice that he was a bit fidgety and uncomfortable for the biggest part of the proceedings, she thought he would probably be glad to get out of the church for some fresh air. When they did eventually emerge from the church, Vera and Bill waited for Pru and John who were circulating amongst the other mourners and were probably inviting them to come back to Bridie's for the wake.

Vera felt it was such a shame that she was returning to Bridie's house for an occasion such as this, it was a place that had been a welcome sanctuary for her at a very difficult time in her life and it would be strange to be there and not see Bridie or hear her lilting Irish tones, and yet she was sure in her heart that she would see her smiling face and hear her soft voice greeting her, she could almost hear her saying.

"Aah there ya are lass, it's good ta see ya, t be sure, come on in n have a cup o tea!"

Inside the house was just as she'd remembered it, today there were a few more chairs set out and the large table had been extended, covered with a fine white Irish lace tablecloth and set out with a massive amount of food, everything from assorted sandwiches to platters of different quiche, pork pie, salad and coleslaw. Bridie's favourite antique 'Belleek' china was in splendid evidence decorating the table in superb style, she always said she would rather them be used when they could be, rather than them just be stuck in a glass cabinet doing nothing. Vera and Bill waited until other people started to partake of the food before they went to the table and helped themselves to some, they then found themselves a couple of free chairs and sat down to enjoy it, they were hungry as it had been a long time since they'd eaten breakfast. There were a lot of nice very friendly people there who took time to say hello and make conversation, it was obvious how well-loved Bridie was. They had spent so much time chattering, Bill looked at his watch and saw that it was half-past two, so he said to Vera that they ought to go as they had some distance to walk and he didn't want Ted to be waiting too long for them. So they said goodbye to the Vincents and the other people they had chatted to and started to walk back to their pickup point. As they neared the place they'd arranged to meet, they could see Ted was waiting for them, he was stood leaning lazily against the side of the car with his face turned to the sun. On the journey back home Ted was enthusiastically telling them about the places he had visited, he said that Ann Hathaway's cottage was beautiful and so interesting to see, as was Shakespeare's Birthplace too; he was so glad to have had the opportunity of seeing them, he felt sure that he would pay another visit as he wanted to go and see Mary Arden's Farm, he hadn't had time to fit that in this visit. Ted dropped them off and said a cheery goodbye and Vera couldn't help thinking what a nice man he was, one of the worlds true gentlemen. Bill had mentioned that he wasn't married and Vera wondered why a handsome polite man like him was still a bachelor, in his late forties, *he'd be quite a catch for someone,* she thought.

Chapter 25

Vera received a letter from a firm of solicitors, Woodhew and Simpson, who were acting on behalf of Bridie Maguire; they commiserated with them over the sad loss of their friend Bridie Maguire; invited them to attend the reading of her will at her solicitor's office in Warwick next Tuesday at 1pm. Vera wasn't the only one who had received a letter asking her to attend, about a week before they were due to go for the reading of the will, Vera's friend Ivy had turned up at Vera's home to tell her that she had also received a letter as she had only met Bridie on the one occasion of Jake's christening, so couldn't think why she was being asked to go. Vera just said that it was obviously because Bridie wanted her there. Vera suggested that if Ivy wanted to, she could come and stay at her house the night before and they could all catch the bus into Warwick together the next day. Ivy thought that this would suit her down to the ground as it would be much more pleasant travelling with company, so it was agreed this is what they would do. They spent several hours together, Ivy happily cuddled Jake and helped Vera prepare the evening meal for when Bill came home. Having been asked if she would like to stay and join them for a meal so that she could tell Bill about her letter, she gladly said yes.

Bill came home and was very surprised to see Ivy there, "Day off from work today then Ivy," Bill said, "you're not ill I hope?"

"Hello Bill, no I'm not ill, I just wanted to come and see you and Vera about something."

Bill looked curious and Vera said, "Ivy's staying for dinner Bill, she'll tell you all about it when you're washed up and we're ready to eat."

"Oh okay, very mysterious indeed," Bill replied.

When dinner was ready and she was about to put it on the plates and Bill was still upstairs, Vera went to the bottom of the stairs and called out.

"Bill, I'm about to put your dinner on the table."

"Okay, love, just coming," he replied, shortly afterwards he came hurrying down. "Oh it smells good, what is it?"

"Wait and see," Vera said, smiling at Ivy.

"Thank you, Ivy," Vera said, "we can sit and have ours now."

Bill and Ivy sat at the table and Vera put their meals in front of them.

"Smashing, cheese, bacon and potato pie, my second best favourite, Bill said rubbing his hands together with pleasure."

"What's your favourite then?" Ivy asked.

Vera and Bill both said together, "liver, bacon and onions," and they both laughed, so did Ivy. "So what's this mysterious news you have to tell me then Ivy?"

"You know the letter you had from the solicitors recently?"

"Yes, what about it," Bill mumbled with his mouth crammed full of food.

"Well, I've had one too, I've been asked to go to the reading of Bridie's will."

"Bloody hell! We'd better organise a coach eh Vera, I wonder how many more'll be going, you'd better come with us then."

"Bill Wiggins you'd make a joke out of anything you would, I can only think that it will be good news for you Ivy, Bridie had a good heart, bless her, look what she did for me. I dread to think how things would have turned out if she hadn't stepped in and rescued me."

"That's very true Vera love, it doesn't bear thinking about."

"When Vera wrote to me and told me what had happened, I couldn't believe it, but I was so relieved that her and her baby to be were safe and away from that awful place. I'll never forget that Matron woman, I could have hit her."

"Anyway, it's all water under the bridge now, everything turned out alright, thanks to Bridie Maguire, God rest her soul."

On the day they went to the will reading Bill told Jake to go up to the farm and stay with Pauline and Ned., while Vera and Ivy finished getting ready. Pauline had agreed to babysit, as Bill had told her and Ned they had some important family business to sort out in Warwick. They caught the bus into Warwick and although they arrived within plenty of time, they made their way to the Solicitors office. It turned out that there were seven people in attendance including the solicitor Mr Woodhew and his secretary, Prue Vincent who was with another woman who Vera didn't know and themselves. Mr Woodhew addressed everyone and said that this was the reading of the last will and testament of Mrs Bridie Maguire and he then proceeded to read its contents to the beneficiaries:

"To my dearest friend Vera Wiggins I leave the sum of £30,000 for her love and loyalty to me in the years that I have known her. This is to ensure that she is never in financial difficulties for her future years." Absolutely stunned on hearing this statement Vera thought she was going to pass out, but mercifully the feeling passed over; she began to cry and Bill put his arms around her to comfort her, but he was obviously as shocked as she was. What Bill didn't know was that on one occasion after he had subjected her and Jake to a beating when he had come back from the pub drunk one night, was that Vera had confided this to Bridie and told her that it wasn't the first time it had happened. Bridie was appalled and said that she would never have suspected or believed that Bill could be capable of such behaviour, and that she didn't have to put up with it. Bridie had said.

"A man isn't worthy of your love if he ill-treats you, a loving man should always cherish, adore and protect you." She was concerned for Vera's safety although Vera had told her that he was remorseful and promised her that he would never do it again as he cried bitterly. They had talked for hours as Bill was at work, Bridie had come on a surprise visit as she had been to Addlestone on business and was in the area. Bridie had broached the subject of the possibility of Vera leaving this abusive relationship and said that she would always be welcome to come and live with her if she did ever want to leave Bill. Vera had told Bridie that she loved Bill despite his lapses into violence; Bridie had warned her to be careful and not to put her safety and the safety of her child at risk. Mr Woodhew, having paused when he saw how upset Vera was, went on to read:

"To my Godson Jake Wiggins I leave the sum of £20.000 which will be held in trust until he reaches twenty-one years of age, I hope he will be mature enough to make the best possible use of his inheritance." Vera and Bill both gasped at this, looking at each other in amazement.

To Ivy Newton, Vera's dear friend I leave the sum of £3.000 for her to achieve her dream of working in a dress shop. She will now be able to open one of her own.

"The residue of my estate which includes the house and grounds, I leave to The Women's Institute for them to use as a conference, events and recreational centre to ensure that young women have the opportunity to learn domestic and social skills to equip them for life. I would like it to be called The Bridie Maguire Centre. Pru, who was there representing the Women's Institute nodded and smiled to the other woman in approval. At the end of the ceremony Mr Woodhew gave Vera two envelopes one with her name on it containing a cheque and one for Jake which had all the trust details, she signed to say that she had received them and she placed them in her handbag. Ivy was also given her envelope, she had been overcome with emotion when she was told about her gift from Bridie and as she signed for it was still dabbing tears away from her eyes. Vera went over to Pru and shook her by the hand and said:

"It's good to see you again, Pru, and I'm so pleased that Bridie had the vision and the generosity to leave her house to the Women's Institute. I know she held your organisation in high esteem and I can't think of the house and grounds being put to better use."

"Thank you very much, Vera, it will be a great asset to us and we will do Bridie's name proud."

As they left the solicitors' office, Vera said:

"I can't believe it, Bill, what a shock, I thought I was going to pass out, fancy Bridie being so generous to us, I'll have to open a bank account now, she said to Bill, perhaps we could call at Addleston on the way back, I don't want to have the cheque hanging around at home and they can keep Jake's envelope in their safe as well."

"I thought you were going to pass out too, the colour just drained from your face, you went as white as a sheet, but it was the shock of it, it ain't every day that you get left a vast sum of money like that love, you're a rich woman now, girl!"

"You mean we're both rich, Bill, and our Jake is, God Bless Bridie Maguire we don't have to scrimp and save anymore, ooer gosh, can I sit down somewhere quick Bill, I've come over all queer again. Bill and Ivy supported Vera as she'd gone all limp, like a rag doll, he spotted a bench just up ahead and almost carried her to it and sat her down.

"Lean forward and put your head between your legs, that'll help," Bill said anxiously.

Just at that moment Pru Vincent and her friend arrived.

"Oh dear is Vera unwell," she questioned?

"Yes she's had a bit of a funny turn," Ivy replied.

"It's the shock most likely, she said, she'll be alright in a minute or two."

"I hope so Bill said, I don't fancy the bus ride home with Vera like this."

"Oh, my cars just around the corner, I can give you a lift."

"That is very kind of you, but are you sure, it's some distance… We'd be very grateful," Bill said, relieved.

"Think nothing of it, it's my pleasure," Pru said.

"Well we're very grateful, Bill said, relieved.

Prus friend suddenly said in a squeaky refined voice.

"Oh it looks like the colours coming back into her cheeks, she's on the mend."

"I'm ever so sorry Vera said, I don't know what came over me."

"I do Bill said, thirty thousand pounds!"

"Sssush Bill," Vera said disapprovingly.

Pru said she would just take her friend home first and then bring the car to them and take them home, she thought that was better than them being squashed together in the car. Whilst they'd gone Vera said to Bill and Ivy.

"You know that we can't tell anyone about the money don't you Bill, Ivy you can please yourself if you want to tell anyone about yours. I don't think Bill and I should tell anyone at all, it wouldn't be safe. I don't want all and sundry knowing about it."

"No, you're absolutely right Vera. I agree, we mustn't tell anybody, we've come into money." Ivy said that she would obviously have to tell her parents where her money had come from but she promised not to tell them about theirs or Jake's.

Chapter 26

Things hadn't been right between Vera and Bill for a long while, their relationship seemed to go downhill a few months after Bridie passed away. Over several years the rows had become more frequent and would flare up over nothing at all and invariably it meant that either her or Jake would take the brunt of his nasty temper either from his verbal abuse or worse. Vera tried her best to get to the bottom of what it was that was bothering Bill and why he had become so brooding and quiet; capable of flying off the handle over the least little thing. She felt that she was walking on eggshells all the time He was certainly drinking more and would go out on his own, never inviting Vera to go with him.

He had taken to gambling too and was continually asking Vera for money and the amounts he was asking for were getting larger, she found it very worrying. Then one evening after Bill came home from the pub drunk, things got completely out of hand and it suddenly became clear from what was said exactly what it was that had changed Bill's behaviour. She didn't know for certain how it had started, all she knew was that she found Bill's manner alarming and she was frightened, it was though he was spoiling for a fight and was picking her up on everything she said. She tried to be pleasant and make conversation asking him if he'd had a nice evening, and he immediately accused her of being sarcastic.

"Don't get bloody funny with me, just because I've been out for a few drinks!"

"I wasn't being funny with you Bill, I was just making conversation."

"Yeah like hell you were, I know sarcasm when I hear it." Vera decided to stay quiet then as she didn't want to antagonise him, she knew she was on a loser whatever she did. She hoped Jake was asleep and wasn't lying awake in his bed listening to his dad.

"Gone all bloody moody on me now then have you, he said, you haven't been the same since you came into that money Bridie left you, and you haven't exactly been generous either, you've hardly spent any of it." Vera didn't feel she could ignore that remark so she asked him.

"Whatever do you mean Bill?"

"What do I mean, I'll tell you what I mean, you've changed, you've gone all hoity-toity as though you're better than me, behaving like 'Lady Muck'."

"That's ridiculous Bill, I don't know what makes you think that, if anyone has changed it's you, you've been really distant with me lately; you don't seem interested in me anymore, and you've certainly no time for Jake."

Raising his voice, he said, "Oh so it's all my fault then is it, well I'll tell you what you can do shall I, you and your spoiled mummy's boy can clear out for all I care, you don't need me anymore."

"Please don't shout Bill what will the neighbours think, and that's your son you're talking about!"

"Oh he's my son is he, I've never been sure about that and I don't give a fuck what any of the neighbours think especially that nosey old hag next door, and don't tell me what I can or can't do, in my own house woman,"

"Bill, Vera said, shocked and upset by his language, you don't know what you're saying, you're drunk, I'm going up to bed."

"That's it you run away off to bed, pleasant dreams," he said sarcastically.

Vera was so worried and upset, she had never seen him like this, or ever heard him say such cruel and hurtful things, surely he couldn't possibly mean what he said about him doubting Jake was his son. She undressed and put on her nightgown, pulled back the bedcovers and was just about to get into bed when the radio began blaring out from downstairs. Vera quickly went downstairs and saw Bill standing there with a big grin on his face, she went towards the radio intending to turn it off but Bill blocked her way. He grabbed hold of her and said:

"Shall we dance?"

Vera managed to struggle free from his grasp and switched the radio off, Bill immediately turned it back on again, she couldn't get past him to silence it again so she went to get down to pull the plug out, unfortunately, she wasn't quick enough and Bill caught hold of the back of her neck and pulled her up violently as he did so he swung his other fist round and struck Vera viciously on the side of her face and sent her sprawling wildly across the room, she landed in a heap, striking her head on the corner of a cupboard.

Just moments before Jake had come downstairs and entered the noisy music-filled room and had seen his dad strike his mother, he went to help her up but she was lifeless, he really thought his mother was dead and he shouted.

"Oh no, Dad, you've killed mam," as he said this Bill lurched towards Jake with a fearsome look on his face as though he intended to do the same to him. So Jake fearing for his life ran out of the house to try to get help. He went to go next door and saw Mr and Mrs Burridge standing outside their front door in their bedclothes along with most of the other neighbours.

"Dad's killed my mam," Jake sobbed hysterically, "what we going to do?"

"Run up to the farm and tell Ned to ring for the police Jake, Mrs Burridge said, He's gone mad."

Jake turned and ran as fast as his legs would carry him down the garden path, out of the gate and up the lane to the farm, he went into the farmhouse door and pounded on it with all his might, Rover the Trenchs' dog began barking loudly.

"Quiet Rover, good boy, go and lie down," Ned commanded. Jake was completely out of breath and puffing and panting as Ned pulled the door open to see young Jake standing there panic-stricken.

"What's happened Jake," Ned asked him.

"It's my dad, he's gone mad and killed my mam, call the police, call the police?"

"Come on in Jake and sit down lad while I call them."

Pauline came downstairs in her dressing gown, saw Jake sitting there distressed; Ned on the telephone and she looked at Ned alarmed and said:

"Whatever's happened, Ned?"

"Look after Jake Poll, he says Bill's gone mad and killed Vera!"

"Oh my lord, Pauline exclaimed, Oh Jake you poor love, you didn't see it happen," she said sitting down next to him and putting her arms around his shoulders. Rover got up out of his bed and came over wagging his tail and sat by Pauline's legs.

Jake looked up at her and nodded his head, then he just buried his head in her bosom and sobbed.

"There, there my love, there, there," Pauline quivered trying not to cry herself as she gently rocked Jake to and fro.

"I thought he was going to kill me as well, Jake said, he had such a terrible look on his face as he tried to get me," and continued sobbing!

"Ssssch there now love, don't think about it, you're safe now."

"Operator, can you get me the police please, there's been a murder at No 2, Wood Lane Cottages, Grendore." After answering a few questions, Ned explained that it was an employee of his called Bill Wiggins and that his son had run to the farm to say that his dad had murdered his mother. The operator took his name, number and address and said that she would send a car straightaway.

Ned replaced the receiver and said, "I really ought to get down there in case anyone else is in danger, Pauline."

"I don't think that's a good idea, Ned, at least wait until you've heard the police arrive, before you go anywhere near, the last thing I want is anything happening to you."

"Yeah, I suppose you're right, and looking at Jake not knowing what to say to him he just stroked his head and said:

"We'll take care of you Jake, everything will be alright."

He thought how stupid that sounded as soon as he'd said it, of course, everything wasn't going to be alright, his mother had been murdered and his father was about to be taken away by the police and locked in prison, the poor lad had lost both his parents in one cruel fell swoop.

They could now hear the sound of police sirens in the distance and Ned waited until he heard them coming down the lane so he put on his coat and shoes, said goodbye to Pauline and left the house. He could hear loud music playing as he left the farmyard and began walking down the lane, then he heard at least two cars screech to a halt, but as he got nearer he saw police officers going into the house. Pretty soon after that, the music went off and he could hear shouting coming from inside the house. He walked up the path towards the group of neighbours, greeted them and said what an awful thing it was to have happened, all of them were looking so relieved that the deafening music had finally stopped.

"I've been expecting something like this to happen, Mavis Burridge said, I did warn the police when Jake went missing and they arrested him before, I told them he was always beating them up but they didn't listen, they should have kept him locked up, then this would never have happened, it's been going on for years, we're fed up of listening to them rowing all the time!" There was more shouting from inside and Bill's voice ranting:

"I'll kill the bloody lot of yer!" Then it sounded as if several of them had overpowered him because they heard him shout, "Let me go, aaagh, let me go."

About two minutes later he was brought out in handcuffs, by two burly policemen, one of which had a bloody nose, he had his head bowed down as he was led past the group of onlookers and taken down the path and bundled into the police car, which quickly took off at speed up the lane. Everyone was wondering what was going on as some police remained inside, but shortly afterwards Dr Carlston's car pulled up in the lane and he got out and rushed into the house. They all presumed that he was there to do an examination of the body and confirm that Vera was dead. Fifteen minutes went by, then they heard the clanging bell of an ambulance which stopped in the lane and two ambulance men came up the path with a stretcher to take poor Vera's body away. Dr Carlston left shortly afterwards.

When they came out they were all so surprised and relieved to see Vera on the stretcher with her head heavily bandaged looking extremely pale, her eyes were open and she saw Ned as he stepped towards the stretcher as they carried her past and he said.

"Don't worry Vera, Jake's with us at the farm, we'll look after him.

It could all have been so different, Ned thought, he had expected to see a corpse on the stretcher covered in a white sheet, thank God Vera was still alive, he just hoped she would be alright, he couldn't wait to give the good news to Jake and Pauline when he got home.

D.I. Melgrove and D.S. Baxter came out of the house some minutes later and a constable remained on guard at the front door, so as to preserve the crime scene. Ned went to have a word with Melgrove but before he could say anything Melgrove said.

"Mr Trench isn't it?"

"Yes, how is she?" Ned asked.

"She has a nasty head injury, it's a bad business this, sir, I think Mrs Wiggins has had a narrow escape, this could so easily have been a murder enquiry."

"Oh dear, poor Vera, what will happen to Bill, will he go to prison?

"He will be held in custody overnight and will go before the magistrate in the morning, I can't really say any more than that at the moment, sir. Where is the son, Jake, was he a witness to any of this?

"Yes he was, he thought Bill had killed Vera and he ran up to the farm to get us to call you, my wife's looking after him at the moment, he's badly shaken up."

"I'll come back with you now, sir, if I may, I need to have a few words with him."

"Do you need to do that now Inspector, he's had a real fright."

"Yes, I'm afraid I must, but I'll be as gentle as I can with the boy, jump in the car and we'll get it over with so the boy can get some sleep. I'll let you go in first and you can tell the lad that his mother is badly injured but is going to be alright."

Ned told Jake and Pauline the good news which was such a great relief to both of them.

When Melgrove saw the boy he was surprised for some reason he had a picture of him in his mind as the eleven-year-old boy that he had rescued from the Miles farm, but Jake had grown, he was now a tall strapping lad of fifteen. He could see that the lad was badly shocked so he didn't ask him too many questions, just, what had he seen and did his father hurt him at all. Jake had told him how he had heard the terribly loud music and come downstairs to see his dad strike his mam and that he couldn't wake her up, so he'd thought she was dead, then his dad went for him, so he ran out; up to the farm to get Ned to ring the police. After he had given his account of what he'd seen Jake asked.

"I won't have to see my dad again will I, I never want to as long as I live after what he did to mi mam?"

"You will see him in court, but you won't have to talk to him and he won't be able to hurt you, but don't get worrying about that now, you need to get some rest."

Melgrove said goodnight to them but as Ned showed him out he said to him:

"You might want to call Dr Carlston to come and examine the boy, just to be on the safe side, you know."

"Yes, I will, Inspector, goodnight.

Ned closed the door, he came back in and said to both Jake and Pauline, the Inspector thinks that we should call Dr Carlston to just come and check you over Jake as you've had a really bad shock with everything that's happened.

"I'm alright really I am," Jake said, reluctantly.

"I know you think you are lad, but we'll let the doctor be the judge of that."

Pauline said, "It's for the best Jake, it's alright, you won't have to go to hospital or anything like that."

"I'll give him a ring then, Ned said dialling the number.

"Oh, hello, Dr Carlston, this is Ned Trench from Wood Lane farm, I'm sorry to bother you at this time of night but Inspector Melgrove suggested I ring you, we're looking after young Jake Wiggins and we thought it might be best if you had a look at him, due to everything that's gone on like."

"That's alright Ned, You were absolutely right to call me, I'll be along shortly."

Half an hour later Dr Carlston arrived and set the dog off barking again, Pauline shushed him and told him to go and lie down as Ned opened the door to let the doctor in.

"Good evening, Doctor," Ned greeted him.

"Good Evening Ned, the doctor said as they walked into the living room, good evening Pauline, and how are you young man, he said leaning over Jake, you've had a bit of a rough time of it, haven't you."

The doctor's sympathy brought on another flood of tears from Jake.

"Now, now, it's alright young fellow, my lad, I'll just take your temperature, pop this in your mouth." He then took Jake's pulse.

"Ah yes he said, I think we need to make sure you get a good, restful night's sleep young man." Looking in his bag he pulled out a bottle of tablets, took the cap off and shook one out.

"If you could get a glass of water please, he waited whilst Ned fetched the water and then he said, just sit up for me Jake and take this tablet please, it will help you to sleep, you will have to have a couple of days off school, but I don't suppose you'll mind that will you?

Jake smiled a weak smile, took the tablet and the doctor tousled his head and said:

"Good man."

"If you could please get him off to bed now and I'll pop in to see him again tomorrow evening."

Pauline and Jake rose from the couch and Pauline took him off to bed, saying:

"Thank you, doctor, come on Jake."

When they had gone upstairs, the doctor said to Ned:

"He will sleep well into late morning and he will be a bit groggy and keep dozing off for most of the day, he's had a nasty shock poor chap."

"How is Vera Doctor," Ned asked concerned?

"She was punched and knocked unconscious when she fell and hit her head against a cupboard, she sustained severe bruising and a nasty gash to her head which will have to have several stitches, her physical wounds will heal fairly quickly, however, I think her emotional wounds will take a lot longer, but she's a strong young woman, she'll be alright, I'm sure, she has two good friends in you and Pauline, thank you for looking after Jake."

"It's the least we could do under the circumstances, we're both very fond of the lad."

"Okay, well goodnight Ned, I'll see you tomorrow, I'll probably have more news then."

"Thank you, doctor, goodnight."

Ned sat down and was contemplating the night's events, Pauline came back downstairs and said:

"Jake's gone to sleep, poor lad."

"Oh good."

"What did the doctor say, Ned?"

"He told me what Bill has done to Vera and how badly hurt she is, he said her body will soon heal but it will take much longer for her to come to terms with what's happened, she's going to need a lot of support Pauline and I'm without a labourer again."

"Well, we'll help as much as we can, I'm still shell shocked over the whole business, I can't believe what Bill has done, but then the demon drink always brings the worst out in people, and we'll have to come up with a solution of getting you some help, you can't run the farm single-handed and the way things are we need to find someone quick!"

Chapter 27

Vera woke up and for a few minutes wasn't sure where she was, she had a pounding headache and her mouth was dry, she looked around and saw that she was in a hospital bed. She tried to get out of bed as she needed the bathroom but as she sat up on the edge of the bed her head pounded harder and she felt very dizzy. She vaguely remembered being examined by doctors and nurses and them doing something to her head which was quite painful, she put her hand up to touch it and felt the dressing they had put on.

"Good Morning Mrs Wiggins, how are you feeling this morning," the nurse who had suddenly appeared beside her asked?

"I'm a bit dizzy," Vera replied.

"Then I think we should get you back into bed," the nurse said as she helped her to lie back down and put her legs back under the bed covers, "you've got a nasty head wound which had to be stitched up when you came in."

"But I need to go to the bathroom," Vera protested.

"That's alright, I'll get you a bedpan, you just relax and take it easy."

The nurse returned with the bedpan and drew the screens around the bed; ten minutes later she was back to remove it and pull back the screens.

"The breakfast trolley will be coming round shortly, please try to eat something," the nurse said gently, "I'll be back later to tidy up for Matron and doctors' rounds."

It was later that morning when the horrors of the night before started crowding in on her, she recalled seeing Ned and him telling her that Jake was alright, then there were flashbacks like moving picture sequences of the dreadful chain of events that had led to Bill violently punching her to the floor and causing her to be in here. Tears started in her eyes as she thought about the way Bill had cruelly treated her for no reason and for the hateful things he had said. Why would he think that Jake wasn't his child, had he always thought that? If that was the case then he must also think that Vera had trapped him into leaving the navy and marrying her. Following this line of reasoning through could only mean that he had always felt bitter and resentful toward her and Jake. These thoughts immediately answered all the doubts she had harboured in her mind as to why Bill could never find time for Jake and why he found it easier to beat him than love him. She knew Jake was different to other boys in that he had a sensitive way about him, was gentle and kind; didn't like playing rough sports and was a lover of nature, he'd rather pick a bunch of flowers for his mam than kick a football around. Bill was a tough man, he would hit someone first and ask questions afterwards, he thought he was a cross between John Wayne and James Cagney and practically modelled himself on his film star heroes. She wasn't sure what she would do but she knew it meant a fresh start for her and Jake. She remembered what Bridie had told her. *A man isn't worthy of your love if he ill-treats you, a loving man should always cherish adore and protect you.* Bill certainly wasn't going to do that, she should have listened to her dear friend. Vera must have drifted off to sleep, she was awoken by an auxiliary nurse clattering as she opened and closed the doors and lifted the lids on the breakfast trolley.

"Would you like some breakfast and a cup of tea dear?" the woman asked.

"Yes, please, I'd love a cup of tea, don't know that I could eat anything though."

"Here's a nice cuppa, and I'll leave you some scrambled egg and tomato, I'm sure you could manage to eat some of it, my dear."

"I will try," Vera replied.

There was some more clattering as the woman closed lids and doors again and moved further down the ward. The nurse came shortly after breakfast and made sure that the ward was free of any evidence of breakfast; she came to ask Vera if she had managed to eat anything and Vera said:

"I was surprised actually, I drank my tea because I was really parched, and then I tried a bit of scrambled egg feeling unsure of whether I wanted it or not, but I ended up eating it all, then I had another cup of tea, and my heads feeling a lot better, hows that nurse?"

"Absolutely marvellous, we'll soon have you fit and well and up and about if you continue like that, now let me smooth your bed out a bit and tuck the sides in, otherwise Matron will throw a fit."

The doctor came to see Vera and examined her, He told her that apart from some heavy bruising and the head wound that needed to heal she was fine, there was no sign of any remaining concussion, however, he said that due to the shock she'd had he would not let her be discharged for a few days at least; he would see her again tomorrow.

After he'd gone a nurse came up the ward carrying a beautiful vase of flowers and said to Vera:

"These have been delivered for you, they came by 'Interflora' aren't they lovely?"

Vera looked admiringly at the lovely mix of carnations, lilies, tulips and green foliage, thinking that they must have cost a fortune.

"Was there a card with them," she asked.

"Well there wasn't actually, we thought it was a bit odd, but we thought you would know who'd sent them."

"I've absolutely no idea," Vera said puzzled and wondering, *I don't think Ned and Pauline would have sent them as I'm sure they'll visit, unless it was Rosemary or Ivy, oh well, I'm sure I'll find out soon enough.*

"Oh, perhaps you've got a mystery admirer," the nurse said smiling mischievously and then thought maybe she hadn't ought to have said that.

Vera asked the nurse if she would be able to get up to have a wash, but the nurse said she didn't think that was wise and would arrange for her to be given a bed bath later, it turned out not to be as bad as Vera thought it would be; it really freshened her up, it made her feel a lot better. An older lady in the next bed said hello and introduced herself as Nancy and told her that she'd had her appendix out.

"What happened to you dear?" she enquired.

Vera thought for a moment, do I tell her a lie or tell the truth, then she thought Oh what the hell, I shouldn't feel ashamed, I've done nothing wrong, so she just came straight out with it:

"I won't lie to you, my husband came home drunk, and set about me, that's the reason I'm here!"

"Oh you poor dear, what an awful thing to have happened, where is he now?"

"In prison, I think, best place for him as far as I'm concerned."

"I should jolly well think so too the brute, do you have any children dear?"

"Yes, a boy, Jake, he's fifteen, he's being looked after by friends at the moment."

"What do you think you will you do, now is it safe for you to go home."

"I'm not exactly sure but I certainly won't be going home, I need to get things straight in my own mind and make some decisions while I'm in here, but I'm determined that from now on, Jake and I are on our own, sorry, I can't believe I'm telling you all this."

"That's alright dear, I don't mind, you obviously needed to get it out of your system, but it sounds to me as though you've made your mind up about that anyway, you must do what's best for you and your boy."

A nurse came then to change the dressing on Vera's head.

"Let's have a look how you doing shall we," she said, gently removing the pad from her head wound?

"Do you think I'll be left with a scar, Vera asked concerned?"

"You certainly will, Mrs Wiggins, but the good news is that it won't show as your hair will cover it, so don't worry, there that's it, all done."

"Oh that's a relief, I would have hated to see a scar every time I looked in the mirror."

The nurse smiled and gently touched her arm:

"You've been spared that, she said compassionately, now you just rest, are you expecting any visitors this afternoon?"

"I don't know," Vera replied and thought about Jake; how he might be coping with everything that had happened, she wondered when she would see him again.

She needn't have worried because that afternoon when visiting hour started at two o'clock; people began filtering into the ward carrying bunches of flowers and bags of fruit. Vera was looking toward the entrance to the ward searching expectantly to see if there was a familiar face. When she saw Pauline and Jake appear she gave an excited wave to show them which bed she was in; when Jake saw her he let go of Pauline's hand and almost ran to his mother's bedside.

"Oh Jake, I'm so pleased to see you, are you alright sweetheart?"

"Yes mam, but I'm glad to see you, I'm afraid I thought I'd lost you for good."

"Well, I'm still here love and I'm fine, so don't you worry."

"Does your head hurt mam, Jake asked, it looks terrible."

"Not so much at the moment Jake, it looks worse than it is," Vera lied.

Pauline reached Vera's bed carrying a lovely basket of fruit, she admired the flowers but never said she had sent them so Vera just said, "Yes they are lovely aren't they."

Jake moved toward the foot of the bed and made room, she smiled at Vera, leaned over the bed and kissed her, saying.

"It's so good to see you, love, we've all been so worried about you, but you are looking well under the circumstances."

"It's really good to see you too," Vera replied, "Thank you for the lovely fruit. I don't feel too bad, a bit bruised and stiff, but the doctor said earlier I'm on the mend, thank you so much for looking after Jake for me."

"Bless you, you're very welcome, he's a good lad, she said smiling at Jake, I hate to ask but have you thought about what you might do when you're discharged from hospital, because Ned and I have discussed it; if you don't want to go back to the cottage you'd be welcome to come and stay with us until you figure out what you want to do, Ned will have to advertise Bill's job as it's drawing near to harvest time and he'll need help. We certainly don't want him working for us after this. Once you have collected your personal things from the cottage, we will clear the place and put the rest of it into storage until you want it."

"I won't be wanting any of it and I've already figured it out, Vera said squeezing Pauline's hand; thank you for you and Ned kindly offering to give us shelter it would be an enormous help as I don't want to have to sleep at the cottage again, you're very kind, yes, we would like to stay with you for a short time until I've sorted myself out, and there's a lot I need to tell you all when I can get out of here."

"I won't be sorry to not go back there, Jake said I like it at the farm and I'm going to love taking 'Rover' for walks across the fields."

Vera and Pauline smiled.

"That's settled then, Ned will be pleased when I tell him you're getting better and you'll be staying with us for a while, how are you for toilet things and money, I didn't think to bring any in."

"I don't have anything Vera replied, it's all at the cottage along with my purse, I think there's about fifteen pounds in it."

"I'll call and collect it for you and bring it in tomorrow, where will I find your purse and is there anything else you need me to bring?"

"Oh thanks, Pauline, you're so kind, it's in my navy handbag in the bedroom, you could bring that and a clean nighty for me."

A bell began to ring to signal the end of visiting time.

"Gosh that hour went quickly, Pauline said, we'd better be going, she leaned into Vera and kissed her, bye love, say goodbye to your mum, Jake.

Jake kissed his mother and said, see you tomorrow mam.

Jake was a bit puzzled as to why the people visiting at the next bed had been staring at him so much, but he passed it off as his imagination.

They walked out of the ward and Jake turned and waved goodbye to his mother. Vera waved back smiling, she reflected on what good friends Pauline and Ned had turned out to be, they had gone above and beyond being employers and landlords.

"It's nice that you've had visitors, Nancy said, is that your young boy, Jake?"

"Yes, it is," Vera replied.

"Is he the young lad that was abducted some while back, such a terrible to do that was!"

"There's no point denying it, his picture was in all the papers, yes it was Jake, but thank God he's got over all that now."

"My son Robert just visited me, it was him who recognised Jake, he said he could swear it was the same lad."

"We had so much trouble just after the police found Jake, he was pestered and hounded by the press and there were so many problems at school with bullying that his school work was suffering so we kept him at home and he was privately tutored, it all died down after that thank God."

"You must have gone through hell my dear, and now this trouble with your husband, such a shame, things can only get better for you now, I hope they do.

"I hope so too," Vera said, giving a big yawn and suddenly feeling tired.

"You sound as though you should try and have a little nap, Nancy said, you look tired."

"Yes, I think I will," Vera said, yawning again; she snuggled down, closed her eyes and went to sleep almost immediately.

She woke after about an hour with a dry throat and desperately wanted a cup of tea, she could hear the tea trolley somewhere in the distance so she guessed she wouldn't have long to wait. She could see Nancy had done the same as she'd done and put her head down for a little snooze, she was fast asleep and gently snoring.

Vera was looking down the ward and saw a man walking up in her general direction, she naturally thought that he must be a member of the medical staff, but then she noticed that he was carrying something and before she knew what was happening he was at the foot of her bed, pointing a camera at her, before she could cover her face, he'd taken a photo and smirked, looking very pleased with himself.

"Would you like to tell us about your husband assaulting you and putting you in hospital, Mrs Wiggins'?

"Get away and leave me alone," Vera shouted.

Nancy woke up and when she saw what was going on she started shouting, "Nurse, nurse!"

Nurse Morrissey, a very attractive staff nurse came rushing toward them and realising the man was a reporter spoke very sternly to him.

"You had better leave now and stop bothering my patients, I shall be making a complaint about you to the editor of your paper."

"It's 'The Addlestone Herald' love, just doing mi job, he said as he started to move out, fancy coming out with me on Saturday night," he said cheekily.

"I wouldn't go out with you if you were the last man on earth, she countered, pointing in the direction of the door, Now go before I really get angry."

The reporter blew her a kiss:

"I'm goin, darlin, I'm goin," he said mimicking looking scared, then he left.

"Are you alright Mrs Wiggins?" Staff Nurse Morrissey asked, looking very concerned for her?

"Yes I'm alright thank you nurse, but I'm not relishing the thought of my picture being in the paper and them raking up muck about us again."

"No, I'm sure you aren't," she sympathised.

"I don't know how they found out I was in here though," Vera questioned.

Nurse Morrisey looked puzzled, "I've no idea either Mrs Wiggins, she answered, but I'll be reporting this to Matron; she will certainly complain to the newspaper."

After the nurse had gone Nancy was so concerned for Vera and did her best to try to cheer her up. She gave her some magazines to read and indicated that some of them had really good stories in them.

Vera was more angry than tearful about the incident and she needed a cup of tea more than ever now to soothe and calm her but she certainly wasn't going to do anymore crying over whatever the newspapers got up to, she'd just have to put a brave face on it and hope it wouldn't come to anything.

She was a bit disconcerted when D.I. Melgrove suddenly arrived and she thought surely he's not come about the incident that had just happened?

"Hello Mrs Wiggins, how are you getting along, you certainly look a lot better than when I last saw you?"

"Hello Inspector, I'm not so bad, just a bit stiff really; my heads healing well and I'm really hoping I might be discharged tomorrow."

"Oh that's good," he said, and before he could say what Vera thought he was going to ask her, she jumped in and said:

"Jake and I are going to be staying at the farm with Pauline and Ned, they've Kindly offered to put us up for a while until we can make other arrangements."

"Oh that is good of them, he said, with a genuine smile, lowering his voice so that people in the other beds wouldn't hear.

"What I came to see you about Mrs Wiggins is to ask you if you will be pressing charges against your husband for assault, I think that you should, but, if you do, it is likely that he will go to prison?"

"I don't think he should get away with how he has treated me and Jake, do you?"

"No I don't he said, so you are prepared to stand up in court and say that?"

"Yes I am," Vera replied.

"Good, you realise Jake will be called as a witness too, because he saw what happened, do you think he's up to it?

"Yes I think he'll be alright," Vera said a little unsure.

"Okay, well, I'll let you know when the case will be heard in court then, in the meantime, you continue to get well, thank you, I'll say goodbye and leave you to rest."

Goodbye Inspector Vera said, as cheerily as she could.

Matron came to see Vera shortly afterwards; asked if she was alright, she was at pains to point out to Vera that the man had not had permission to enter the ward, he had snook in behind the nurses' backs when they were busy and she would make sure that he was reprimanded by his editor.

"Whatever you do don't let it upset you Mrs Wiggins, you rest and have a nice cup of tea now."

"Thank you, Matron, I won't," Vera said.

Over a nice cup of tea and a 'Rich Tea' biscuit, Vera and Nancy chatted about all and sundry, completely avoiding that topic of conversation. Nancy told her all about her son Barry's achievements and how proud she was of him, he had passed all his exams when he was at school and on the strength of those results had managed to get a trainee assistant managers position with a firm of prestigious chartered accountants, Bradstock and Chalmers in Haneaton, she said that they thought very highly of him there and he was destined for great things in the company. He had found himself a very nice young lady too called Alice it looked as if it was serious and they would end up getting engaged later on, she came from a good family, they owned the milliners 'Miss Chic' in Persey Street, which her mother ran, they sold the most adorable hats there Nancy cooed. Vera said she knew the one but she didn't really have any cause to buy a hat.

Before they knew it the meal trolley was wheeled into the centre of the ward and the patients were being asked what they wanted, there was usually a choice of two options. Apparently, today's menu was braised steak or steamed fish, Vera opted for the braised steak with mashed potato, cabbage and carrots, which smelt delicious, she had found the food here to be very good, bread was served with it too, and there was always a nice pudding for afters. Vera was so hungry, she had such an appetite, she really enjoyed her meal and had jam sponge for dessert. There were some people on the ward who were always complaining about the food, she thought the standard was very high and couldn't understand why they were always moaning about it, but there you are, you can please some of the people all of the time. Nancy agreed with Vera that the meal was very good, she said that she was expecting Barry and Alice to come in and see her at visiting time, she was looking forward to that.

When visiting time did arrive Pauline and Jake were the first to walk into the ward and they came and kissed Vera, asked how she was; commented that she looked so much brighter and asked if she thought the doctor might discharge her tomorrow. Pauline said that she had brought all the things she had asked for and gave them to her; Vera thanked her. Pauline said.

"I've got a nice room all prepared for you, we can move what things you want from the cottage as soon as you're ready."

"Oh that's wonderful, it's so kind of you Pauline."

"It's the least we can do, Pauline said, it will be nice to have a bit of female company while Ned's out working."

Suddenly there were raised voices, it was Nancy and her son Barry.

"What on earth made you go and do a nasty thing like that for Nancy asked, obviously outraged?"

"I don't know what you're making such a fuss about mum, I just thought I'd let them know, people need to know what's going on around here."

"Oh very public-spirited of you I'm sure, have you any idea the hurt you've caused the poor woman."

"I didn't think."

"Well, what did you do it for then, Nancy saw the look of shame on Barry's face as he lowered his head, you didn't take money for the story did you, she dreaded to ask?

Barry didn't answer, he just looked very guiltily at his mother.

"You did didn't you, I just don't believe that of you Barry, I didn't bring you up to do things like that, how could you stoop so low?"

"What's going on, Alice asked as she arrived and saw the both of them and felt the charged atmosphere?"

"Ask your darling Barry," Nancy replied, disgusted.

"What is it, Barry?" Alice asked him.

"I contacted the newspaper and told them that the mother of the boy who was abducted had been beaten up by her husband and was in hospital."

Vera couldn't believe what she was hearing, Jake put his arm around her for comfort, and Pauline was gaping in astonishment, all three of them continued watching the drama play out.

"Why did you do that?" Alice asked.

"I needed the bloody money that's why!" he exclaimed.

"Don't swear Barry, I can't believe it, well, you certainly don't need me then Barry Tilsley, you're not the man I thought you were, that's it we're through."

"Don't say that Alice, I'm really sorry."

"I'm sorry too, Barry, but that's the lady you really need to apologise to, Alice said pointing to Vera, I'm sorry Nancy, Goodbye."

"Goodbye love," Nancy said, now crying.

Staff nurse Morrisey turned up then and said, "Please keep the noise down, or I will have to ask you to leave, she said indignantly, this is a hospital ward not a circus!"

"I'm sorry, nurse, Nancy said, she looked at Barry who was absolutely crestfallen, I want you to apologise to Vera; then you'd better go after Alice and see if you can change her mind."

Barry looked over to Vera's bedside, "I'm really sorry, I didn't mean any harm, it was a stupid thing to do please forgive me."

"It looks as though you've had your comeuppance already, I hope she gives you another chance, I should go if I were you," Vera said pityingly.

"You were far too lenient on him, Nancy said, but I won't let him forget it in a hurry I can tell you, whatever must you think of us?"

"It isn't your fault Nancy, let's forget it ever happened shall we, I'm afraid it's been one of those days."

Pauline and Jake who had both remained quiet throughout the whole debacle both showed their sympathy for what had happened, Jake said.

"I knew he'd recognised me earlier mam, I'm sorry."

"You don't have to be sorry about anything Jake, you've done nothing wrong son, Vera said, perhaps you ought to take him home please Pauline, all this has made me feel rather tired."

"Of course, love, we'll come and see you again tomorrow, you can tell us what the doctor said, goodnight love, you get a good night's sleep."

"Goodnight mam, Jake said giving her a kiss, everything will be alright."

After they had gone Vera said to Nancy, "I just want to say that you were no way responsible for what Barry did, I hope everything turns out alright for him."

"You're a saint you are, Vera, goodnight dear."

"Goodnight, Nancy."

Chapter 28

The next morning Vera woke up knowing exactly what she was going to do today, she had lain in bed last night churning everything over and over in her mind. It didn't matter whether the doctor said that she was fit to go home today or not, she was determined that she would go anyway, with or without his say so. She felt well in herself; she'd had enough of lying in a hospital bed, she just wanted to get out now, especially after the events of yesterday. She would wait to hear what the doctor had to say but she had definitely made her decision, if he didn't discharge her she would discharge herself. In a strange way, Bill putting Vera in hospital had finally brought her to her senses, she could see him for what he now was, a thug of a man with no heart. Bill in a warped and twisted kind of way had done her a favour. She was certain in her own mind now that after what he had done to her she would not go back to him, that was it, it was all over. She wasn't sure what she would do but she knew it meant a fresh start for her and Jake. She got up to go to the bathroom, she saw that Nancy was still asleep and wondered if she'd had trouble getting off to sleep because of what had happened. One of the nurses said good morning to her and smiled pleasantly as she passed her in the ward, she was taking a bedpan to somebody, Vera thought, *thank goodness I've seen the last of those things.*

When Vera came back to her bed Nancy was wide awake and sitting up in bed.

"Good morning Vera love, how are you this morning?"

"I'm fine, thank you," Vera replied.

"Oh good and I'm so relieved you're still speaking to me after what Barry did yesterday."

"It wasn't your fault Nancy, and I really don't feel angry at Barry, I hope he made it up with Alice."

"Well serves him right if she meant what she said and didn't want to see him anymore, silly fool, if he needed money he only had to ask me."

"People don't always do what's expected of them though Nancy, but I hope you'll forgive him, I have."

"You're a dear sweet woman Vera," Nancy said with tears in her eyes.

"I've got something to tell you, Nancy, I'm leaving today, I lay in bed thinking about so many things last night and I just need to get myself out of here and start planning what I'm going to do with my life. I've been putting things off because I was fearful about the future; I've been in a kind of limbo, confused, not knowing what I wanted to do, but my confusion has disappeared, I'm absolutely clear in my own mind now, I know what I have to do."

"I'm so pleased to hear that Vera, you deserve to be happy."

"Another lady once said that to me, you're both absolutely right, I do, but for some reason, I've been denying myself that right, but not anymore. Thank you for saying that Nancy."

"I haven't done anything, Nancy said looking at Vera amazed, you've solved your own puzzle, my dear."

"Goodness, Vera said, I could eat a horse, I hope breakfast's on the way."

When the doctor came to examine Vera he said that her progress had been remarkable and he could see no reason why she shouldn't go home. He told her that her doctor would visit her to examine her head wound and he would arrange to take her stitches out once he thought the wound was sufficiently healed. The doctor said he would arrange for a prescription for her to get dispensed at her local pharmacy, this would include some ointment, dressings and codeine for pain relief if she needed it. He would also write a letter to her G.P., Dr Carlston, so that he knew that she had been discharged.

"Well good luck Mrs Wiggins, you take good care of yourself and that boy of yours." Vera took this as a distinct sign, the doctor hadn't mentioned her husband, it was confirmation that the decision she had made was the right one, he was out of the equation.

Nancy had overheard that the doctor had discharged her, she said that she was pleased for her but she would really miss her company.

After the nurse had gone she sat chatting to Nancy, she asked her how long she thought she would have to remain in hospital; Nancy said that she wasn't sure, her appendectomy scar was being a bit troublesome and was weeping a lot, the doctor was a bit concerned that there was some infection in it which could possibly be an abscess. Vera said how sorry she was to hear that and hoped they would be able to treat it quickly and get her better. Lunchtime came and went, and when visiting time finally arrived Vera was so pleased to see Pauline arrive, she was on her own Jake wasn't with her. Pauline hugged Vera, immediately telling her that Jake was ok, he was helping Ned on the farm.

"How are you love?" Pauline asked.

"Ready to go home with you she replied, I've had my stitches out and they've given me all the things I need to take home with me, so other than say my goodbyes to everyone, there's nothing to keep me here."

"That's wonderful Vera, I'm so pleased, Ned will be too, but no one will be more pleased than Jake."

"If you don't mind waiting I'll just go and say goodbye to staff nurse Morrissey before she goes off shift."

"That's fine, you go ahead Vera."

Vera went off down the ward to the nurses station, Pauline sat on the chair next to Vera's bed and Nancy spoke to her.

"I'm going to miss Vera so much, she's such a lovely young woman, it's so sad what's happened to her, I hope she will be safe when she leaves here."

"Please don't worry about her, I can assure you she will be, she's coming to stay with us and as you probably know her husband is on remand and waiting to go to the Assizes."

"Yes, Vera did tell me, I hope they throw the bloody book at him."

"He will be dealt with properly I'm sure.

Having said her goodbyes to the staff nurse Vera came back to say goodbye to Nancy.

"Well Nancy my love, I'm going now, you just get yourself well, and you'll soon be on your way home too. I'm really going to miss you, Oooh, don't cry darling or you'll start me off as well."

"Not half as much as I'll miss you my dear, cmon, give me a hug."

Vera came to the side of the bed and leaned over and gave Nancy a hug and kiss. Nancy handed Vera an envelope:

"That's my address in Haneaton, if you're ever passing, and if you ever feel like a chat my phone numbers in there as well."

"Thank you, Nancy, I will certainly keep in touch, I'll just get my case from under the bed and we'll be off."

Pauline bent down and pulled Vera's case from under the bed, she stood up and said:

"I'll carry this for you."

"Vera looked at Nancy grabbed hold of her hand and said, goodbye darling, I hope Barry is coming to visit you, and walking on down the ward she gave Nancy a wave before walking out."

Pauline and Vera were walking along the corridor and they saw Barry and Alice coming towards them as they reached them Vera said.

"Hello Barry, Hello Alice, I'm glad I've seen you and I just want you to know that I don't bear you any ill will, it's nice to see you together.

"Thank you, Mrs Wiggins, Barry replied, you might like to know that the only way Alice and I are together is because she made me do the right thing and hand the money back to the newspaper. I'm sorry for what I put you through, please forgive me."

"I already have Barry, All I ask is that you two look after one another, and look after that lovely mother of yours too."

"I will," Barry said, Alice said.

"We will, thank you, Mrs Wiggins, goodbye."

'Goodbye."

Vera and Pauline left the hospital, as she breathed the fresh air and felt sunshine on her face Vera said, "What a great day to make a brand new start."

"Yes, I suppose it is," Pauline replied, looking a bit puzzled at Vera's remark and wondering exactly what she meant.

Vera had a good talk to Pauline as they were driving back home, she told her that she intended to leave the area and make a fresh start somewhere else, where, she didn't know as yet, but she hoped she would be able to come to a decision within the next few weeks. She needed to speak to Jake, to find out whether or not he would want to leave the place where he had lived and grown up for years. That was the only obstacle that she could foresee that might hinder her plans.

"I can fully understand why you would want to move away Vera, Pauline said, there are too many painful memories associated with this place for you, we will miss you terribly if you do go, but you know we will support you whatever you decide to do."

"Thank you, Pauline, I know you will, I'll miss you and Ned too, you've both been so kind to Jake and I."

The next day the headlines in the local weekly paper 'The Addlestone Herald read:

MISSING BOYS MOTHER BEATEN BY HUSBAND

They had printed the awful photograph that the rogue photographer had taken of Vera in hospital with her head bandaged, Vera looked at it and saw how dreadfully ill she had looked. The article went on to say that there had been an argument which had ended in Vera being beaten by her husband Bill Wiggins, the father of the boy who had been abducted four years earlier. It raked up all the old story of Jake's disappearance, Bill's arrest, Arthur Miles death, everything. Vera wasn't happy about it at all, but philosophically she just passed it off, thinking, *you won't hurt me, and while you're writing your rubbish, I'm getting on with my life, I'm a survivor and so is Jake.*

Chapter 29

As Pauline drove the car into the farmyard and they got out of the car, Jake came running over to his mother.

"Welcome home mam, he said, flinging his arms around her and kissing her, I've been helping Ned clear out the barn ready for the barn dance and harvest supper."

"Glad you're making yourself useful Jake, she said making a fuss of Rover who had come to greet her."

Ned came from the direction of the barn then, he hugged Vera.

"It's good to see you, Vera, how are you feeling, I must say you're looking a lot better than when I last saw you?"

"It's so good to be out of the hospital and breathing fresh country air again Ned, they were marvellous and I couldn't have wished for better treatment."

"Come on inside, Pauline said, I'll make us all a nice cup tea."

"Oh that sounds lovely, Vera replied.

They all enjoyed sitting and chatting over a cup of tea, then Pauline took Vera upstairs to show her to her room and get her settled in and Jake and Ned went back out to carry on with their work

Vera took an opportune moment to speak to Jake about them moving away that evening after he had finished work, she was somewhat surprised at his answer when he said emphatically that he didn't want to leave as he liked working on the farm. He said it was no good her trying to convince him to go with her, his mind was made up as long as Ned and Pauline were prepared to let him stay. So they decided that they would speak to them that evening after dinner.

Pauline had prepared a delicious meal of steak and kidney pie with mashed potatoes, carrots, peas and gravy, they were all enjoying it when Pauline said.

"You're very quiet this evening Jake, is everything alright?" Jake looked at his mother unsure of how to respond so Vera saved his embarrassment and said:

"Well actually we need to talk to you, but we were waiting until after we had finished eating before we said anything."

"Well you might as well tell us now, Ned said smiling, I'm sure nothing you're going to tell us will spoil our dinner."

"You know that I want to leave the area and move to pastures new, well, I asked Jake if he wanted to come with me but he said he would rather stay here and carry on working on the farm, so really, we wanted to ask if you would be happy with that arrangement?"

"There's no denying Jake's a good hard worker, he has a natural affinity with the land and the animals; he picks things up very quickly, I've no doubt that he will make an excellent farmer one day." Ned looked over at Pauline and said:

"I'll have to tell em, love," Pauline nodded in agreement and Ned continued, "you see we're not exactly sure about the future of the farm, financially it's not looking good and the way things are going it looks like we might have to give it up. We had a poor harvest last year which hurt us a lot, I'll be completely honest we are in a lot of debt and I'm on the verge of bankruptcy."

"Oh no, Vera said in astonishment looking from Ned to Pauline, I had no idea, how awful for you both."

"Well there's no reason why you should have known," Pauline said, "but now you see why it wouldn't really be fair to let you go away and leave Jake here when the future of the farm is so uncertain."

"Yes, I do, absolutely," Vera replied. Ned then added.

"We weren't going to tell you at all because you've been through enough recently without worrying about our troubles, we thought you and Jake would move away to start your new life and we could just get on and weather the storm as best we could, we have approached the bank for a loan but we're not very hopeful."

"So let's just say for a moment that you manage to get your loan, or you somehow secure the money from somewhere else, imagine that your financial problem is completely solved, would that mean that there would still be a future for Jake here on the farm?"

"Why bother imagining, I don't think for one moment that my bank manager will give me any money when he's gone all through the books and can see the state we're in, we've just had so much bad luck, what with having to buy a new tractor and other equipment because the old stuff wasn't fit for purpose; then the bad harvest, the money isn't suddenly going to appear, I honestly think we're sunk. Sorry to disappoint you, Jake, if the future of the farm was not in question, I would have said without a doubt that you could stay and work with me, you're a good lad."

"Please forgive me for asking, I don't want to appear rude, but what sort of money are we talking about to put the farm back into the black and keep it going?"

Ned didn't see any harm in telling Vera now that she knew the situation, he paused as if he was doing mental arithmetic and said:

"I would think about five thousand pounds would put us in the clear and keep us going."

"I see, Vera said smiling, so ten thousand pounds would mean that all your problems were over?" Ned thought that perhaps Vera hadn't fully understood what he'd told her, after all, else why would she be smiling the way she was and doubling the figure he had given her.

"I don't think you understood me," Ned said perplexed.

"Oh I understood you perfectly well, Ned," Vera said, smiling again as she said it, that's why I'm going to give you ten thousand pounds?"

Ned, Pauline and Jake were completely thrown by Vera's statement, "I think they all must have thought that she was still suffering from concussion as a result of her recent head injury."

"Are you alright Vera?" Pauline asked her concerned and looking at Ned.

"Yes I am thank you, it's alright Pauline, I haven't gone mad, and it isn't the knock on the head I had either. If you would let me, I would like to give you the ten thousand pounds."

"Mam, don't be silly, you don't have any money, are you sure you wouldn't like to lie down?"

"Bless you Jake, but I'm perfectly well and rational, Vera was almost laughing now but she controlled her impulse to dissolve into hysterics and said:

"Please let me explain, some time ago I was left a large sum of money by my dear friend Bridie Maguire, far more money than I will ever need for myself, it's some of this that I would like to share with you my friends, I can't think of nicer people that I could give a gift to."

There was a stunned silence that seemed to last for ages until Pauline said.

"This is incredible, I can't believe it, can you, Ned?"

"No I can't, it's the stuff dreams are made of, are you absolutely sure about this Vera, you'd really do that."

"Of course I will, it isn't an entirely altruistic gesture anyway, if it's the means to ensure that Jake has a secure future with you on the farm, then I'm only too happy to do it, but I would still have given you the money anyway, even if Jake wasn't involved. Would you like me to write you a cheque now?"

"Are you happy about this Jake, are you sure you want to stay here and help me on the farm, because I can't take your mother's money unless you're serious?"

"Of course, I'm serious, I love working with the animals and being out in the fields all day, if you're happy with my work, I'd grab that cheque if I were you!"

Ned smiled, "I couldn't be more pleased with your work Jake," and he stretched out his hand and they shook hands.

"Yippee, Jake shouted excitedly, which instantly woke Rover up and made him start barking as he came over to Jake wagging his tail enthusiastically, Jake patted and made a fuss him, good boy."

Ned turned to Vera and shook her by the hand, then felt that under the circumstances a kiss was more appropriate, so he kissed her soundly on the cheek and said:

"I can't believe your generosity, Vera, you've made us so happy."

"You have that my love, Pauline said, embracing and kissing Vera, you know there'll always be a home and a job here for Jake, and you too, if you ever decide you want to come back here."

Vera went to get her handbag from upstairs, and returned to find Ned, Pauline and Jake in animated conversation about the surprise windfall. She sat at the table, put her chequebook on it and said:

"I presume I make the cheque out to you Ned, Vera asked with her pen poised?"

"Yes please, Vera," Ned replied.

"N-e-d T-r-o-u-c-h," Vera pronounced in a drawl as she wrote his name, dated and signed the cheque and gave it to him, "there you are."

"Thank you so much Vera, you've saved the farm you have love, and made three people very happy into the bargain, Pauline and I are eternally grateful to you."

"My pleasure Ned, but I make only one proviso, I do not want anyone to know that I have given this money to you."

"I understand, Ned said, I won't tell a soul."

Everyone could see that Ned was very emotional and on the verge of breaking down, he put his hand up to his mouth and left the room to go upstairs. Pauline was visibly upset as she said:

"I'll leave him on his own for a bit, it's a lot for him take in, we really thought we were finished as far as the farm was concerned, thank you from the bottom my heart Vera, I don't know what would have happened if it wasn't for you my love."

Vera put her arms around Pauline and hugged her without saying anything, no words were necessary. Later that week Dr Carlston telephoned the farm and asked if Vera would attend the surgery tomorrow morning. When he saw Vera he said how well she looked, he removed her dressing and examined her head and was very pleased to see that it had healed sufficiently for him to remove her stitches, he removed the eight stitches, Vera found it a bit painful, but she gritted her teeth until was all over and done with. She found it almost an emotionally cleansing thing, she thought to herself, *that's the last pain you're going to cause me, Bill Wiggins.*

He said that she would no longer need to keep a dressing on it as he would like the air to get at it and dry it out. He told her not to wash her hair for a few days to give it a chance to heal, Vera thanked him and left.

The postman delivered three very official-looking letters which were stamped from the county court assizes, one for Vera, one for Ned and the other for Jake. Jake took them from Charlie the postman and called his mother from downstairs. He knew what was in it before opening it and reading what it said. He was summoned to the court of the assizes in Hanworth to appear as a prosecution witness at his fathers trial. As much as he was dreading it, he knew he would have to go, but the thought of it sent shivers down his back and covered him in goosebumps. He showed it to Vera when she came down, she read it and guessed that her letter contained exactly the same.

On the day of the court case, they were both very nervous, Ned and Pauline had brought them in their car, because Ned would be called by the defence lawyer as a character witness for Bill. When they walked into the town hall in which the assize courts were held they had to sit on a wooden bench outside the court and who should be sat there but Mavis Burridge, the last person any of them expected to see, she said hello to Jake but ignored everyone else. After the initial shock of seeing her, Vera realised that Mavis was also going to be called as a witness for the prosecution as she had made a statement about Bill's violent behaviour to the police just after Jake went missing and he was arrested.

The first person called was Ned, when he saw Bill in the dock he was shocked at his demeanour, he had his head bowed down all the time he was giving evidence. He was asked by Bill's defence lawyer as his employer to make a statement as to Bill's character and conduct at work. Bill basically stated that he had always found his work to be completely satisfactory, he was a good willing worker and a strong dependable man, but he had got a bit of a temper. The lawyer practically dismissed the bit about him having a temper by saying:

"Well, we've all got a bit of a temper haven't we, we wouldn't be human if we hadn't, but as his employer, you got along with him well?"

"Yes," Ned said.

"Thank you Mr Trouch, that's all my questions for this witness m'lud."

The prosecutor then stood and asked Ned, "What did you mean when you said that the accused had a bit of a temper?"

"Just that, Ned replied, if you ever chose to disagree with Bill about anything you could be asking for trouble."

"Would you like to say what you mean by 'asking for trouble'?"

"He could be fiery, we took on extra help last year and one of the extra hands didn't see eye to eye with Bill about something and told him so, Bill didn't argue with him he just knocked him to the ground, luckily the bloke wasn't hurt and didn't retaliate, he walked off the job."

"So would you say that the accused is the type to hit first and ask questions later?"

"I suppose so, certainly on that occasion, yes."

"Thank you, Mr Trouch."

The defence lawyer then read parts of Bill's naval record and discharge papers out to the court. These showed that he had always been of good conduct and had no stains on his character.

The next person to be called for the prosecution was Vera who felt her legs nearly buckle as she walked into the court and stood in the witness box. She looked over at Bill and thought he looked ill and gaunt, he gave Vera a pitiful glance but kept his head down for the rest of her testimony. Vera tried not to look at the jury too much as they were all staring at her. After she had answered to her name and sworn on oath to tell the truth, the whole truth, and nothing but the truth, so help me God, the prosecutor then asked her.

"Mrs Wiggins, I know this is probably going to be painful for you but would you be so kind as to tell the jury about the events that happened on the night of Saturday 30th June, 1962, as you remember them."

"Jake and I were both at home, Jake was in his bedroom and I was downstairs reading, it was getting late and I was waiting for Bill to come home from the pub."

"I see, and Bill is the accused, your husband who is standing in the dock?"

"That's right, yes."

"Alright you may carry on Mrs Wiggins."

"Well, when he did finally come home, at about ten-thirty he was in a dreadful state, he must have had quite a lot to drink as he was staggering and slurring his words. I'd made him a bite of supper but he snapped at me that he didn't want any bloody supper. I could see that he was in one of his moods so I tried to make pleasant conversation by asking him if he'd had a nice evening?"

"What did he say to that?"

"He said I was being sarcastic because I'd asked him if he'd had a nice evening out, he told me not to be 'funny' with him just because he'd been out for a drink."

"What happened then, Mrs Wiggins?"

"I thought it was best to keep quiet, but when I did he said I was being moody, I couldn't seem to do anything right. He accused me of being different since I'd been left a legacy in my friends will, he said I had been mean with the money and was 'stuck up', no sorry, 'hoity-toity'," he said.

"This money, Mrs Wiggins, was it a large sum?"

"Yes, it was."

"I'm not going to ask you how much it was, just if it was in your opinion a 'life-changing' amount?"

"Yes, it was," Vera replied.

"And it was left to you, not to the both of you?"

"Yes, but I never saw it like that, it was our money for our future."

"Like bloody hell it was," Bill shouted out angrily.

The Judge hit his gavel on his desk and shouted.

"Silence in Court, I will not tolerate any further outbursts from you, Mr Wiggins, if there are, you will be taken down and tried in your absence."

Bill glared and grimaced at Vera but didn't say anything more.

"Please continue my learned gentleman," the judge said.

"I would like you to continue to tell us about the events on that evening please Mrs Wiggins, what happened after he had accused you of being different since you were given the money by your friend?"

"I told him what he was saying wasn't true, if anyone had changed it was him. He started shouting loudly and I asked him to lower his voice because of the neighbours, he said he didn't give a ****, sorry I don't like saying the four-letter word he used, about the neighbours. I felt he didn't love me anymore, and he didn't seem to care for Jake, he was always arguing and hitting the two of us, he said some very cruel things, even suggesting that Jake wasn't his child, I still can't believe he said that, you only have to look at Jake and you can see Bill in him."

"So the accused hit you both on numerous occasions?"

"Yes he did, sir."

"Carry on Mrs Wiggins."

"I tried to calm the whole situation down by saying I was going upstairs to bed, then he said '*run off to bed then, pleasant dreams*', sarcastically. I got undressed and was just getting into bed when the radio came on downstairs very loudly, so I went back downstairs in my nightie to turn the music down. When Bill saw me he grabbed me and tried to get me to dance, I went towards the radio but he stopped me so I tried to reach down to pull the plug out of the wall. He got hold of my neck and pulled me up, then he hit me and sent me flying across the room, I fell badly and hit my head on something which knocked me unconscious, the next thing I remember was waking up in hospital."

"You had to have stitches in the head wound that you sustained from the attack I understand?"

"Yes eight of them, I still get bad headaches now."

"Thank you, Mrs Wiggins, that will be all."

Vera looked up at the people in the public gallery, she could see Ivy, Rosemary and Pauline who were there to support her which made her feel a bit stronger, Earnest Burridge was there as well, they were the only people she knew, oh, she hadn't recognised him at first but Ted Beavis was there too.

The barrister for the defence stood up, looked at Vera and said:

"Would you say you were an argumentative sort of person, Mrs Wiggins and that you tended to nag your husband, the accused?" Vera was slightly taken aback by this question.

"No, I wouldn't say that," Vera replied indignantly.

"What I'm trying to say Mrs Wiggins is that it takes two to argue doesn't it, it's not a one sided thing, so all the blame can't be levelled at the accused, I put it to you that perhaps he was goaded and severely provoked by you, on this and other occasions."

The prosecutor jumped to his feet, "I strongly object m'lud, Mrs Wiggins is not the one on trial here, she is the victim in this affair!"

"I agree with you, and suggest that our learned friend should modify his line of questioning!"

"I do apologise m'lud, the defence barrister replied."

Vera became visibly upset at the remarks made by the barrister and blurted out, "That's not true."

"If you're saying that it's not true Mrs Wiggins, why do you think the accused behaved the way he did towards you on the night in question?" Vera was trying to hold back her emotions and not cry in front of everyone, but obviously upset, she said.

"Because he'd had too much to drink and was in a bad mood, that's why."

"Would you say that when you met your husband he liked to just have a social drink, or that he has drunk more since he married you?"

"Once again m'lud I object to the honourable gentleman's line of questioning, he is inferring that the witness is responsible for the accused's behaviour."

"I won't tell you again, the judge said addressing the defence barrister, kindly temper your questions!"

"I apologise again m'lud, I have no more questions for the witness." The judge looked at Vera and said:

"You may stand down now Mrs Wiggins."

Vera left the witness box and went out to see how Jake was, when she saw him she could see he looked really nervous so she tried to reassure him that all he had to do was tell the court the truth, just exactly what he'd seen.

Jake asked Vera how she was feeling; she just smiled and said:

"I'm fine love and you'll be alright too, when you're called it'll all be over before you know it, I'll be sat in the gallery supporting you, you don't need to be frightened of your dad, he can't hurt you."

They heard the ushers hollow dignified voice intone:

"Call Detective Sergeant Melgrove."

D.I. Melgrove entered the courtroom and stepped into the witness box after he had given his oath he was asked by the judge to give his account of what had happened on Saturday 30th June, 1962.

Melgrove began after asking the judge if he could refer to his notes of that evening. We received an emergency call from Mr Ned Trench of Wood Lane Farm who said there had been a murder at the home of Bill and Vera Wiggins, We were toldVera Wiggins had been killed. On reaching the premises we were assailed by extremely loud music blasting from the radio, on entering said premises we immediately turned it off. We saw the accused in a very drunken state slumped in a chair burbling to himself, he became aggressive when my officers attempted to arrest him and had to be overpowered, restrained and handcuffed. We saw Mrs Wiggins lying on the floor, to all intents and purposes dead, but on examination by Dr Carlston she was found to be alive but seriously hurt. An ambulance was called on the police radio and Mrs Wiggins was taken to Haneaton Hospital; Mr Wiggins was taken to Addlestone Police Station and charged with assault and causing grievous bodily harm. In custody the prisoner was uncooperative and belligerent throughout until was transferred to H.M. Prison Birmingham on remand.

The judge thanked D.I. Melgrove for his account and asked him to stand down.

"Calling Mavis Burridge."

Mavis took the stand with a very self-righteous look on her face, placed her hand on the bible and read out the words of the oath on the card, stressing the last four words as piously as she could:

"So help me God."

The barrister for the prosecution asked.

"Are you Mavis Burridge of number 3 Wood Lane Cottages, Grendore?"

"Yes, I am."

"And you are the neighbour of the accused and his wife Mr and Mrs Wiggins?"

"Yes that's right," she said, almost as though someone had waved something smelly under her nose.

"Can you describe to the court what you saw and heard on the evening of Saturday 30th June, 1962?"

"I most certainly can, well my husband Earnest and I were getting ready for bed when we heard Bill Wiggins shouting next door, we could hear everything because he was so drunk and angry. He was shouting at Vera, Mrs Wiggins, telling her she'd changed since she had been given some money, she was very mean with it and had gone all 'hoity-toity'.

Later he said he didn't care about his neighbours and he used that four-letter word that seems to be getting used so prevalently these days, absolutely disgusting."

"Oh what word was that Mrs Burridge."

"Oh, oh mm, I couldn't possibly say it, Mavis said, looking appalled and going bright red and getting all flustered."

There were a few titters in the public gallery at her obvious embarrassment.

"That's alright Mrs Burridge, but in your opinion, it was an obscene word?"

"It most certainly was, I've never heard such language."

"Then what happened after that?"

"Well all of a sudden there was the most dreadful noise with loud loud music blaring out from next door, it was absolutely deafening. We got dressed and went outside to see what was going on, all the other neighbours came out to see as well. It was shortly afterwards that young Jake came running out of the house in a dreadful state poor lad, saying that his dad had murdered his mother. We told him to run to the farm and get Ned Trench to call the police. When the police arrived they went inside, thank goodness the music was switched off then, we couldn't see what was going on but we could hear Bill Wiggins shouting at the policemen saying that he was going to kill them all, they managed to overpower him, brought him out in handcuffs and took him away. Then Dr Carlston arrived and later the ambulance came; they brought poor

Vera out on a stretcher, she looked absolutely awful, we were afraid for her life poor woman."

"Thank you for that excellent account, Mrs Burridge, I have no further questions."

The defence barrister said, "I have no questions for this witness, m'lud."

"I would like to call Jake Wiggins to the witness box, m'lud," the prosecuting barrister said.

The usher calls out, "Jake Wiggins to the witness box please."

Jake is ushered into the court and takes his place in the witness box, he swears on the bible and the prosecution barrister, who can see Jake looks nervous, asks him.

"Don't be nervous Jake, please tells us in your own words what you witnessed on the evening of Saturday 30th June.1962."

Jake looked across at the dock and saw his father sitting there glaring at him as if to say, *you watch what you say about me*, he looked up at the public gallery and saw his mother smiling encouragingly at him; he began to speak very quietly, "I was in bed…"

The barrister said with a gentle smile, "Can you please speak louder Jake so that everyone can hear you?"

"Sorry sir, I was in bed, I'd heard my dad come back home from the pub then a while later I heard him and my mam arguing, I heard my mam come upstairs, then suddenly loud music started playing, I thought it would stop, but it didn't so after a while I got dressed and went downstairs. When I opened the living room door I saw mam crouched down; my dad grabbed her by the back of the neck, pulled her up, then he lashed out and sent her flying backwards across the room. Mam was just lying there on the floor and I thought she was dead because she wasn't moving, I shouted at my dad that he'd killed my mam and he started to come after me, he had such a terrible look on his face and his eyes were bulging. I was so scared I ran out."

Jake paused then and it looked as if the telling of his memories of the events and the ordeal of the courtroom had all suddenly become too much for him.

"It's alright Jake, you're doing really well, would you like a glass of water?"

"Yes please, Jake said, looking up at his mam."

The judge spoke to Jake directly as he could see he was in difficulty with the whole business.

"Would you be more comfortable if your mother were to come and stand next to you?"

"Yes I would, sir."

"Little mammy's boy," Bill taunted from the dock."

The Judge then banged his gavel down hard in front of him and bellowed.

"Take the prisoner down, you will come back when the verdict is delivered Mr Wiggins."

Bill was escorted down into the cells; the judge then directed Vera to come and stand alongside Jake. Vera quietly said:

"You're alright I'm here," and she took hold of his hand and squeezed it as the judge said.

"You may continue now."

Jake coughed and started again.

"When I ran out Mrs Burridge told me to run up to the farm and get Ned Trench to call the police, I stayed up at the farm then and Pauline looked after me, I was in a state because at that point I really believed that dad had killed my mam. I can't really tell you anything else other than the first I heard that mam was still alive was when Ned came back and told us."

"Thank you, Jake, you're doing very well, the barrister said, I now just want to ask you a couple of questions about your relationship with your father. Would you say that you have a good relationship with him?"

"No, we don't get on, he has always hit me and my mam."

"Why do you think he hits you both?"

"I have no idea, I just don't think he likes me, he's never had much time for me while I was growing up, my mam will tell you that."

Vera nodded her head in agreement and gave Jake a hug, she had tears in her eyes.

"Now Jake, young boys usually get hit by their fathers if they've done something wrong or if they are particularly naughty and need correcting. Would you say generally that you are well behaved?"

"I often can't understand why dad hits me, I think he does it because he wants to, or he can't help himself, all I can tell you is that even when I was small he didn't hit me like you would a small child, he laid into me, thumping me, I was sometimes black and blue with bruises."

Vera once again was nodding in agreement.

"Thank you, Jake, I don't have any more questions, you have been a very good witness."

The defence barrister stood up and said:

"I don't have any questions for the witness, mi lud," and sat straight down again.

The judge then said, "You may both stand down, thank you, I would now like to call Dr Carlston as a witness."

Dr Carlston entered the court, stood in the witness box, read the oath and waited to give his testimony. The judge asked him in his expert opinion to describe the extent of the injuries that Vera Wiggins sustained in the assault so that the jury could be clear as to what their verdict would be. So Dr Carlston clearly and in layman's terms outlined all Vera's injuries, he stated that the physical injuries as serious as they were, would heal, but the emotional and psychological damage inflicted on both Vera and Jake would be longer-lasting. He added that despite everything that they had both been through, in his personal considered opinion they were strong people and would eventually overcome the trauma that they had suffered."

The judge thanked him and asked him to stand down.

He then addressed the jury and summed up the case directing them to consider all the facts of the case with understanding and compassion, he also asked if they had appointed a jury foreman and for the person to stand. The man stood up, he was a stout man with a bald head and a moustache; wearing a brown striped suit. The judge pointed out that when they were sent out, they were to try to reach a unanimous verdict as to whether the accused was guilty of assault and battery causing grievous bodily harm or not, if they were unable to reach a unanimous verdict, then he would accept a majority one. The jury were then dismissed to consider their verdict and the court was adjourned.

Vera and Jake left the courtroom and went out into the lobby and were met by Ivy and Rosemary who both said how well they had done in the witness box, Ivy held a bag of 'pear drops' open and offered it around for Vera and Jake to take one. After they had talked amongst themselves for a while, Vera couldn't help noticing that Ted Beavis was looking at her, then he beckoned her over to him so she excused herself and walked over towards him.

"Hello Vera, what a terrible ordeal for you and Jake, I'm so sorry this has happened to you. I couldn't believe it when I heard what Bill had done to you, he said kindly, I wanted to come and visit you while you were in hospital but I thought it best to just send you some flowers!"

"Oh so you're the phantom flower sender, they were lovely Ted, but they were such a mystery, why didn't you attach a card with them?"

"I did."

"You did, I don't understand that then, unless the nurses inadvertently lost it or threw it away, because I asked the nurse that brought them to the ward if there was one and she said that there wasn't. Oh well never mind,

I know now, so what did you put on the card, Ted?"

"I wrote, *Sorry to hear about what happened, please get well soon, your friend, Ted Beavis.*"

'That was so kind of you to do that Ted, they cheered me up, and the mystery surrounding who had sent them took my mind off dwelling on my injuries."

"I am so glad Vera, I wanted to write so much more, I hope you won't be offended by what I'm going to say, and now might not be the best time to say it, but, I know you are married and you probably still love Bill even after the cruelty he's inflicted on you and Jake.

"Ever since that day I gave you both a lift to Stratford I haven't been able to get you out of my mind, I just thought you were so beautiful and what a lucky man Bill was to have you as his wife. Now I know that he doesn't deserve you and all I will say, as I think we are about to be called back into the courtroom is, if you want a friend who desires to treat you the way you should be treated, like a lady, then I will be waiting for you."

Ted took hold of her hand and held it tenderly. Vera was pleasantly shocked yet touched by his simple honesty, she smiled at him and said:

"I'll remember that Ted, I think we need to go back in to court now," and she gently pulled her hand away from his she could see Jake urgently beckoning her to come on. He asked her quickly before she dashed off:

"Can I call on you Vera, perhaps we could go for a drive or go to the pictures or something?"

"Yes, okay, Ted, but I'm not at the cottage, I'm at the farm now."

"Right, I'll call round next week then."

Vera had dashed away then, Jake caught her by the hand, "Come on mam, we've got to get in."

They joined behind everyone filing back into the public gallery, the jury was brought back into court and Bill was brought back up from the cells and resumed his place in the dock, flanked by two burly policemen.

The usher instructed everyone to, "All rise," as the judge re-entered to preside over the final proceedings.

The barristers and court officials nodded their heads in deference and the judge took his seat and said:

"Have the jury reached a verdict?"

The Jury foreman stood up and said, "Yes, we have, 'Your Honour'"

"Have the jury reached a unanimous verdict?"

"Yes, we have, 'Your Honour'"

"Is your verdict to the charge of assault causing actual grievous bodily harm, guilty or not guilty."

Guilty, 'Your Honour'."

There were gasps, smiles and hugs being shared in the public gallery, then it went very quiet and still as the judge was about to pass sentence.

"Will the accused please stand, you have heard the verdict of the jury. This was a most vicious crime that only by chance did not result in the murder of the victim, your wife, who you were supposed to cherish and protect. The way you have conducted yourself in court indicates to me that you show no remorse for your callous actions. Therefore the sentence that I am about to pass takes all that into account, you will be sent to prison for five years, which is the maximum sentence I can give you, take the prisoner down."

Bill shouted out, "You lousy buggers, you'll pay for this, I'll see that you do." He was hustled away back down to the cells, the rest of what he was shouting was muffled as he descended below.

Chapter 30

Over the next few days Vera began to formulate in her own mind what she wanted to do, she didn't have to think long and hard about where she wanted to move to and settle down, she had always wanted to live near the sea and for some unknown reason one place kept popping into her mind, Brighton, then she remembered, Rosemary had told her that she had been on a lovely holiday there with a girlfriend one summer they had stayed in a caravan on the south downs near Rottingdean and they'd had a wonderful holiday, Rosemary said that she would love to go back there one day.

Now that the awful experience of the court case was over and done with and Jake was settled on the farm; Ned and Pauline were free of the worry and anxiety that had been with them for over a year, Vera now felt able to take herself off and begin to sort her own life out.

She was sorry that Bill had been sent to prison for five years, he had hurt her deeply both emotionally and physically but she wouldn't have wished that on him. She hadn't really thought too much about what sentence he might get when Inspector Melgrove had told her that he could possibly go to prison when he visited her in hospital, fleetingly she'd imagined he might get twelve to eighteen months, which she felt would be sufficient to teach him a lesson and bring him back to his senses. His own conduct in the courtroom hadn't helped his case though, as the judge had said, his outbursts of temper had only served to compound what she and the other witnesses had testified.

Despite all this, she still felt sorry for him and made an appointment to see her solicitor as she wanted to ensure that Bill had the means to look after himself financially when he was released from prison. She wrote a letter, a letter that she found very difficult to write, after several failed attempts at getting the wording just the way she wanted it, she was satisfied that it now read:

Bill,

I have arranged for my solicitor to visit you in prison shortly before you are released to give you some money to help you find accommodation etc. The amount he has been instructed to give you is sufficient to meet your needs until you get back on your feet. Use it wisely as there will not be anymore.

I have left the cottage in Wood Lane and moved away from the area, it has now been re-let to someone else.

I wish to have no further contact with you and I will be filing for divorce on the grounds of physical and mental cruelty, you will get the papers from my solicitor in due course.

Jake does not want any contact with you either, you are to forget about us and get on with your own life.

Vera.

Vera had decided that the amount she would give Bill would be £1000 pounds, she felt that this would be enough to look after him until he found himself employment. She didn't want to be overly generous due to the way that he had been behaving by drinking heavily and gambling, she wasn't prepared to give him unlimited funds for these types of activities, if he frittered away the thousand pounds then that was his lookout! She wasn't prepared to take the chance of giving him more than that after all, she doubted that Bridie would have approved of her giving him any money at all.

Chapter 31

On the Friday of the week following the court case, Pauline and Vera were at home preparing the evening meal, Ned and Jake were out working in the fields, it was about two o'clock when the doorbell rang, Pauline answered it and was surprised to see Ted Beavis at the door.

"Hello Ted, she said, sounding surprised, what can I do for you?"

"Is Vera in?"

"Yes she is, come on in, would you like a cup of tea?

"Yes please, I hope I'm not disturbing you,"

"No, of course, you're not," she said as she led him through the hall and into the kitchen.

"Vera, Ted's here to see you."

"Oh hello Ted, how lovely to see you."

"Make him a nice cup of tea will you Vera, I've just got to go and see to those chickens."

Pauline thought it best to make the excuse about looking after the chickens to leave them on their own and let them have some privacy, Vera had told her that Ted had spoken to her when they were in court and how charming he'd been; how she had discovered that he was the sender of the mystery flowers and he'd promised that he would call round this week. *Well here he was true to his word,* Vera thought.

Ted ploughed right in and asked her.

"Would you like to come out to the pictures, tomorrow night, they're showing 'Carry on Cruising' at the Rialto in Addlestone, I thought a good laugh might do us both good."

"Oh that would be very nice Ted, I love the 'carry on' films, they're really funny."

"Oh, that's marvellous, I didn't know if you'd come out with me or not after what I said when I saw you last."

"From what I remember you were very sweet and a perfect gentleman, you mentioned that I might still be in love with Bill, all I can say is that he killed any love that I had for him several years ago, all I feel for him now is pity, Ted."

"That's only to be expected under the circumstances, you're free of him now though."

"Technically I'm not, there's still the little matter of a divorce, but I've set all that in motion, here you are, let's take our tea through into the living room."

They sat opposite each other in the easy chairs, Vera smiled at Ted and thought how very good looking he was, he had light brown hair, was of stocky build with strong muscular arms, his lips were thick and beautifully formed, she kept having to tear her eyes away from them, they looked so inviting, she hoped he hadn't noticed.

"It was good of Pauline and Ned to offer you and Jake a place to stay, they're good sorts."

"Yes they have been true friends, Jake's going to be working for them, he really loves the outdoor life that farming gives him, I thought he would come with me when I move away but he's determined to stay here." Ted looked really crestfallen:

"You're moving away, where will you be going?"

"I'm thinking of going to live on the south coast, possibly Brighton."

"Oh I'm really sorry to hear that, I was hoping we might spend more time together and get to know each other better, sorry, that's very presumptuous, what must you think of me?"

"I'll tell you what I think of you Ted, you seem a very nice man, and I very much like the idea of you getting to know me better, and I you, but Brighton isn't the other side of the world you know, let's just take things slowly and enjoy each others company while I'm here and see where that takes us eh?

Ted smiled and his face brightened a little, "Yes, that would be nice, it just came as a bit of a shock that's all, but I should have realised you'd want to see the back of this place after all that's happened."

"That's right Ted, I do, living here is a constant reminder."

"How long will it be before you leave?"

"I'm not sure, it depends how long it takes me to find a suitable property. I've contacted a few estate agents down there and told them the kind of place I'm looking for, they are going to send me some details of what they have, it's all very exciting really."

"I'm sure it is, if I can be of any help, you only have to say."

"That's very kind of you Ted, You might be sorry that you said that as I'm going to hold you to that."

"Oh that's good, well, I'd better be going, I'm really looking forward to tomorrow night, I'll pick you up at five-thirty if that's alright."

"That's fine Ted, so am I."

He stood to go, so Vera stood up to show him out and they walked towards the back door, he stepped out and turned round taking hold of her hand, then he leaned in and gave her a gentle kiss on the cheek, "Goodnight Vera, see you tomorrow."

Vera was still enjoying the wonderful feeling that Ted's kiss had awakened in her as she replied, "Goodnight, Ted, yes, see you tomorrow."

Pauline came in just after Ted had left, "Well," she said, "you're looking happy, what happened?"

"He's asked me to go out to the pictures with him tomorrow night."

"Oh smashing, I hope you said yes?"

"Of course I did silly, he's really nice, he gave me a peck on the cheek as he left."

"Yes I know, I was watching from round the corner of the barn, he is such a sweetie."

"Oh spying on me were you, only joking, yes he is, isn't he!

Pauline suddenly realised the time, "Here, come on, we'd better get a move on, the men will be home soon wanting their dinner."

After dinner, Pauline, Ned, Vera and Jake sat talking about their arrangements for the harvest supper and barn dance, this would be the first one that Pauline and Ned had organised and they would be trying to enlist the help of as many people as they could to bring it about and make it a success. They would have to empty the large barn of the binding machine and thresher and give it a good clean out; put large trestle tables up in the far end, they could arrange hay bales around the walls for seating and place a few small tables around for people to put food and drinks on, leaving a large area in the middle for dancing.

Ned would find someone to sort the music out and fix up some speakers to run from the record player, Pauline said she could get all her WI ladies to organise the food and non-alcoholic drinks, she would get them to do buffet finger food rather than have to use knives and forks to eat. Ned said he would take care of the stronger stuff, it would be mostly beer, but they would have to have some spirits as well, whisky and gin should be enough. He would have to beg, steal or borrow some strings of lights from somewhere to brighten the place up a bit and transform it from an ordinary barn into something special.

Pauline was busy writing all the ideas and comments down so that she wouldn't forget anything and everyone could refer back to it later if they needed to. Ned set the date for Saturday, September 15th when he hoped that all the harvest would be safely in, the main reason of the barn dance was to celebrate that and bring people together, those who had worked hard to get all the wheat and barley cut and threshed; put in the silo and bagged up ready for selling, the men and women who had helped with the potato picking, those people who were specially invited, like Dr Carlston, Graham Davis the local vet and those villagers who wanted to come and very importantly it could serve as a leaving party for Vera and give her a good send-off. Ned thought it was going to be a lot of work but if they all pulled together each doing their little bit, it would soon get done; it would be a great evening for everyone.

Chapter 32

Ted drove into the farmyard and tooted his horn, he saw Vera coming out so he got out of the car and opened the passenger door for her, she was wearing a pink and white plain shift dress, a pink cardigan, white shoes and a white handbag.

"You look gorgeous," he said, pecking her on the cheek again.

"Thank you, kind sir," Vera replied feeling very flattered that he liked the way she looked.

He drove away and on the journey, Vera was able to find out a little more about this man. She had asked him what he did for a living and was quite surprised by the answer he gave.

"I'm a draughtsman, I make technical drawings for the aeronautics industry."

"That sounds very interesting and very important work."

"Yes it is, I enjoy it, it gives me a great deal of satisfaction, and it pays well too."

"Where is the office you work from?"

"That's in Coventry, but one of the joys of my job is that I am not office-bound, I can work from home a lot of the time."

"Oh that must be good to be able to do that."

"Yes it is, it means that I can see more of you before you disappear off to Brighton, if you want to?"

Vera didn't see why on earth not, just being close to Ted made her pulses race, and the deep timbre of his voice was so sexy, she wondered if he realised just how much she fancied him.

"I'd like that Ted," she said coyly.

"That's good," he said and took his hand off the wheel to gently squeeze her hand, then he continued driving to the cinema.

When they entered the cinema and went to the ticket booth Vera said that they should go dutch, but Ted said, "This is my treat," so she didn't make fuss about it.

"Two Upper Circle please, he said, to the woman in the booth who was 'dolled up' with heavy foundation make-up, her dark hair marcel waved like a film star and her ruby red lips flashed as she said in a manufactured upper-class voice:

"That will be Three and Tuppence please, sir."

Ted thanked her.

Before they went into the auditorium he escorted Vera over to the confectionery counter and bought a box of 'Black Magic' chocolates and two 'Kia-Ora' orange juices, he gave the chocolates to Vera as they walked upstairs to the posh seats in the upper circle.

The usherette shone a torch at their tickets and guided them to their front row seats in the balcony just as the 'Pearl and Dean' music started up. They watched the different advertisements and Vera opened the chocolates, she whispered in Ted's ear:

"You're spoiling me, Ted, have a chocolate."

He took a chocolate from the box.

"I haven't even begun yet," he whispered tantalisingly, causing Vera to say:

"Oooooh, lovely."

The main film started playing and as it did Vera felt Ted's arm slip across her shoulder and his large hand rested on her bare arm. She thought to herself how much she had missed a man's closeness for such a long time, she found it soothing and reassuring, she inclined her head towards his and they settled to watch the film. It was just the tonic she needed, she had laughed so much at the film it had given her the stitch in her side. Ted had really enjoyed it too, as they left the cinema they were discussing the characters and the parts they had enjoyed the most. It felt like the most natural thing in the world as Vera slipped her arm through Ted's to walk to the car. As they approached the car Ted asked:

"Have you eaten, are you hungry, I know this lovely little restaurant that does the most delicious food?"

"How did you guess, I could eat a horse," Vera said.

"I don't think they'll have that on the menu," Ted quipped, and they both laughed.

They drove back out into the country to a quaint little thatched place called 'Le Petite Escargot' which had low oak beams and horse brasses everywhere and an inglenook fireplace. Vera thought the name sounded romantic.

Ted told her that it was wonderful in the winter when they had the log fire blazing and especially so at Christmas when they had the decorations up.

"It's absolutely charming, Vera said, thank you so much for bringing me here, she thought to herself, *Bill never took me out anywhere, let alone to wonderful places like this.*

Ted smiled, "I knew you'd like it, he said, you wait until you taste the food, it's heaven.

The waiter greeted them courteously showed them to a table near a window; gave them a dinner menu and a wine menu and left them to make their choices.

"Do you like red or white wine," Ted asked her.

"I don't know, I don't usually drink wine, Vera replied, but I would love to try some, I'll let you choose something nice."

"In that case, I know the very one, Ted said enthusiastically, I'm sure you will like this one, I'm not a wine buff by any means, but I know what I like."

The wine waiter came over and Ted ordered a bottle of wine that Vera thought she wouldn't even be able to pronounce.

"Now what would you like to eat, we could start with Pate de fois Gras…."

Vera butted in and giggling said.

"Ted I've never been to a French restaurant before in my life, and I don't understand French so will you please order for me."

"Of course I will, he said, in that case we are definitely having the fois gras, followed by 'Trout Meuniére Amandine', then we could have 'Crépes Suzette' for dessert, how does that sound?"

Vera was amazed at how sophisticated and intelligent Ted was, she said:

"It all sounds great, I can't wait to taste it."

The waiter came to take the food orders as he'd seen Ted put the menus down on the table.

Ted reeled off the order in his accomplished way, Vera was watching his every move she was totally captivated by him, this was a side of Ted she hadn't seen; hadn't expected and she liked it, he was spoiling her; making her feel really special.

They chatted away so easily over the glass of wine that the waiter had poured for them, Ted asked her.

"I hope you don't mind me asking but what will you do down in Brighton, will you get yourself a job or will you be a lady of leisure?"

"I haven't really had any experience of work other than the first job I had in the factory, I certainly don't want to do that again. I quite like the idea of running a little tea shop, I'd be my own boss and I'd get to meet people, so I wouldn't be lonely."

"That is a good idea, but I don't think you'll ever be lonely Vera," he said with a smile.

Their foie gras arrived, so they began to eat Vera loved it, in fact, she couldn't fault any part of the meal, not that she was trying to, it was all exquisite. She was feeling warm and mellow from the two glasses of wine she had drunk and couldn't remember the last time she had felt so happy, Ted was such easy company to be with and so attentive and charming.

When they had finished their meal and had coffee, Ted paid the bill and they went out to the car and started to drive home. When they reached Grendore at the top of Wood Lane, Ted asked Vera:

"Would you like to come back to my place for a nightcap and see what the place is like?"

"Yes, please Ted, I'd like that."

Ted drove past the farm and stopped further up the lane outside his cottage, they walked up to the door and they went inside, Ted switched on the light. It wasn't what Vera expected at all, she thought it was going to look very lived in and maybe a bit untidy. Men! On their own didn't always take willingly to domestic chores. The place was immaculate, there was a very comfortable looking three piece suite in a light creamy colour, a large bookcase crammed full of books' side table with a ceramic lamp that had Chinese figures and flowers all over it, and there was a lovely rustic stone and wood fireplace.

He certainly looked after the place, unless he had a cleaner come in and do for him of course?

"Well, what do you think of the bachelor pad, he said, turning on the table lamp and switching the main light off, which made it look even more cosy?"

"It's very nice Ted, you look after it well."

"What would you like to drink, he asked?

"I'd really like a nice cup of tea Ted, I think I've had enough alcohol for one evening."

"Cup of tea coming up, maam," he said as he walked into the kitchen.

Vera sat herself down on the settee and felt the plump seat cushions cradle her in comfort, she thought about the wonderful evening she'd had and was stillest in those thoughts when Ted came back in with a cup of tea on a tray.

"Do you take milk and sugar?" he asked.

"Just milk thanks, I'm sweet enough," she said

"You certainly are," he replied, he put the cup down on the tray, sat down beside her and before Vera knew what was happening he was kissing her, which is exactly what she was hoping he would do, those thick warm sensuous lips were caressing hers and she briefly felt the tip of his tongue gently flutter over her mouth. She wanted more but she didn't want to appear too forward. Her slight nervousness caused her to make a humorous comment.

"This is the most beautiful cup of tea I've ever had."

Ted thought that he should be bold now or the moment would be lost.

"I think we should take the tray upstairs, don't you, but tea was the last thing he wanted now? He stood up, took her hand and pulled her gently to her feet, he wrapped his strong arms around her and once again his soft lips crushed hers with passionate desire, he led her upstairs and into the bedroom, kissing her again he began to take off her cardigan and unzip her dress, she started to unbutton his shirt, her dress fell to the floor she stepped out of her shoes and dress at the same time. Their kisses were getting more passionate and breathy and she was feeling the mass of hairs on his chest. They quickly finished undressing separately and got into bed. They lay facing and his hands were exploring her whole body, cupping her breasts, he moved his head down and played his tongue over her firm breast and onto her nipple, then gently sucked it as his hand descended to her crotch, Vera was squirming with pleasure, he kissed her again, this time his tongue went deep into her mouth as his fingers gently explored her vagina, he slipped one inside and felt the inviting moistness. Vera could feel his large cock pressing against her thigh, she put her hand down and felt his two enormous hairy balls, then the thick shaft of his penis with its bulbous throbbing knob. He broke from the kiss then and his lips went to her ear, as he whispered tenderly.

"I want you so much, Vera."

All Vera found herself saying in a swoon was. "Oh yes, Ted, yes."

Chapter 33

Lying in the sunshine on the terrace alongside Ted at their lovely bungalow in Saltdean, Vera looked back on the first blissful time that he had made love to her, it seemed an age away, so much had happened since then. She would never have believed how much a person's life could change; that five years on she would have a new husband and be so blissfully happy. It was at the barn dance that Vera had discovered that she was hopelessly in love with Ted and was determined not to let him get away, the barn dance, coincidentally, had also served to bring Rosemary happiness.

Vera and Ted had a whirlwind romance and all their friends were so happy for them when they realised it was serious and they wanted to be together forever. They chose the house they were living in, having both fallen in love with it the moment they saw it. It was an art deco style property with those large square windows so obviously of that period and it had a lovely rambling garden with large expanses of lawn and lots of trees and shrubs. Ted had put his cottage on the market and it had sold very quickly to a young couple who wanted to move from Coventry to the countryside. Whilst Vera was searching for a property, Ted had said that he couldn't bear the thought of her moving away from him, he wanted to be near to her all the time, spend the rest of his life with her. He proposed so romantically in the time old fashioned way, going down on one knee and presenting her with an antique diamond and sapphire engagement ring that had been his grandmother's. Vera's 'Decree Absolute' had been granted three years ago, so there was nothing standing in their way, they were married at Haneaton Registry Office, Pauline and Ned were witnesses. Amongst the wedding guests at the reception were Rosemary with her new husband Dr Jeremy Carlston, Vera and Ted had been guests at their wedding three months ago. Ivy was with her fiancé Philip, Jake, Nancy, Barry and Alice were also there. Ned was Ted's 'best man', the reception was held in the best hotel in the town, 'The Mount Pleasant', the rest of the guests were friends and relations of Ted's, his Mother and Father who were lovely and absolutely adored Vera, but there were a lot of Ted's friends there who Vera hadn't met before so it was nice to be introduced to them. Talking to Ivy at the reception she had told her that the shop was doing really well; she was forever indebted to Bridie for making it possible for her, what a wonderful legacy she had left for them all, she said that if the baby she was expecting turned out to be a daughter, she was going to name her Bridie, Vera was so touched by that. After the reception Vera and Ted had honeymooned in the South of France, visiting places like Monte Carlo and Nice, a beautiful experience that Vera would never forget.

A month after they came back from their wonderful honeymoon, they visited Jake, Pauline and Ned at the farm just to see how everything was going, sadly their dog Rover had died two weeks earlier so they were reminiscing about what a wonderful companion he had been and how they were all missing him. Vera had said that she could just see him now with his tail wagging bounding up to visitors that came to the farm. As they sat together talking over a glass of wine, Jake suddenly said that he wanted to say something to everyone, they were all intrigued as to what he was going to say as he looked very serious and was obviously nervous.

"There is something very important I have wanted to tell you all for a long time so while I have all of you together, the people who mean everything to me, I have to take the opportunity to let you know something that may come as a shock to you, it's something I could never have said a year ago as I wasn't fully aware enough then and wouldn't have had the confidence to say anything anyway." Jake paused and took a gulp of wine from his glass, as you can see I'm not finding this easy, I'll have to just say it and get it over with, I'm a homosexual, or 'gay' as we call it. I've felt different since I was a young child but it was around the age of eleven that things began to be difficult and confusing, I know it must be a shock…

"It isn't a shock to me at all Jake, I've known for a long time but I didn't think you wanted anyone to know, I love you dearly and all I want is for you to be happy, I've seen the struggle you've had and I can see how you've suffered over keeping it a secret, well, it's out in the open now and I'm so proud of you." Jake went to Vera and embraced her:

"Thanks, mam, I knew you would understand."

"I think what your mother has just said goes for all of us Jake, Ted said warmly, and I couldn't love you more if you were my own son, he tugged Jake towards him and hugged him, now you just have to get on with your life and do what makes you happy."

"I've had an inkling this day would come, and I'm glad it has for your sake, you can't go on living a lie Jake, you have to be true to yourself, I've known ever since that day two years back when I took that lad Mike on to help us with the harvest, I saw the way you looked at him and how you behaved when you were in his company, I suspected that something had gone on too, but we won't talk about that," Ned said laughing.

They all laughed, even Jake who was very red faced with embarrassment, Pauline said quietly to Jake:

"If I'd had a son, Jake, I would have wanted him be just like you, you're a very special person, who deserves to be happy."

Vera felt that this was finally the right time to tell Jake about the gift that Bridie had left him, it would be something for him look forward to in a year's time when he came of age. Vera said.

"I've got something important to tell you too, Jake. I think you might need to sit down, I've waited until an appropriate moment to tell you this. You know all about your Godmother Bridie leaving me a lot of money, but what you don't know is that she also did the same for you, she left twenty thousand pounds in her will to be given to you when you reach the age of twenty-one, next year son you are going to be a very rich young man, you are going to have to think carefully and sensibly about what you will do with it!"

Jake couldn't believe what he was hearing, it was a lot to take in.

"She must have been a wonderful woman mam, I wish I could have known her."

"She was, son, if it hadn't been for Bridie, you might not have even been here, I'll tell you all about that one day."

The rest of the evening was spent in laughter with a few more bottles being drunk in celebration of Jake's good fortune and him having 'come out'.

Chapter 34

The shadowy figure crouched low as he approached the house, he went past an outbuilding hoping that no dogs would hear him and give him away by barking, he could see a light on in the kitchen and assumed that they would be in there. He crept around the house and reached the french windows, the curtains were drawn but there was a chink of light coming through a gap and he was able to look inside to see if anyone was in the living room. It was empty, and by a stroke of luck when he gently tried the handle of the door, he found it was unlocked, opening it very quietly he went inside.

The door from the living room into the kitchen wasn't closed shut, he could hear them talking and plates rattling, so he guessed they were at the sink washing up, that meant that they would have their backs towards him as he entered the kitchen, he carefully picked his way across the room so as not to make a sound or knock anything over. He braced himself and pulled open the door springing into the kitchen and pointing the rifle straight at them.

Pauline saw him first and screamed, "Aaaaah, Bill."

Ned turned in astonishment and as scared as he was said gently so as not to spook Bill into firing at them:

"Put the gun down Bill, we can't do you any harm, what do you want with us?" Bill shuffled from one foot to the other in a state of excitement and agitation.

"You've already done me what harm you could Ned Trouch by what you said in the witness box, five years I've had to think about what you and those other buggers said, but my grievance ain't with you, by the way, I think Pauline should sit down, she's gone as white as a sheet. Ned pulled a chair out from the table and helped Pauline sit down. No, all I want from you is the whereabouts of that bitch of an ex-wife of mine, she's got to pay for what she did to me, I ain't going to hurt you not as long as you tell me where she is, if you don't I'll blow your bloody brains out.

Pauline said hesitantly, "She's started a new life now Bill, we're not going to tell you where she is, why can't you just leave her alone."

"I want her to suffer like I've bloody suffered those five long years in prison, thinking about her living it up with all her newfound wealth, wanting for nothing and living in luxury no doubt. She had the bloody gall to try to pay me off with a measly one thousand pounds, well she's gonna be paying more than that and I don't mean money either."

Ned tried to appease him by saying.

"Why don't you forget it, Bill, we can give you some money if that's what you want, you don't want to get yourself into any more trouble do you."

"I ain't after no bloody handouts from you, and I don't need your advice either I've told you what I want, and you know what I'll do if I don't get it.

A familiar voice spoke from the door that led into the hallway.

"You're getting nothing from any of us."

Jake had heard Pauline's scream from up in his bedroom and then heard her say *Bill,* he had silently crept downstairs avoiding the one on the turn that creaks, he had heard Bill's threat to shoot them so he'd opened the gun cupboard took out his favourite 12-bore shotgun that he used to shoot vermin and loaded it with a cartridge.

Bill swung around violently and his rifle exploded with a loud bang, Jake had anticipated that he would do just that and had skilfully avoided being shot by shielding himself with the door, but he had to make sure Bill didn't get a chance to re-load his rifle, before Bill could do anything Jake stepped purposefully into the living room aimed and fired and the cartridge hit Bill full in the chest, leaving a gaping wound, he dropped to the floor with a groan, there was no way that he would ever hurt anyone again. It had all happened so quickly and yet for Jake it was as if it had been in slow motion like something out of a dream.

Pauline screamed again absolutely horrified by what she had just witnessed she buried her head in Ned's waist and sobbed hysterically. Ned soothed her hair trying to comfort her and looked over at Jake who looked as though he was about to collapse.

"It's alright now, Ned said to Jake, sit yourself down, I'll have to call an ambulance and the police, I'll let your mam know what's happened as well."

Jake didn't reply he just buried his head on his arms on the kitchen table and cried. He wasn't crying for Bill or even for himself, he was crying at the relief of knowing what horrors he had saved his mother and Ted from. He couldn't believe that Bill was so crazy and eaten up with bitterness that his only thoughts were of wreaking revenge on his mother, who had never done him any harm, his mind must have been so twisted by his experience of serving time in prison that the only thing he could focus on was getting even with those he thought had caused his torment, when all along, in reality, the person who had done that was himself.

Pauline had calmed down sufficiently to come to the other side of the table to be with Jake, she did so without looking at the body of Bill lying in a pool of blood on the kitchen floor.

"Get me an ambulance and the police please, Ned said urgently to the operator on the other end of the line, there's been a shooting at Wood Lane Farm, Grendore." He put the receiver down and dialled Ted and Vera's number, it was Ted who answered the phone.

"Brighton 453790."

"Ted it's Ned," Ted could immediately tell from Ned's voice and the lateness of the hour, that something was amiss.

"What's wrong, Ned? Has something happened?"

"Yes, I'm afraid so, prepare yourself for a shock, Bill came here with a shotgun, I'm afraid he's dead, Jake shot him, you'd better come over right away."

"What, oh my God no, yes we'll be there as soon as we can, Jake's not hurt is he, and you're both alright?"

"Yes, we're all ok, apart from the shock of being held at gunpoint by a madman, we'll see you in a while, drive safely."

The ambulance arrived and after they had taken the body away and the police had taken a statement from all of them they were exhausted. Inspector Melgrove could not believe that these fine people had been subjected to such an ordeal, he pondered on what the Brighton police would have encountered and had to deal with if Bill Wiggins had been able to find out where his ex-wife was living and had gone to find her, it didn't bear thinking about, thank God she had been spared this nightmare, she had been through enough trauma in her life, according to what Jake had told him she was happily settled with a new husband and a new life, good luck to her.

By the time Ted and Vera arrived at the farm, the police had taken all the photographs of the scene they needed and Ned had mopped the kitchen floor of blood with disinfectant and they were all reasonably calm. Inspector Melgrove had told them that Jake would not have to face any charges over the matter as it was obvious to anyone that he had shot his father in self-defence, but he would probably have to attend the Coroners Court and give evidence, but he saw this as just a formality. He left asking Jake to kindly give his mother his very best regards.

Ted and Vera arrived very quickly Ted must have driven at a frantic pace to get to the farm so soon. Vera went straight over to Jake asking him if he was alright and what had happened. Jake told his side of the story and Pauline and Ned recounted how Bill must have got in through the French windows and then suddenly burst in on them from the living room and was pointing a rifle at them demanding to know where you lived.

"We had no intention of telling him, Ned said, but God knows what might have happened to us if Jake hadn't come to our rescue, I think he saved our lives tonight!"

"I'm so sorry you had to go through this horrendous experience because Bill was looking for me, if I'd still been living at the cottage it wouldn't have happened."

"No, you'd be dead mam," Jake said.

"He's absolutely right Vera, you can't blame yourself for this, Bill was obviously completely deranged, if you had seen the look in his eyes it was horrible."

"Well, I don't know about anyone else, but I could do with a stiff drink!"

"I think we all could," Ted agreed, he poured three large whiskies for Ned, Jake and himself and two brandies for Pauline and Vera.

"I hope you realise that you saved Pauline and Ned's life tonight Jake, what you did was in self-defence, you're in no way to blame for Bill's death, here you are brave man, drink this, Ted said handing him the glass of whisky."

"Thanks, Ted, Jake replied, he took a large gulp of his drink, there was no other option, he wasn't going to listen to reason, especially not from me!"

The next day the local newspapers had got wind of the story and came to the farm asking questions, but they were told to go away as no one wanted to make any comment, when they became a nuisance by being persistent, Ned pointed out to them that they were on private property and if they didn't leave immediately he would call the police and have them for trespass, they finally left them alone.

The day after that the shooting made headline news, they had obviously somehow gleaned all their information from a police source.

FATAL SHOOTING AT LOCAL FARM
Abducted boy shoots his father

The account was absolutely sensationalised and made Jake look like he murdered his father intentionally. They dug up all the history of the abduction from 1958 as though it was all linked, they even inferred that it was a revenge attack by Jake because of the way his father had treated him and his mother. They played down the fact that if it hadn't been for Jake there could have been a double murder.

Chapter 35

Two weeks later Jake, Vera, Ted, Pauline and Ned left the Coroners Court after the Coroner had pronounced a verdict of Justifiable Homicide on the grounds of self-defence. He had completely exonerated Jake as totally blameless in the affair and had spoken to him directly with great warmth and empathy, telling him that he should not blame himself and do his utmost to put the whole matter behind him.

In actual fact that is exactly what Jake did, he felt no guilt whatsoever over Bill's death, but there were strange mixed feelings of sadness, regret, hurt and anger that accompanied his death, almost a kind of mourning for the dysfunctional relationship that he and his father had had. He felt that he had never really known who he was, it was always a strained relationship, there was always a distance between them, he was like a stranger. He blamed his father for a lot of the problems he'd had, his self-consciousness, his inability to mix and socially interact when he was younger, instead of nurturing him as a loving father should have done, he had almost imprisoned Jake within himself, he blamed him for all of that, but now he was free.

Jake was contacted by the firm of solicitors, Woodhew and Simpson, to inform him of the legacy that had been bequeathed to him by his Godmother Bridie Maguire and had been held in trust for him until he reached the age of twenty-one. They requested that he call at their offices in Warwick with proof of identity, where he would then receive a cheque for £20.000.

Later that week he telephoned the solicitor's office and arranged to go in the following day to collect the cheque, he would then call at his bank to deposit the cheque into his account. Ned kindly said that he would be happy to give him a lift to Warwick and drop him at his bank in Addlestone on the way back, before returning home.

Jake came out of the solicitors' office with the envelope containing the cheque safely put away in his inside jacket pocket, he was all of a tremble, Ned's car was parked right outside. He jumped into the car, took the envelope out of his pocket and opened it just so that he could look at it again and show it to Ned.

"Bloody hell Ned, I'm rich, he said elated, look!"

"You certainly are Jake, but all I ask is that you look after it, spend it wisely, whatever you do don't fritter it all away."

"Don't worry I won't, this is my future, Ned," and he kissed the cheque.

"Thank you, Bridie Maguire," he said as he put it back in his pocket.

Chapter 36

Pauline and Ned had been talking, they were getting worried about Jake, for a few weeks he had been going out a lot after work and coming home in the early hours of the morning, they appreciated that he was young and needed to have leisure time, but in his job he had to make early starts, he just wasn't getting enough sleep and Ned said that it was beginning to affect his work; he was going to have to have a word with him about it. He couldn't run the risk of him causing an accident or getting hurt due to his lack of concentration, being in charge of machinery and looking after livestock carried a big responsibility.

Ned did things properly, as Jake's boss he didn't speak to him front of Pauline, he asked him to come into the office and he told him of his concerns, giving Jake an opportunity to have his say as well. Ned was somewhat surprised by the fact that Jake agreed completely with everything he'd said and knew he was in the wrong and needed to buck his ideas up. He apologised, they left it at that, and Jake got on with his work.

There was something troubling Jake though, Ned and Pauline were his friends as well as his employers, he was experiencing a conflict of interests, he needed to tell them what was really going on and he wanted to tell them when they were together as friends, All day at work he thought about how he was going to tell them, it wasn't going to be easy.

He had decided that there was no point putting it off, he would speak to them that evening after dinner.

Pauline and Ned were both stunned and disappointed at what Jake had just told them, yet at the same time, they fully understood why he didn't want to work on the farm anymore and had made up his mind that his future lay elsewhere.

He was going to live in London, as much as he loved the work he did, he wanted to have new experiences while he was young, there was no nightlife around here that he was interested in, the nearest place where there was a gay scene was Coventry, and that was only when the pub shut after hours. That's why he'd been coming home in the early hours of the morning. He admitted he was lonely and there was very little chance of him meeting anyone around here that he could have a stable and meaningful relationship with, his only hope was to move away and make a new life for himself and be amongst people who were like-minded. After all, it was Ned who had told him that he should be true to himself. Thankfully he was responsible enough to tell them that he would continue working on the farm serving notice until Ned had found a replacement for him, but.

HE WAS DEFINITELY OFF TO LONDON.

Acknowledgements

Thank you to my friends Barbara, Gill, Carmel and June who all read the manuscript and gave me their thoughts, encouragement and enthusiastic approval to seek to get *Jake* published.

About the Author

Keith Bond was born in Stratford Upon Avon, Warwickshire, and was educated at Grendon Church of England Primary School until the age of eleven, when he commenced at Secondary Modern School in Atherstone.

When he left school, he was employed at Tamworth Industrial Cooperative Society as a shop assistant in the drapery department, where he was able to put his artistic talents to good use in dressing the store window display.

He lived with his Mother, Father and younger sister in a cottage in Farm Lane, Grendon, then on a council estate in Baddesley Ensor for a while, before moving to Polesworth, where his parents and sister continued to live for many years.

Keith has had an interesting and varied career, living and working in London, Brighton, Southampton, Bournemouth and Birmingham, doing various jobs, ranging from a coal miner, to assistant stage door keeper at The Royal Opera House, Covent Garden.

He gained a Social Work Degree in 1990 whilst working for The Salvation Army, and has worked with homeless adults in residential care, as well as frail elderly in sheltered housing.

Keith is now retired and lives with his partner in Hampshire, where he is now able to devote his time to writing, which he loves.

Available worldwide from

Amazon

---

www.mtp.agency

www.facebook.com/mtp.agency

@mtp_agency

Printed in Great Britain
by Amazon

27882421R00118